Praise for *New York Times* bestselling and award-winning author Christopher Rice's sixth acclaimed novel, a page-turning mix of New Orleans atmosphere, bayou chills, and heart-pounding suspense. . . .

THE HEAVENS RISE

"A masterful coming-of-age novel. . . . Rice's characters are complex and real, his dialogue pitch-perfect, and his writing intelligent and strong. He builds suspense beautifully . . . amid enduring philosophical questions about what it means to be human.

—*Publishers Weekly* (starred review)

"Christopher Rice is a magician. This brilliant, subtly destabilizing novel inhales wickedness and corruption and exhales delight and enchantment. Rice executes his turns, reversals, and surprises with the pace and timing of a master."

—Peter Straub, #1 *New York Times*
bestselling author of *Mrs. God*

"Christopher Rice has written an amazing horror novel with more twists and turns that a mountain road. You'll think you know your destination . . . but you'll be wrong."

—Charlaine Harris, #1 *New York Times*
bestselling author of *Dead Ever After*

"Christopher Rice has crafted a rich and haunting world in *The Heavens Rise*. This story of a tormented family and the events that have led to their destruction and onward into the future is tense, tight, disturbing, and made very real by a very talented author who obviously knows his way around the Big Easy. An excellent read!"

—Robert McCammon, #1 *New York Times*
bestselling author of *I Travel by Night*

"Creepy, chilling, and almost impossible to put down. . . . A page-turner."

—*Booklist*

"With rich, multi-layered characters merging into the lush backdrop of pre- and post-Katrina south Louisiana, Rice had my attention from the start. . . . Every twist and unexpected revelation fell into place smoothly and kept me engaged. . . . Looking forward to the next amazing story."

—*Suspense Magazine*

"A creepy, intriguing, and dangerously addictive supernatural novel."

—*The Sun*

"Rice's best book to date . . . rich storytelling that will raise the hairs on the back of the neck. It rivals the best of Stephen King . . . and sets a standard for psychological horror."

—*Louisville Courier-Journal*

"An eerie tale of the supernatural set against the backdrop of the swamps of New Orleans. Christopher Rice does a marvelous job. . . . So chilling . . . I can't recommend *The Heavens Rise* enough!"

—*Fresh Fiction*

"Rice draws upon his New Orleans roots to create a Louisiana that may seem familiar but is a bit more terrifying, bringing about a perfect blend of s pooky and memorable. . . The depth of character, chilling atmosphere, and moral dilemma are all marks of a superb story."

—*Shelf Awareness*

"Tense, gripping, gory at times."

—*Huffington Post Books*

"Entertaining and chilling."

—*BookReporter*

ALSO BY CHRISTOPHER RICE

The Moonlit Earth

Blind Fall

Light Before Day

The Snow Garden

A Density of Souls

THE
HEAVENS
RISE

CHRISTOPHER RICE

G

GALLERY BOOKS

NEW YORK   LONDON   TORONTO   SYDNEY   NEW DELHI

G

Gallery Books
A Division of Simon & Schuster, Inc.
1230 Avenue of the Americas
New York, NY 10020

First Gallery Books trade paperback edition July 2014

GALLERY BOOKS and colophon are registered trademarks of Simon & Schuster, Inc.

For information about special discounts for bulk purchases, please contact Simon & Schuster Special Sales at 1-866-506-1949 or business@simonandschuster.com.

The Simon & Schuster Speakers Bureau can bring authors to your live event. For more information or to book an event contact the Simon & Schuster Speakers Bureau at 1-866-248-3049 or visit our website at www.simonspeakers.com.

Designed by Jill Putorti

Manufactured in the United States of America

10   9   8   7   6   5   4   3   2   1

Library of Congress Cataloging-in-Publication Data is available for the hardcover edition.

ISBN 978-1-4767-1608-4
ISBN 978-1-4767-1609-1 (pbk)
ISBN 978-1-4767-1610-7 (ebook)

For
Sid Montz
and
Christian LeBlanc

CONTENTS

THE
HEAVENS
RISE

FROM THE JOURNALS
OF NIQUETTE DELONGPRE

I'*m not sure how long it was down there.*

The soils beneath South Louisiana are constantly shifting; a mass of alluvial sands deposited over hundreds of thousands of years by the Mississippi's flow. It could have worked its way up from deep within the earth, possibly pressured by the nearby upwelling of one of the many salt domes that dot the bottom of my home state.

Or it could have been drawn to the surface by the work of some retired and forgotten oil well. I've studied old survey maps. There were two within a five-mile radius of our property. But they were capped and abandoned decades ago.

I remember when my father got the call that the contractors had discovered some kind of artesian well just a few yards from where they were laying the foundation of the new house. I remember how excited he was as he breathlessly explained the possibilities to my mother and me. The cost of running a larger pipe between Elysium and one of the parish's main water lines was considerable; that's how isolated the place was. But after a little investigation, the aquifer turned out to be woefully small, an isolated pocket beneath layers of bedrock that had long ago been cut off from its original source.

Still, Dad wanted to put it to some kind of use, even if it was only temporary.

We had so many excited conversations about that well. I can remember us all sitting around the dining table speculating on the ornate uses we could put it to. A fountain, perhaps. A koi pond was my idea. "Too California," my mother protested.

She was the one who had named the property years before I was born. Elysium, a final resting place for the heroic and virtuous. It was an odd name for an isolated acreage of mud and cypress that was a good ten-minute boat ride from its nearest neighbor. But my mother had an obsession with Ancient Greece that stemmed from the pagan-themed Mardi Gras parades that ruled our lives each winter. The significance of the name ended there, though. The house my father eventually built on the property wasn't even Greek Revival. It was a raised Acadian cottage, with wraparound screened porches and a one-story brick foundation to protect it from floods. Still, if there was one thing my father worshipped more than his lifelong dream to construct an elegant idyll in the swamp, it was my mother, so the name stuck. Back when he was a college student, and the place was just two trailers, a long oyster-shell driveway and walls of deep, dripping shadows on all sides, my father proposed marriage there beneath ropes of string lights he and his fraternity brothers hung that afternoon. A photograph of the happy couple taken on that night, surrounded by several of my father's brawny accomplices, hung on the wall of our front parlor for years.

A swimming pool. That's what my father wanted. If the well eventually did run dry, we could always feed the pool from the main water line, he insisted.

I was resistant at first. The idea of a gurgling, classical French fountain surrounded by all that wild foliage appealed to my teenage love of the Victorian gothic. But my father used a very simple and cogent argument to change my mind; I loved to swim, but with my mortal fear of snakes, I'd never so much as stuck a toe in the thick finger of black water that snaked through our property like the waterlogged path of some giant jungle serpent. But if I had a cool, perfectly clear pool of pure water, direct from the source . . .

Eventually, I gave in. Of course my father still asked for a show of hands, which seemed like a silly formality to me, but I cast my vote anyway. A swimming pool it was.

It was a decision that destroyed our lives.

I

MARSHALL

1

The patient in Room 4 was named Marshall Ferriot and he couldn't dream.

Instead he experienced vivid eruptions of memory that came from the center of what he perceived to be his person. After the terrifying fall that landed him at death's half-open door when he was only seventeen, he lost all sense of his physical body.

Only rarely was he given some sense of the passage of time and, when it came, it was always accompanied by the jarring realization that his home was a dark, purgatorial place where dreams and memories, all those aspects of human beings people consider to be intangible, took on discrete wavelengths before they were stripped from those human souls they once defined.

In these moments, he could feel himself dragging against a current of souls broken down to their raw constituents—a quantum flow of hopes, nightmares and memories—and it made him feel like shark bait

being towed through open sea. While he had no sense of his limbs, he
knew he was still too fully formed to be worn down and passed through
this pulsing refinery of the spirit.

Then, a moment of stultifying blackness would arrive, stealing the
passage of time, an intermittent distortion that turned a march of ten
years in the conscious world into an endless tape loop of revelations
lost, rediscovered and lost again.

Sometimes he could hear the nurses. Their whispers and their
shouts would come in at equal volume and, with them, a dim awareness that they spoke of him often because they were afraid of him.

But, for the most part, Marshall Ferriot's consciousness fluctuated
steadily between vivid memories of the time before his fall and a terrifying awareness of his paralysis at the edge of death.

And the memories were growing stronger. They had come to include rich sensuous details that suggested an awakening of some kind
might be close at hand. But first they carried him back to New Orleans,
the city of his birth, and to the swamps of Tangipahoa Parish and a
place called Elysium, where he'd been granted his first and last taste of
a beautiful girl with cat-eyes and honey-colored hair, a girl whose very
name filled the remnants of his soul with sustaining rage.

Niquette Delongpre.

2

Her motivation was revenge, he was sure of it. And that was fine with him. At seventeen, Marshall Ferriot prided himself on being a young man who could recognize opportunity when it arrived and, with the fiery end of the passionate romance between Niquette Delongpre and Anthem Landry, opportunity arrived at Marshall's doorstep with bells on.

He had wanted her since they were sophomores, after her breasts had swelled to fullness over the course of one summer, after her walk had acquired a swaying, adult confidence, probably 'cause she'd given up her virginity to that stupid fathead she'd fallen head over heels for the minute he'd transferred into their class. Since then, Marshall Ferriot had spent hours watching Nikki glide gracefully through the hallways of Herschel B. Cannon School, all the while wondering what the skin around her nipples tasted like, or how much pressure he'd have to bite down on them with before she let out a pained yelp that would curl his toes with pleasure.

He'd concocted a few plans over the years, most of them intended to get her white-trash boyfriend kicked out of school and sent back to Jefferson Parish where he belonged. But it was clear the two of them were too much in love to be driven apart by such a meager separation, so Marshall had even thought about cozying up to that little homo she was best friends with, maybe letting the guy give him a BJ or two if he promised to do Marshall's dirty work. But Ben Broyard, pipsqueak that he was, always looked at Marshall as if there was a stink coming off of him, as if he could detect the dark thoughts Marshall nursed about people who made him angry and thought they were kind of stupid, even if they did involve knives and rope.

What Marshall had been waiting for was a golden opportunity, a sign that the stars had aligned on his behalf, and it didn't come until the last months of senior year. There had been plenty of girls to occupy his time along the way, of course. There were the real girlfriends, the ones befitting a young man of his stature and breeding, classically pretty, with first names that were more often used as last names for men—Chesley, Whitney, Preston—girls who never let him go below the waist unless he got them shitfaced on Zima. And then there were others. The ones who could keep secrets. The band geeks and the computer dorks. The ones so grateful for any kind of attention from a guy like Marshall they'd let him use things like beer bottles and staplers.

But Nikki Delongpre, she was the prize. The ultimate. Everybody agreed; there was something *different* about her. Like the fact that she'd been the only freshman ever to make varsity cheerleading, and then had ditched the squad a few months later because, as she told everyone who asked, she thought she was too young to have an eating disorder. Stuff just didn't get to Nikki the way it got to the other girls at Cannon; she wasn't a gossip, she rarely drank. And until Anthem's betrayal, she was rarely swept up in some tearful drama over something somebody might have said about her three weeks ago. Marshall had overheard two teachers talking about her once and their words had seared themselves into his mind. While the first asserted *the Delongpre girl* had a wisdom beyond her years, the second—in the same kind of superior tone Marshall's mother used to discuss the moral failings of Democrats—asserted that Nikki was a perfectionist, and if she was ever going to really grow up, she would have to stop planning her life and actually begin living it.

And there it was, the opening. The way in.

He could show her how to start living.

When he asked her out the first time, she made him meet her at some ratty coffeehouse over in the Faubourg Marigny that was full of hippies and fags. And even though the whole thing made him feel like some cheap man-whore, the way she was keeping their meeting a secret from everyone on their side of town, he knew better than to complain.

And there was no getting her to talk about the great betrayal that had ended her three-year relationship to Anthem Landry, but it didn't matter. The story was common knowledge by then anyway.

Poor Nikki. She had planned her entire life down to the last detail, without giving any thought to the type of man she'd selected to make the trip with her. Davidson College had been her school of choice: North Carolina was just far enough from home to get them away from her boyfriend's sprawling, overbearing family, but not so far that they couldn't fly home for every holiday. The problem, of course, was that everyone except for Nikki knew that her boyfriend didn't have a snowball's chance in Houma of getting in, not when he couldn't be bothered to memorize anything besides old Saints scores. But Niquette Delongpre—planner and perfectionist, daughter of one of the most respected maxiofacial surgeons in the country—wouldn't be deterred by her boyfriend's rejection letter. Obviously, Anthem should move with her to North Carolina anyway. Get a job to support himself, maybe find a community college and gets his grades up to where he could reapply. Anthem's response, heard by most of the Cannon campus during lunch, *"You expect me to fuckin' pump gas all day while you sit in a classroom talking about poetry?"*

The lawns outside the cafeteria had certainly paid host to worse lovers' quarrels. But a few days later, the news broke that after consuming half a bottle of Southern Comfort, Anthem Landry had somehow wound up in the arms and accommodating mouth of a doe-eyed junior, Brittany Lowe, who was well known among her male classmates for having tiny, unobtrusive teeth. That's what the girl said, anyway. Anthem denied the charge with shouts, and more than a few tears, to anyone who would listen. Nikki chose to believe the worst.

And for Marshall Ferriot, that was very good news. Especially when you considered the story was a complete lie. Turns out Brittany Lowe was willing to do pretty much anything Marshall wanted her to do, as long as he supplied her with a bottle of Vicodin out of his mother's medicine cabinet.

Despite his success so far, Marshall knew better than to speak ill of the man in question to Nikki's face, even if he did think the guy was a worthless piece of Lakefront trash. Anthem Landry came from a family of riverboat pilots and those assholes were the worst, a bunch of drunken slobs who had bought all kinds of political power in Baton Rouge so they could keep the entire port hostage with their ridiculously high salaries. He should know; his father ran one of the most successful cold storage companies on the Gulf Coast. Men like his dad kept the city running, his family always said, while lazy niggers threatened to take the whole thing down.

And what the hell kind of queerbait name was Anthem anyway? It chapped Marshall's ass that the guy never caught any flack for it at school. Let Marshall belch in the wrong direction and he'd end up with some stupid nickname he couldn't live down for months.

Of course he didn't say a word of this to Nikki.

Instead he started talking about his desire to travel the world, to make big bucks in a city like New York and Chicago after he graduated from Duke (which was, by the way, not too far from Davidson). He thought he was being subtle, but maybe he wasn't. After three more coffee dates, Nikki's smiles started to seem a little indulgent. But she listened to him ramble on, and then, finally, just when he feared he might have lost her, she invited him to Elysium.

3

They moved the patient out of Room 4 when animals started dying outside his window.

The squirrels came first, a slightly disjointed row of them that appeared in a single day, just a few feet away from the window ledge: furry tails limp and snakelike, chests sealed to the patchy lawn with dead weight. Two of the three nurses who gathered at Room 4's window that afternoon blamed the live oak tree nearby; some sort of awful fungus must have laced itself all through the branches overhead, then Alvin and his poor buddies took a few nibbles and *plop, plop, plop.*

But Arthelle Williams wasn't sold on this scenario. It would have been five plops in all, and not a single one of the squirrels had landed on its back. Was that even statistically possible? The thought of there being statistics related to random squirrel deaths made her laugh so hard her breath fogged the glass.

She volunteered to go outside and take a closer look. It was a marvel, she thought, that her coworkers could empty a bedpan without so much as a wince, but the idea of getting within a few feet of a dead rodent turned them into squealing little girls.

They watched her from the window as she poked at the furry carcasses with a stick. There was no sense in pushing Marshall Ferriot's wheelchair to the window; he wouldn't be able to see any of it anyway. The boy hadn't seen a damn thing for eight years. But the new girl, Emily Somethingorother—the little blonde who'd watched too many TV shows about hospitals on her daddy's flat-screen and was always asking them silly questions about *their mission*—was so upset about the dead squirrels she hadn't managed to peel her hands from her mouth for the entire time it had taken Arthelle to walk outside. Tammy Keene, the other nurse who'd discovered the gory scene, finally gave in to the girl's histrionics and curved one arm around Emily's shoulders while she gave Arthelle a pointed look that said, *If I'd wanted to deal with children today, I would have stayed home and looked after my own.*

"Some of these new nurses," Arthelle had said to Tammy earlier that morning, "they make it hard to tell who the patients are." The joke hadn't been one of her best. If they had been working at a real hospital, it might have earned her a cackle or two. But here at the Lenox Hill Long Term Care Center, it was always possible to tell the nurses from the patients, because none of the patients could walk or speak. A high-end vegetable garden; that's how Arthelle had heard more than one visiting physician refer to the place. And it was a pretty apt description: a place for the rich to stash their brain-dead invalids until pneumonia or a virulent infection did them in for good. Of course, the brochure didn't word it quite so succinctly.

Arthelle dropped the stick she'd been using to prod the carcasses when she realized the other end had sunk into exposed brain matter. The squirrels hadn't tucked their heads underneath their bodies as she'd first assumed. Their skulls had been smashed in. By what exactly, she had no idea. If it had been a tool wielded by a man, the blows were amazingly precise. The poor guys weren't that big, and the rest of their bodies were undamaged.

Not smashed. That's not right either. Exploded.

Childhood horror stories about seagulls being killed by Alka-Seltzer pellets swirled in her head, but it was the stomach that got blown out in that scenario, wasn't it? Not the skull. Not the *brains*. And from their respective poses, it looked like the squirrels had been crawling straight for the window when the event in question had reduced each of their heads to little mounds of gore. And it didn't look as if it had all happened at once. Some of the poor little guys . . . well, they looked *fresher* than the others.

There was a perfectly logical explanation, she was sure of it; gruesome, to be sure, and a very valid reason to get the hell away from the furry little devils and report the whole mess to security, but logical nonetheless.

God knows, they didn't need any more weirdness around Marshall Ferriot. That was for sure.

Spend your day working around mannequins and you were bound to believe one of them had turned its head in your direction when you weren't looking. This was normal, and to be forgiven. But it was also to be *contained* and dealt with responsibly. This was the lecture Arthelle gave Tammy Keene, Emily New Girl and the other nurses who had joined them for dinner that evening at one of the malls in Buckhead. The squirrel slaughter was common knowledge by then, and Arthelle figured the last few women who had invited themselves along were after gruesome details, not comfort food.

For a moment or two, it seemed as if her lecture had worked. Arthelle's fellow nurses responded with bowed heads and the dull clinks of spoons hitting cast-iron skillets as they all devoured their macaroni and cheese.

"He killed them."

It was Emily who'd said it, of course; Emily, with her doe eyes, and that squeaky, cartoony voice Arthelle just knew was an act designed to get men to take care of her. Little Emily New Girl, her head full of childish ideas that would never provide her with a grown-up life. And even though she looked away quickly from Arthelle's fearsome glare, the sight of it wasn't enough to keep her mouth shut.

"He can make you do things . . . he *can*. If you look into his eyes, he can make you . . . And when it's over, you don't remember doing any of it."

No one said anything until the waiter brought the check.

The bird was next. It happened early in the morning and, while no one saw the event itself, everyone who was on the wing at that moment heard the loud *thwack* the crow made as it flew right into Room 4's window with enough force to crack the glass in two places. And because there had been no witnesses, no one could tell if the bird's compact skull had cracked open during the collision or just moments before.

And even though there was no evidence that young Marshall Ferriot had been disturbed by the event—or any other event that had taken place in his immediate vicinity for the past eight years, for that matter—he was moved to another room later that afternoon, this one featuring a view of a barren service alley with a Dumpster tucked at the far end.

"Somebody better pop the lid on that Dumpster a couple times this week," Tammy Keene said after she and Arthelle had tucked Ferriot into his new bed. "Make sure the rats are doing okay."

"Hush your mouth, girl," Arthelle whispered. "I'm tired of this nonsense."

Sick to death of the whole subject was more like it. The poor boy was a vegetable, for Christ's sake. And she was coming to hate how quickly the women in her life would give their heads over to superstitious gobbledygook. Sisters, in particular. Almost every girlfriend of hers from childhood had grown up to be some crazy Bible-thumping church lady. Arthelle sometimes felt like the only black woman in the South who wanted to live a life of the mind.

There was also the fact that she didn't feel like telling Tammy, or anyone else for that matter, about how badly she'd gone off on Little Emily when she caught the girl rooting through Ferriot's file that morning. So some trust based at a New Orleans bank paid for the boy's care? So what? None of it was proof that the boy was some kind of witch or warlock or whatever else little Emily was making him out to be to the other nurses.

He was a patient just like all the others and, if he gave Emily the creeps, she should stay out of his goddamn room and stop making trouble. Otherwise, Arthelle would have her ass fired.

They had a job to do, and it wasn't to make up stories.

4

TANGIPAHOA PARISH
APRIL 2005

After they crossed Lake Pontchartrain, Marshall used his fake ID to buy them a milk carton full of frozen strawberry daiquiri and, when they were passing through Madisonville, a tiny hamlet that sits right at the spot where the Tchefuncte River slides free of Lake Pontchartrain's northern shore, Marshall reached across the gearshift and took Nikki's hand. For several agonizing seconds, her 4-Runner thudded over the steel girders of the town's tiny drawbridge before she closed her fingers around his. And even though she wouldn't look at him, he sprouted a painful hard-on in his jeans.

"Watch out for snakes!" Nikki said as they walked up the oyster-shell driveway to the property. It was the third time she'd warned him about a possible reptile encounter since they'd stepped from her car. Snakes didn't bother him much, but they sure as hell got to her. He found himself taking note of this fact, lingering over it, wondering if perhaps he could put it to some kind of use. For her own good, of course. *If I can cure her of a terrible fear, just think of the things she might let me do to her.*

Like most children who'd grown up in Louisiana, she'd probably heard that old story about the water skier on the bayou who lost his balance and started screaming, "Help, I'm in barbed wire!" Only, according to the story, it wasn't barbed wire. When the boat circled back, the friends pulled the man from the water to find him festooned with thick, black serpents. An entire school of water moccasins! Maybe if he told her that he'd found the story listed in an anthology of debunked urban legends or that, while water moccasins were certainly aggressive, they had terrible aim when it came time to bite, she might like him even more.

He followed the beam of her flashlight, which she kept angled on the mud underfoot, across the broad lawn that sat between the house and the dark, gurgling rectangle of the swimming pool. The entire property was plated in deep darkness that became impenetrable at its wooded borders, and the fact that she wasn't leading him into the house, or in the direction of any shed that might contain light switches, sent shivers of delicious anticipation racing up his spine.

This is what you get when you work hard enough, he thought, as he listened to their intermittent gasping breaths. *If you sit through enough bullshit coffee dates, if you're a man of promise and resources, you can get a girl like Nikki Delongpre to take you to her secret love nest under the cover of darkness.*

Even better, he was one of the first people to see this place in its current incarnation. The house had been finished only a few weeks before, and the contractors had filled the pool just a day or two ago. There was some kind of party planned in the next few weeks, probably a housewarming, but she got fuzzy on the details as soon as she brought it up, probably because she wasn't ready to invite him. He'd floated some details about the shitty fund-raiser at the Plimsoll Club that his parents were forcing him to attend in a week, just enough to see if she wanted to be his date, but she'd gotten vague and distant then too.

But none of that mattered in this moment. He was here! Elysium!

She dropped the icy milk carton onto a lounger he could barely make out in the darkness. They were standing on flagstones now.

"Let me get some cups, turn some lights on," she said, already turning for the house.

He took her gently by the arm and held her in place.

"Don't leave me . . ." he gently whined.

Her laughter was more breath than anything else, and he couldn't see her face, just that she had bowed her head slightly to keep their mouths from meeting. Lights meant more chatter, more feelings and more bullshit. The dark promised him the taste of her neck, the heft of her breasts and the heat between her slender thighs.

"It's too dark," she whispered.

"What are you afraid of? Snakes?"

"Seriously. Don't even . . ."

But in her rush to make this point emphatic, she'd lifted her lips to within inches of his, and he seized the moment. Their connection was instant, moist, her mouth yielding, her body going limp as he curved his arms around her back. She was as hungry for this as he was. At least it seemed that way for about three minutes, and then she started to stiffen. He needed to make another move, and fast.

He lightened up on the kissing, allowed her to breathe for a second or two, but he kept his arms wrapped around her as he walked them closer to the pool's dark edge.

"You don't have to be afraid of anything," he whispered. "I'll protect you from all of it."

Then he hurled them into the pool.

The water was so cold it hit them with the force of an anvil, and only then did Marshall remember what she'd said about its being fed by some kind of artesian well. But he kept her locked in his embrace, even as she coughed and cursed him and sputtered.

"I've got you . . . I've got you . . ." he said over and over again, and after trying to pull away from him, she finally relented. When she held to him with fresh childlike desperation, he realized it was her total fear of their dark, rippling surroundings that had sealed her body against his. She would rather cling to him in the freezing cold than dog-paddle a few feet through water she couldn't see the bottom of.

And so he went back to work, with more force now, attacking her neck, peeling her soaked shirt up above her stomach, palming her breasts and then kneading them, and the whole time he kept waiting for her bone-rattling shivers to come to an end, for the warmth of desire to fill her as it was filling him. But she kept shivering in his arms, no matter what he did to her. And when he went to lift her shirt up over her bra, when her arms became caught halfway overhead inside her soaked sleeves, he realized she wasn't helping, she was resisting, trying to pull her arms free while kicking herself away from him at the same time.

"Hey," she said, and her voice was as cool as ice, without a trace of desire in it, and just this simple word told him she was feeling none of what he had just felt. None of the desire, no loss of control.

There was a deep, resounding thud against the stone nearby. Marshall felt it in his chest, then he felt it in his outstretched arms, and realized he'd been the cause of it. In the darkness, he could just make out the white's of Nikki's eyes. He had taken her by both shoulders and slammed her head into the side of the pool.

"Marshall," she said quietly. But there was a trembling edge to her words that sounded like both a question and a challenge. Just by saying his name she was asking him how much further he was going to go. *That Nikki Delongpre, nothing gets to her. Not even concrete.* But he had gotten to her, all right. She was terrified. Paralyzed, hardly hysterical, but terrified nonetheless. And for a moment he thought about doing something to her, something really bad, something he'd never done before. But she wouldn't keep it a secret, not like the other skanks he liked to play with. And if she wouldn't keep it a secret, that meant whatever he did would have to be . . . final.

"Marshall, I'm going to get out of the water now." Soft, gentle and condescending, like she was talking to a man with a gun. And wasn't she, in a way? After all, he was taking stock of certain things, like the fact that she'd kept everything between them such a secret. Had she even told anyone she was out there with him? How far away was the nearest neighbor? A ten-minute boat ride?

Too much work.

That's what it came down to in the end.

He allowed her to slide free of his grip and hoist herself up onto the flagstones. As soon as her feet were on solid ground, she grabbed for the flashlight and wheeled on him. "You son of a—" but the words died in her mouth when she saw what the beam had landed on.

The pool was full of them.

At first he thought it must be some kind of plankton, or maybe even sawdust left over from the construction. But these things weren't the color of wood, they were the color of skin, and they were everywhere, clustered together in beige clumps that looked like shredded human flesh. And they were drifting through the water with determination, driven by currents he couldn't feel.

Then darkness descended over him as Nikki took off running, the bouncing beam marking her path toward to the driveway. He could hear the jangle of the keys she'd already pulled from her pocket, could see her furiously wiping her other arm across her shirt, too frightened of him to stop and see how many of the crawly little things from the pool were still clinging to her.

He was still hoisting himself out of the pool when the 4-Runner's engine sputtered to life and the headlights swung out into the swamp's darkness and disappeared.

He wiped his arms in the darkness for a few minutes. But he didn't care. And he didn't care that she'd just abandoned him either. No, what mattered most to him, what would cling to his soul most forcefully about this night in the days to come, was the realization that he'd allowed her to escape, a realization that now felt as overpowering as discovering you had cancerous tumors all through your body.

I decided not to kill a woman because it sounded like too much work.

Finally he forgot about whatever the pool was full of and just stood there, letting the water run down his body and onto the flagstones. And what steadied his breaths, what chased away his memory of her flashlight beam bouncing off in the direction of her 4-Runner, was a new series of images that came to him unbidden.

Nikki Delongpre was staring up into his eyes as he held her to the mud a few feet away from where he stood now. One hand was around her throat, the other was drawing a paring knife up the length of her torso, slicing the flesh over her breastbone, drawing a red thread past the breasts she had refused to reveal to him. In this vision, Nikki did not scream or cry out or beg for him to stop. Rather, she gazed right into his eyes as a flowing, crimson seam opened in the center of her chest, her stunned, moist-eyed expression radiating a silent, awestruck recognition of his newfound power.

He was not a sick man. A sick man would have craved the sound of her screams, and those did not figure into this little fantasy of his. In fact, he was immensely proud of the cleanliness of this vision, of its lack of common violence, of his own ability to be perfectly content with just this focused display of pure physical dominance and its flowing, unstoppable result.

He tried to apologize, but she wouldn't let him.

In the days that followed, before he made a decision that changed everything, she vanished wherever he appeared, out a side door in the locker room, into the warren of rooms behind the theater during lunch.

The injustice of this began to bore into him more deeply than her rejection of him out in the swamp. It was as if she'd sensed the bloody fantasy that had coursed through him as she'd run for her car and was determined to let him simmer in it. Not just simmer. Drown altogether.

He blamed her for the deep throbbing ache in his jaw that alerted him to the fact that he'd been gritting his teeth for an hour. He blamed her for the sickness that had come over him later that night, even though he knew those disgusting little crawly things in the pool were probably to blame. (The chills and the nausea had gripped him while he was still in the car on the way home with his father. Of course, his dad hadn't pressed for an explanation; he lived in such terror that his only son would turn out to be a bone smoker, Marshall could talk his way out of anything with even the vaguest story implying he'd been alone with a member of the opposite sex.)

And then came the final and most crushing blow.

They were back together. Nikki and Anthem, Cannon's most perfect couple. After all the work Marshall had done, trust had been restored. How was it even possible? As he lay awake at night, seething with rage, those footsteps up the oyster-shell driveway toward Elysium's darkened pool seemed like the last few seconds before an Olympic diver hit the water at a contorted angle, the chance of a medal rippling out away from him as he plunged under the surface. But the moment he couldn't wash from his mind was the last words Nikki had said to him before fear had gripped her entirely.

Watch out for snakes.

The Delongpre residence was a two-story Greek Revival on Prytania Street, just a block from Lafayette Cemetery. The second-floor porch was big enough for a swing, and a high wrought-iron fence protected the front yard. But the driveway, an expanse of red brick, was open and exposed to the street, and that's where the family's hunter-green Ford

Explorer sat with its cargo door half open, the dome light sending a soft spill of light over its leather cream-colored seats.

Half a block away, Marshall sat behind the wheel of his father's BMW, watching Millie and Nikki Delongpre load their overnight bags and groceries.

In the locker room at school, he had overheard talk of a party, a birthday party for Nikki's mother. But it wouldn't just be a celebration of Millie Delongpre's forty-seventh. It was also the first social occasion Anthem and Nikki would be attending together following their reunion, their official coming-out-after-coming-apart party. So far, there had been no sign of the man of the hour, no glimpse of Anthem Landry's cherry-red F-150 pickup truck. Maybe he was meeting them tomorrow. At almost nine o'clock, the Delongpres were certainly getting a late start.

The party would be held at Elysium the following evening, and when Marshall imagined the place with lanterns strung from its cypress branches, when he thought of well-dressed guests standing and chatting in the same spot where he hurled Nikki into the pool, he was filled with a silent, focusing rage that distracted him from the stapled-shut grocery bag shifting on the passenger-side floor of his father's BMW.

If he waited in the car any longer, he would lose his opportunity.

He could still hear Nikki's parents calling to each other inside the house when he lifted the Explorer's cargo door by about two feet and set the grocery sack in between two Louis Vuitton satchels and a crate of Beaujolais. Then he took his car key and made three quick cuts in the side of the bag, each one large enough for the inhabitant to work its way through when it decided it was time to emerge.

By the time he was back to the BMW, he heard the back door to the Delongpre residence close with force, followed by the family's excited laughter. Nikki was recounting some childhood story about how her father had once screwed up his fishing line and hooked a lump of her hair in the process.

Marshall slid behind the driver's seat of his father's BMW and waited. He waited until the Ford Explorer pulled out of the driveway and headed down Prytania Street. He waited until the red taillights turned the corner, leaving him alone with a steady, rasping sound. At first he thought it was coming from the grocery bag next to him—he had spent most of the day with the thing—but then he remembered that his gift had been delivered, that it had been tucked inside the SUV that had just driven past him into the night, leaving him with the desperate rattle of his own strained breaths.

5

A rthelle was at the drink machine when she heard the screaming. She'd know as soon as she rounded the corner up ahead if the commotion was coming from Ferriot's new room. *Please, God. Let it be anything else. A rat or a mouse loose on the hall. Anything. Just let it be alive!*

Things had been quiet for a week now, probably because Emily had steered clear of the boy, and there'd been no more strange animal deaths outside the center either. The only one to raise the subject of Ferriot at all had been Tammy Keene, and only to Arthelle. Tammy had two kids she had to support on her own, which meant no time to fill her head with stupid books about UFOs and doomsday prophecies; in other words, she was as eager to keep Emily in check as Arthelle was.

Emily was the one screaming, all right. She was standing outside the open door to Ferriot's room, bent at the waist, hands to her mouth as she wailed. Other nurses had come running too. They also stumbled in their tracks when they saw the bloody footprints Emily had made around the doorway.

Ferriot was in his wheelchair, just like he was every morning, staring into space with the same slack-jawed expression that made him look like he'd been trying to remember someone's phone number for years.

Tammy Keene was on the floor, curled into a fetal position, back to the doorway, the blood flowing from her chest forming a dark curtain across the linoleum. Arthelle hit the floor on both knees, rolled the woman onto her back and saw her wide, staring eyes, radiating nothing but shock over the fact that the box cutter she always carried on her hip when she was doing gift distribution was embedded in her chest. The other nurses started pouring into the room, but not Emily. She was still screaming.

"I told her not to! But she didn't believe me. I told her not to look into his eyes!"

Once she pulled Tammy's bloodstained shirt up over her bloody chest and saw the extent of her wound, Arthelle started cursing under her breath, bloody fingers trembling as she traced a gash that started just above Tammy's navel and made a straight, gurgling line right up to where the box cutter's blade had caught on the underside of her rib cage. The blood was everywhere. Tammy's lips moved, but nothing came out except weak, hissing breaths. Everyone around them was sliding into action, and that was good, because Arthelle was paralyzed, stunned, trying to put it all together.

No blood on Emily's hands or face. None at all. But the only screams she'd heard had come from Emily, not the gutted colleague the other nurses were now rushing to save. And the window was closed and Ferriot was right in front of it, so how could someone have scrambled out into the alley without knocking the poor boy out of his wheelchair?

These thoughts were assaulting Arthelle from all sides, reducing her to a quivering wreck in one corner of the room while her colleagues tried to stop the flow of Tammy's blood, ignoring as they worked the fact that Tammy's eyes now stared up at the ceiling with the glaze of death.

An alarm screamed. But it was the wrong one, not the steady honking of the Code Blue alarm meant to summon all of them to a patient's room. This was the old *whoop and wail,* as the girls called it; the shrill, screaming fire alarm. *An alarm's an alarm,* she thought. *And what does it matter now? She's gone. Tammy's plum gone.*

Emily was halfway across the room before Arthelle sprang to her feet. The crazed girl had hauled the fireman's ax back over one shoulder, its red and silver blade glinting in the fluorescent light. The nurses working on Tammy were too busy to see what was about to happen, but Arthelle did. The ax blade struck the arm of the wheelchair a few inches from Marshall Ferriot's limp right hand. By then, Arthelle had driven Emily face-first into the floor with enough force to knock the wind out of the crazy little bitch.

Thanks to Arthelle Williams, they had all been spared two gruesome deaths at the center that day. But as soon as Arthelle felt a surge of triumph, she looked up and saw Tammy Keene's blood sliding toward them across the linoleum, making the victory feel as empty as the patient sitting a few feet away appeared to be.

FROM THE JOURNALS
OF NIQUETTE DELONGPRE

*A*nthem Landry came to us in the middle of sophomore year, a transfer student from an all-boys' Catholic high school in Jefferson Parish, where he'd been required to wear a khaki uniform to class each day. That's why he showed up for his first day of class at Herschel B. Cannon in acid-washed blue jeans and a black T-shirt with the phrase PAIN IS WEAKNESS LEAVING THE BODY printed on the back in paint-splatter font. Obviously he thought the absence of an official dress code meant he could attend his new school looking like he was about to go fishing with his brothers.

If he hadn't been almost six feet tall, there might have been a few snickers as he made his way to the nearest empty desk. But the other students in our English class that day registered his size and his outfit with the same stunned silence.

What I remember even more vividly is the look he gave me once he took a seat and sensed me staring holes in the back of his thick, olive-skinned neck; a look of such unguarded fear that my breath caught in my throat. At first, I was filled with pity for him—there's nothing worse than being the new kid. If Ben and I hadn't had each other the year before, I'm not sure what we would have done. But then I found myself dizzy from a strange combination of desire and opportunity. I wasn't used to seeing that kind of vulnerability in a boy of his size and good looks, and I couldn't help but see it as an invitation.

That afternoon, Ben and I found him sitting alone in the central courtyard, a few yards away from the giant oak tree where most of the freshmen and sophomores gathered during lunch, inhaling a plate of turkey tetrazzini as if it were the first meal he'd consumed in months.

I think I was the first one to speak. So your name's Anthem, huh? That's kinda cool.

And Anthem said something like. My mom's got a thing with names. My brotha says she likes tuh name her kids like we all celebrities or royalty or something.

Ben and I exchanged a look as we heard the guy speak. The accent was way too Jefferson Parish, that was for sure: 100% yat. (And yat, by the way, is a derogatory nickname for working-class folk who live along the lakefront, folks who see crawfish boils and hair spray as a religion, folks who dress their toddlers in Saints gear every game day and speak with what is essentially a Cajun accent deprived of its French lilt and turned into something you might hear in the South Bronx.) We could fix the clothes with a few trips to Perlis or the Lakeside Mall. But the accent might be hopeless. Or so we thought. At the time, we underestimated how several years surrounded by genteel Uptown drawls would soften the edges of it dramatically.

Anthem went on to explain how his older brother Charlie had really been named for King Charlemagne, and Merit, his next oldest brother—he had five in all, a figure that astonished Ben and me into deeper silence— thought he'd been named for good character but the rumor in the family was that his mother had just been a fan of Merit Ultra Light cigarettes before the doctors had told her not to smoke during her many pregnancies.

They were a family of riverboat pilots—the men were, at least—and most of them lived within several blocks of one another near the spot where Avron Drive dead-ended with the Lake Pontchartrain levy. Anthem's dream was to join the ranks of the New Orleans–Baton Rouge Steamship Pilots Association just like most of his brothers had done, pulling down $300,000 a year piloting massive cargo ships and container vessels up and down the treacherous curves of the Mississippi.

His father, also a pilot, had died the year before in a car accident and the payout from his life insurance policy had allowed Anthem to transfer to what was arguably the most prestigious private school in all of Louisiana. When Ben revealed that his father was also dead, I could practically feel every muscle in Anthem's body relax a bit, and the moment of silence we all shared seemed strangely comfortable given the subject of Ben's admission. The confines of adolescence excused any of us from coming up with some empty, comforting platitude to soothe the pain of a lost parent. Shared pain, unresolved and beating inside each of us like a second heart, formed our initial bond with the strikingly handsome new kid from the wrong part of town.

After what felt like an appropriate amount of silence, I brought up the idea of a shopping excursion after school, as if it would be as spontaneous and innocuous as a trip to CC's Coffee House. I can't remember exactly how I phrased it, but I tried to be diplomatic. Something about getting him some stuff to wear that would make him feel more comfortable. He played dumb; he admitted as much later. But I took the bait.

Comfortable? Did he look like he was uncomfortable? The jeans fit pretty nice, didn't they?

Finally I blurted out something like, You're not going to win over a bunch of new friends with that shirt, okay?

He gave us both a big grin and said, Looks like it won you two over just fine.

It seems inevitable now, that Anthem and I would end up together. But when I remember those first few weeks after we became a trio, I can still *feel the constant fear that he would leave us, that his imposing physical form would demand that he turn into one of the brutish jocks Ben and I so despised.*

He fell in love with me instead.

Our first kiss was at a Mardi Gras parade. Several nights before Fat Tuesday, the Krewe of Ares rolled through Uptown, and Ben and I invited Anthem to join us at our regular parade watching spot at Third and St. Charles Avenue, in front of an old florist shop and surrounded by Greek Revival mansions, their front porches crowded with other drunken revelers.

Ben had stolen a bottle of scotch from his mother's liquor cabinet and the three of us had been sharing sips out of his secret flask. Anthem took every opportunity to get closer to me as we were jostled by the crowd of parade-goers, their arms shooting skyward as papier-mâché floats rolled past us belching diesel fumes. The masked riders on board tossed handfuls of glittering doubloons and plastic beads into the night and the giant heads of Greek gods and goddesses at the head of each float just missed scraping the thick oak branches overhead. Once he'd found the courage to press his chest up against my back, and once both of our arms were raised at the same time, Anthem Landry wrapped his fingers around both of my wrists, turned me as if we were going to dance, and kissed me with a gentle determination that made me lose my balance and fall against him.

I had known the bonds of friendship before that night. I had known loyalty and unshakable commitment of a certain chaste kind. And while there had been a few fumbling experiences where I'd let boys get to second base, pure romantic affection had been unknown to me until that very moment. Until Anthem Landry took me in his powerful arms and kissed me, I had never known what it was like to become briefly lost in someone else's desire to know your smell and your taste. And that's what I became; blissfully, irretrievably lost.

Bloodred plastic beads bearing the Krewe of Ares logo—a spear and Spartan helmet—slammed to the pavement all around us, some of them snapping upon impact. From a few yards away, Ben watched, slack-jawed with amazement. But I was lost to everything except the scotch-sharpened breath of my first and only real lover.

Ironic, I guess, that I experienced this kind of intimacy for the first time at a Mardi Gras parade named for an ancient god of violence and war. Or perhaps not, considering everything that came later.

II

BEN

6

Anthem Landry considered it a miracle that Nikki took him back, and every hour since that fateful phone call, he felt like an electric-chair-bound convict rescued by the governor's pardon at the last possible second. He'd turned into one of those chatty, cheerful jackasses who could make conversation about almost any topic with any clerk in any place of business. His older brothers, who only rallied around him when he was down, had taken to calling him Cool Whip, which was really just a version of the term *pussy whipped* that they could use when their mother was in the room.

For Anthem, the real discovery was that none of the begging, none of the sobbing late-night phone messages and none of the long letters he had tucked under the windshield of her Toyota 4-Runner, letters in which he had pled his innocence to kingdom come, had done the job.

Once again, it was Ben who had come to the rescue. The kids and teachers who'd observed their little trio from a distance over the years always wrote Ben off as their third wheel, the nerdy hanger-on Nikki stayed loyal to because they'd been besties since birth. It was horseshit, and Anthem told them so whenever he got the chance.

Ben Broyard was their glue, their rational mind, the provider of their few deep breaths. And in the past twenty-four hours he'd averted the end of Anthem's whole world. Sure, he was barely five foot two, and had a high-pitched nasally voice that wasn't about to get him work on WWL radio, but when the little dude set his mind to something he could marshal as much wallop as a hurricane. And for the past two weeks the most important project in his life had been getting Brittany Lowe to admit that her story about hooking up with Anthem was a complete crock. How he'd done it, Anthem wasn't exactly sure. All that mattered was that he'd tape-recorded the lying skank's confession and played it for Nikki.

And the rest, as they say, was makeup sex.

"Why?" Anthem had asked Ben after things were reconciled, after a night spent inhaling the scent of Nikki's perfume and feeling like he'd been pulled up and over the edge of a cliff by one arm. "Why'd she lie?"

"I'm workin' on it, A-Team" was Ben's cryptic reply.

That had been three days ago, and now the two of them were flying across the Lake Pontchartrain Causeway, bound for Elysium. Of course, someone was missing, and in light of recent events, Nikki's absence from his pickup truck that night left knots of tension across Anthem's upper back. It wasn't just a housewarming party they'd be attending in the morning; it was also Miss Millie's birthday, so she had every right to demand that her daughter ride out to Elysium with her and Mr. Noah. But still, it made Anthem nervous, like the weekend away was actually an audition rather than a welcome back celebration.

It was *neither,* Ben pointed out about three times after they got on the causeway, probably because it gave him an excuse to turn down the volume on the Cowboy Mouth CD Anthem had been playing on repeat for about a year now.

"This is a birthday party for her *mom*," Ben said, with that maddeningly parental tone that sometimes made Anthem want to pop him one. "Don't make this all about you. God knows. The Anthem and Nikki Show has had enough cliffhangers this season."

"It's just good that we're going, right?"

"Absolutely."

"I mean, if she wasn't sure, we wouldn't be going at all. And they sure as hell wouldn't let us come out the night before like this and sleep in the guest room, so—"

"You know, we've really covered this, A-Team."

"I know, I know. I'm just saying."

"Yeah, well, less saying. More driving. The causeway cops are all bored a-holes."

"You're a real gift in my life, you know that?"

"You're kidding, right?"

"Totally bullshitting."

"Yeah, I figured."

But he wasn't kidding. And he figured from the way Ben had gone quiet, his hands clasped between his bony knees, his gaze straight ahead so that the dashboard lights glowed in his circular-framed glasses, Ben knew he wasn't kidding but didn't want to talk about it. The older they all got, the more sarcastic and uncomfortable with touchy-feely moments Ben got. And, Nikki insisted, the less interested in girls he got. But Anthem figured that was just because most of the girls Ben was hot for were the pretty, popular types who weren't all that interested in a nerdy bookworm who wanted to write for a newspaper someday. *Right,* Nikki would answer, *the ones he knows are out of his league so he doesn't have to worry about*— And Anthem would change the subject or cut her off because the idea of his best buddy being a bone-smoker felt oddly like some kind of betrayal, and worse, Nikki's insistence on bringing it up all the time told him she was trying to prepare *him* for the possibility, and not herself.

But none of that mattered now. What mattered was, his passenger's frosty silence notwithstanding, that everything suddenly felt like a gift to Anthem Landry. They had just entered that spot in the middle of the causeway where it was impossible to see land and, for the first time, he knew complete contentment. Or at least what he thought contentment should feel like; it was such a grown-up word, so superior sounding and so removed from the hormonal mood swings of adolescence.

What Anthem Landry felt that night was the sense that he and the two people closest to him were living in a sacred space between great moments in their lives. And for years afterward, whenever he was in pain or trapped in the dark minutes of another sleepless night, he would exert all the effort he could to return to that lone, blissful hour. To Fred LeBlanc's voice singing about how the morning mist arises through a crack in the glass after another sleepless night of wishing someone would take him back to New Orleans. To the hot wind ripping through the half-open windows and the briny smell of the moon-rippled lake water. To that eternal, frozen hour, buffed and polished to perfection, a lens focused perfectly on past promise.

For years afterward, the sound of oyster shells cracking under tires ignited a low flame in the pit of his stomach because that was the sound that brought an end to so many things. That sound, and the sight of Elysium's long curving driveway, empty and deeply shadowed behind the padlocked cast-iron gate. He tried Nikki on her cell but got her voice mail.

That didn't mean anything, Ben insisted. Coverage on this part of the North Shore was always spotty.

Twenty minutes. That's how long they lasted, twenty minutes of listening to the ticking sound of the truck's cooling engine mingling with the moist undertones of the swamp, before Anthem pointed out the strangeness of the situation.

"This is weird," Anthem said. "They should be here by now." And Ben started right in with all the assurances, all the elaborate possibilities as to where they could have stopped along the way and why. Gas stations, grocery stores. Maybe a flat tire or two or three. Never mind that Ben had spoken to Nikki on the phone just as the family was heading out the back door, over an hour before Anthem had left Metairie to pick up Ben at his parent's house Uptown. Never mind that Mr. Noah was a taskmaster who defined punctuality; if he knew the boys were joining the family tonight, which he most certainly did, he would have had the house open and blazing with light to greet their arrival.

After an hour, and four calls to Nikki's cell, Ben ran out of explanations.

After an hour and a half and no return call from Nikki, Anthem ran out of patience.

He made a three-point turn in the rutted road and drove back to the highway. There was a gas station next to the turnoff and Ben wanted to see if anyone working there had seen the Delongpre's Lexus SUV.

Later that night, they'd both learn that if Anthem had kept driving for about another half mile on Highway 22, they just might have noticed the mangled stretch of guardrail through which the Delongpre family had disappeared.

7

NEW ORLEANS

*P*lease God, Marissa thought. *Not another endless conversation about what did or didn't happen to the Delongpres.* But as she walked the perimeter of the carpeted ballroom, she realized the other guests that evening were mostly white, well-fed Uptown folk, just like the missing family in question, and that meant Marissa Hopewell would have a better chance that evening of avoiding a conversation about the weather.

Noah, Millie, and Niquette Delongpre had vanished exactly a week ago, leaving behind only pieces of their Lexus SUV along the banks of Bayou Rabineaux. Forget about the five young black men, two of them teenagers, who had been gunned down in cold blood just a few blocks from where Marissa lived with her mother in the Lower Ninth Ward. Apparently, the Delongpres made for better television. Or at least their ironically cheerful family photographs did.

Even so, Marissa had still combed through all the articles on their disappearance. Hell, she'd even started a file on the case to see if it had the makings of a good column. But for now the details were too sketchy, the concerns a little too Garden District for her taste. And she found herself jumping to the same conclusion as the other women who worked at her paper; the father, one of the top surgeons in his field, had made enough money over the years to stash plenty in bank accounts throughout the world if he'd wanted to. He'd probably staged the whole thing, maybe even offed his wife and daughter so he could run off with his exotic, foreign mistress. That, or the whole thing was just some weird tax evasion stunt that would come to light as soon as the police finished combing through Noah Delongpre's files.

It never ceased to amaze Marissa how often rich white men ran afoul of the IRS.

As she searched for the table number printed on her place card, she saw that while she wasn't the only full-figured black lady in the room—five in all, including her, and not counting the servers—she was the lone pantsuit in a sea of tuxedos and off-the-shoulder cocktail dresses. For the most part, the guests looked jovial and carefree, despite the strange disappearance of three of their own. Maybe coming out en masse to support a scrappy little French Quarter theater now in its seventy-fifth year of operation made Uptown's best and brightest feel spiritually connected. Or maybe the special Sazeracs mentioned on the invite were going right to everyone's head.

The event's organizers had dressed up the Plimsoll Club for the occasion, although Marissa was having trouble figuring out the exact theme. Flowing blue drapes imprinted with stars and lightning bolts framed the walls of plate-glass windows, and the view stretched all the way from the Mississippi River Bridge to the Central Business District's humble cluster of buildings. They were thirty-one stories above the spot where Canal Street met the river, inside the circle of steel girders that sat atop the World Trade Center, an X-shaped skyscraper that was a little too heavy on the concrete for Marissa's taste. (And a little too sixties and out-of-date to hold such a prominent place in the city's skyline, if you asked her. But nobody had. And it wasn't like some Fortune 500 company had offered to tear it down and build something nicer in its place.)

All of the waiters and strolling performers were dressed in flowing medieval costumes Marissa couldn't quite put a label to. Were they supposed to be at a circus or a Renaissance festival? *Venetian Carnival,* read the invitation in her hand. Not quite, she thought, but that certainly explained the bejeweled, feathered masks that covered their faces. She wasn't there to pull a Tom Wolfe on the night's proceedings, but that didn't stop her from taking mental notes on everything.

Her boss had slid the invitation into her hand earlier that day because the theater was honoring its first (and only) black executive director, and well, that seemed like something that might fit well in Marissa's weekly column. The man's smile was just tense enough to acknowledge the strange place Marissa occupied as the only black columnist at *Kingfisher.* The paper was a household name in New Orleans and a formidable rival to *The Times-Picayune.* But it was staffed largely by do-gooder white kids, and even after three years, most of them reacted to her as if she was an intelligent life form from another planet. Fact was, most white people in New Orleans weren't equipped to deal with a black woman who didn't speak in the halting, drawling patois of the housekeepers who had helped raise them. Take away the accent altogether, add a bachelor's from the University of Chicago and three years at the *Chicago Tribune* and oh, lordy! They practically quaked in their books thinking she was going to demand reparations on the spot.

When she saw the Ferriots seated at her table, each step across the plush carpeting seemed to place an even greater strain on her calves. Marissa had expected to spend the night feeling out of place. But the Ferriots were Garden District, King of Carnival–style rich, the kind of family that made weekly appearances on the society page of *The Times-Picayune* because they just couldn't stop handing out piles and piles of their own hard-earned money.

When Marissa took the empty seat across from her, Heidi Ferriot glanced up from her wineglass as if she'd heard a short, high-pitched sound from somewhere across the room, just sharp enough to have been a nuisance but not loud enough for her to investigate with more than a frown. (A frown intended to make someone else, preferably someone who worked for her, do something about it.) Her black velvet dress had a sloping white collar that made her look like a calla lily stuffed inside a black stocking. Next to her, Donald Ferriot looked their way with a wan smile; he'd been turned around in his chair, studying one of the costumed jugglers weaving expertly in between the tables. The man's explosion of downy salt-and-pepper curls and oversize bow tie made him look like a mad scientist attending the Bride of Frankenstein's wedding. (If the Bride of Frankenstein had decided to get married in Monaco.)

And then there was the son. Marissa had trouble remembering his name at first. Maxwell? Meyer? No. Marshall.

That was it. Strange kid. For some reason, he couldn't bring himself to look up from the designs he was tracing in the white tablecloth with his dinner fork. (The kid's slow, repetitive motions reminded Marissa of some Hitchcock film, something with Gregory Peck and ski tracks in the snow.) He was far more handsome than both of his parents, with his high, sculpted cheekbones and his jet-black hair, slicked back like some 1950s matinee idol.

"Careful, folks," Donald Ferriot said, with a tip of his wineglass at Marissa. "The press is here."

She was embarrassed by how pleased she was to be recognized, especially by a man of Donald Ferriot's alleged stature. But she tipped her glass in return. "Just here to cover the awards ceremony. All comments at this table are officially off the record."

There was a light ripple of laughter from the other guests, but not one of them bothered with an introduction. Heidi Ferriot, on the other hand, gazed at Marissa mirthlessly.

"I know everyone who works on the society page at the *Picayune*," she finally said. "And I don't remember you."

"You wouldn't. We've never met."

"Yes, that I gathered."

"Also, I don't do society columns and I don't work for the *Picayune*."

"She writes for *Kingfisher*," Donald Ferriot said.

"Ah," Heidi Ferriot said, and the sound was more breath than syllable. "That makes sense," she whispered.

Because Kingfisher *is more liberal than the Picayune. And you're black. And not the kind of café-au-lait, is-she-or-isn't-she kind of black my kind of white lady is more comfortable with. And oh, by the way, how the hell did your* black ass *end up at my table?*

Marissa told herself to cut it out, to stop letting the voices of her own insecurities masquerade as insight. Sometimes being the odd one out meant you had to give other people the chance to show you they weren't always—

"And what do your people do?" Heidi Ferriot asked.

"I'm sorry. My *people*?"

"I'm sorry. I didn't say *you* people. I said—"

"I heard what you said," Marissa answered. "My mother's retired now."

"And your husband?"

"Haven't met him yet."

"And your mother. What did she do before she . . . *retired*?" There was too much emphasis on the last word for Marissa's liking. It suggested that in Heidi Ferriot's world, black women didn't retire, they just went on the dole.

"She was a dance teacher."

"So at some point, presumably, she was a *dancer*?" Heidi asked.

"When she was younger, yes. She taught children, mostly. Through church groups and the like. She had her own studio for a while but she gave it up when I was a girl."

"But not on Airline Highway. And not with a *pole*, I presume."

The brittle silence around her seemed to confirm it: *Yes*, the bowed heads and pinched mouths of the other guests seemed to say. *That bitch just called your mother a whore.*

Marissa was not an investigative journalist, but she was a columnist, and columnists lived off of access just like anyone else in the business. And you didn't get access by shooting off your mouth at fancy parties and taking things too personally. And yes, this may not have been the most significant event of her career, and the end of the night probably wouldn't deliver the makings of more than a passable column. But still. But still, but still, but *still* . . .

"Marissa?"

It took her a few seconds to realize it was the kid who'd spoken. And he'd used her first name as if they'd been lifelong friends.

"I asked you if you knew your snakes."

Asked. How long had he been speaking to her before she'd heard him? Was she on the verge of having a stroke? Was she really *that* angry?

"My snakes?"

"Yes. Your snakes."

"I'm not sure what you mean. I don't own any snakes."

Marissa was surprised to see that Donald and Heidi were looking not at her but at their son, and their expressions were suddenly tense. Were they afraid he was about to divulge some terrible family secret to this black journo? Or were they just afraid of their son in general? Too afraid to pull that fork out of his hand and slap some manners across the back of his head?

"I guess I should be more specific," Marshall said, but he was staring down at the table. Marissa thought, *The way he's working on that tablecloth, I'd bet he'd be just as happy doing that to his own leg. Or mine.* A strange thought, but the guy was plenty strange. "If you were confronted with a snake, would you be able to determine whether or not it was venomous?"

"That depends," Marissa said.

"On what?"

"I grew up here. So I know the snakes in this area. But if you dropped me in Texas, I'm not sure I'd be of much use on that front."

"I think it's important . . . in *life*, I mean, to be able to tell the difference between a snake that can actually kill you and a snake that just scares you. Don't you agree?"

"Well, maybe . . . but what if you're not afraid of snakes at all?"

"Are you not afraid of snakes, Marissa?"

In a low voice, Donald Ferriot said, "What's this about, Marshall?"

The kid was barely eighteen years old and talking to Marissa like she was his kindergarten teacher.

"Now, don't lie just for the sake of argument," he chided her. "That wouldn't be very polite, now, would it?"

"To be honest, Marshall, I'm more afraid of the snakes I might meet every day."

"I don't understand."

"The snakes I might be forced to have dinner with, for instance."

The silence around the table was as stilted and pained as it had been after Heidi Ferriot fired the first shot. Marissa was about to say something to lighten the mood but Marshall was suddenly staring straight past her head with such wide-eyed intensity that her words left her. One of the costumed waiters, or possibly one of the jugglers or mimes, had caught the kid's eye. Caught *both* of his eyes in one tense fist was more like it. The longer Marissa stared at him, the more it became clear that Marshall Ferriot had gone entirely still, so still it felt as if the air pressure around them shifted suddenly. As if Marshall had been rendered so rigid and devoid of life, the air itself was literally avoiding him.

"What's the matter?" Donald Ferriot asked his son. "Are you getting sick again?"

In response, Marshall got to his feet and started walking toward the nearest plate-glass window. He picked up an empty metal folding chair a bartender had been resting his feet on a few minutes earlier. The chair had heavy cushions on the back and seat, so when he lifted it in both hands, the seat's weight forced it to fold automatically.

"Oh shit," Marissa whispered. She was convinced the kid was about to do something truly, truly stupid, probably in some kind of sick retaliation for Marissa's crack about snakes. When Marshall was still several paces from the plate-glass window, he swung the chair back over one shoulder as if it were as light and slender as a baseball bat.

He'll just try to make a commotion, Marissa thought. *He'll hurl the chair at the window to get the entire room's attention and then—*

The first crash got everyone's attention all right. But Marshall didn't stop there. He slammed the chair into the glass again and again and again, with a ferocity and determination that kept everyone glued to their chairs. The room was a sea of frightened expressions and napkins brought to mouths. Around the fourth strike, the kid had managed to punch several large holes in the plate glass, and the cracks radiating out from each one looked poised to bring the entire window apart.

Then Marshall tossed the chair to one side and took several steps backward. He had backed up almost to the nearest table when a terrible realization of what he was about to do swept the room. There were several small screams. Then Marissa was on her feet.

If she'd thrown herself at Marshall, tried to tackle him to the ground like he was a quarterback, she might have been able to prevent what happened next. But the kid was a good two feet taller than her. And it was a moot point anyway because when she reached for his shoulder, she missed.

Marshall hurled himself face-first into the perforated glass. *Like something out of a goddamn cartoon,* Marissa thought. The collision made a deep, bone-rattling thud tinged with the violent metallic rattle of the giant window's frame.

But the window held.

The kid's right shoulder was wedged inside one of the holes he'd punched with the chair; it looked to Marissa like he was trying to pry himself free. He was dazed and disoriented, his forehead sprouting blood from a dozen different cuts. But when he looked back into the room, his eyes found Marissa and she saw utter lifelessness in them. It was as if the kid's spirit had literally been drained out of him.

In the years to come, Marissa would try to convince herself that it was the impact with the window that had knocked Marshall Ferriot's senses from him, but that look—the emptiness of it, its *soullessness*—would stalk most of Marissa's quiet moments for the rest of her life.

The group of tuxedoed men who had gathered behind her and Donald Ferriot froze where they stood. The glass Marshall was plastered against was too fragile for anyone to make a sudden move, she realized.

Marshall's jaw went slack. His Adam's apple jerked in his blood-splattered throat.

"I . . . I . . . put a . . ."

And as soon as his son's words seemed to sputter out into ragged breaths of delirium, Donald Ferriot broke free from the group and lunged for his son. And even though the men all around him could sense Donald's terrible mistake before he made it, none of them got to him in time.

Donald crossed the carpet with too much speed and force. He stumbled in his final steps, pitching forward into his son's body. And for a few seconds, it seemed like it would just be a slight nudge, that's all. But as Donald Ferriot threw his arms around his son's waist and prepared to pull him free of the glass spiderweb he'd hurled himself into, the window gave way right in its weakened center and both men became a single tangle of limbs that vanished in an instant.

Then it sounded to Marissa like all the chairs in the room had gone over at once. Silverware and glasses were knocked from the tables as everyone jumped to their feet at the same moment. The screams came next; a single piercing wave of them that said the shock of what they had all witnessed had worn off almost instantly.

To Marissa it felt like a stampede, and in the midst of it somehow, Heidi Ferriot ended up in her arms, her knees going out from under her, the bellows coming out of her a blend of rage and agony. Marissa wanted to lift her hands to her ears to blot out the terrible sound; instead she held tight to the shuddering wreck of a woman who was making them.

8

The oak branches outside Ben Broyard's window cast dancing shadows on his bedroom ceiling. Night had fallen hours ago, but he was too exhausted to reach for the bedside lamp. This wasn't just exhaustion, he knew, but a bone-deep sense of loss that felt completely alien. Not just alien. *Adult*. That was the thought he kept returning to; that what had happened this week to him, to Anthem, to *all* of them, was an *adult* thing, more significant and lasting than graduating high school or having sex for the first time.

Loss. Grief. Words that had tumbled off his tongue too easily over the years but which he'd learned the real meaning of only that week, when his best friend was replaced by a yawning, fathomless darkness surrounding miles of empty swamp road. He'd always been the mature one, the one who said the adult thing in every situation, but now he realized that to be mature, you had to know more than the dictionary definition of words; you had to know what it felt like when those words hit you in the gut.

Ben was only ten when his father died, an aneurysm during dinner that dropped the man to one knee next to the kitchen table, and then face-first into oblivion. And what he remembered most about that time was how Nikki's parents let her sleep in his bed because her prolonged embrace was the only thing that allowed him to get through the night without waking up in tears. He could remember how everyone had closed in around him en masse; his best friend, aunts, uncles, cousins, even his mother, who'd just been made a widow in her late thirties—they had all worked in concert to protect him, the baby, the only child of a good man gone too soon.

How many times had he heard those two words back then? Too soon, too soon. Well, *eighteen* was also too soon, right?

Still, everything about this week was different. He wasn't the baby anymore, for one, and he had no special status amongst all those who had gathered on the banks of Bayou Rabineaux, spreading grid maps of Tangipahoa Parish across the hoods of their sun-baked cars, loading into fantail boats to assist in the fruitless search. No one left behind was special or more significant than any other. That's what the sudden disappearance of an entire family could do; it sent out a pressure wave that leveled all their loved ones with the same explosive force, rendering them incapable of caring for the man, woman or child standing next to them.

At times, he'd found himself praying to a God he wasn't sure he believed in and asking the simple question, *Is this how you would have me grow up? Not with a great love or some accomplishment, but the sudden unexplained absence of the person I cared most about in the world? Is this how you would have me start in the big wide grown-up world?*

Nikki, the only person in his life who'd taken him aside and told him she would always be there, no matter who he turned out to be. No matter who he fell in love with. And what had he done? Just nodded and smiled as if she'd offered him a ride home after school that day, as if he didn't understand what she truly meant. *Yeah, thanks, Nick. Hey, that new cheerleader's kinda hot, maybe I should ask her out, huh?*

Down the hall, his mother had turned up the volume on the TV just enough to let him know she was parked in the living room a few feet from the front door. And because their house was a small shotgun cottage, that meant she had the back door in plain sight as well. So he was basically under house arrest. Again.

If she hadn't called and made them come home when she did, he and Anthem would probably still be traveling back roads, hanging missing-persons flyers all over the state. But it had been a hell of a first day, that was for sure.

They'd started around dawn and managed to hit every gas station window and restaurant bulletin board from Madisonville to Gonzales. They had a flyer for each of them. Nikki, Mr. Noah and Miss Millie. And for most of the day, it had felt good. They were *doing* something. Being proactive, as Ben's mother liked to say.

But after she ordered them home, their adrenaline surges subsided, and as they were driving back on Interstate 10, the setting sun a blood-orange bonfire behind them, each too consumed with thoughts to turn on the radio, that's when Anthem exploded with the first sobs he'd let lose since Nikki vanished. And they were snotty, choked things, desperate wheezes combined with terrible, gut-clenching whines, and Ben could only rest his hand on Anthem's shaking knee lest he lose control of his car. And after a while, he managed to speak again. "I was going to go. I was going to go with her, to North Carolina. That's what I was . . . That's what I was—" *going to tell her that night,* Ben knew; Anthem didn't need to finish.

Now, as Ben watched the dance of shadows on his ceiling, he envisioned the flyers the two of them had left all over the state that day. He saw the black-and-white faces of Nikki, Mr. Noah and Ms. Millie staring out at night-shrouded highways, their frozen smiles abandoned to the reluctant company of bored gas station attendants and grimy shelves of junk food.

Better to see these things, he guessed, than to imagine what might have become of their SUV that night. The scraps of evidence they'd been left with could be easily assembled into a nightmare: the mangled guardrail scraped with banners of black paint that matched their Lexus, two cracked pieces of rear bumper, one half of the SUV's rear window that had been recovered from the mud a good distance from where they went off the road. All he had to do was run through this list in his head before he saw Nikki trapped inside the sinking car, fists pounding the windows, black water rushing in to fill her screaming mouth.

It was the third or fourth ring, he couldn't be sure which one exactly, that stopped his tears.

"It was him," the girl on the other end said as soon as Ben picked up.

Not Nikki. And he wondered if he'd be sidelined by this realization for the rest of his life, whenever the phone rang unexpectedly. But he did recognize the girl's voice. After the hell he'd put her through, and the confession he'd wrung from her, he figured Brittany Lowe would never speak to him again, but here she was.

"You asked me why I did it," Brittany said. "The story, about hooking up with Anthem. You asked me why I—"

"Why you lied. Yeah, I remember."

"He wanted me to."

"Anthem?"

"No! Jesus. Aren't you watching the news?"

"I'm kinda tired, you see, my best friend, she disappeared last week and we're still looking for her so—"

"Marshall Ferriot," she said, unwilling to be the victim of his sarcasm. "The guy who just jumped out a window at the Plimsoll Club?" Ben was stunned silent. "He's the one. He's the one who asked me to lie,

all right? I figured I'd just tell you now since, you know, it doesn't look like he's going to *live* and all."

When Ben didn't respond, Brittany Lowe let out a long, pained sigh and hung up, leaving Ben staring at the hardwood floor, rings of sweat beading in between his face and the phone that was now trembling in his right hand.

9

"You're a liar!"

The boy couldn't have been any older than sixteen, but his outburst left Marissa Hopewell standing gape-mouthed a few steps from the entrance to her office building.

She was as startled by the kid's physical appearance as she was by his shrill accusation. Business-casual pedestrians weaved around him as his thick patch of sandy-blond hair danced in the hot wind, the same wind that kept turning her breasts into a boat's prow under her flapping peasant dress. He was older than he looked at first glance; it was his height—five foot two, tops—that made him look like a child, and an angry one at that. The rest of him was all milk-white skin, a small, round face dominated by huge blue eyes—bloodshot from hours of crying, it looked like—and a full-lipped mouth so generous it made him look like he was constantly sneering.

He looked vaguely familiar, too. Like a child actor she'd seen play bit parts in movies over the years.

Bev Legendre, *Kingfisher*'s ad sales director, put a protective hand on Marissa's shoulder, while the other ladies they'd just had lunch with hovered close by, deciding whether or not to call the security guard.

"I'm sorry. But I don't know who you are," Marissa tried in her best maternal voice. But the kid screwed his eyes shut and shook his head as if her soothing tone was enough of an accusation to rival the one he'd just made.

"You had a fight with him. Before he did it. Before he jumped. But you just left that part out, didn't you?"

"*Young man,* how 'bout you calm yourself down and—" Bev cut in, with a tone of whiskey-voiced authority. Marissa placed a hand on the woman's shoulder and gave her a slight nod. Bev withdrew and went to join the other women, a few of whom were now stationed inside the lobby doors, pretending not to stare and doing a bad job of it.

"You're a friend of Marshall Ferriot's?"

Instead of answering, the kid said, "I talked to everyone who was at the table that night and they said your column was crap!"

"Well, there's no accounting for taste."

"How about lying? Is there any accounting for *lying*?"

She'd regretted her wisecrack as soon as it was out of her mouth, but when the bundle of hostility a few feet away reacted with that dreaded accusation yet again, she had to work to unclench her fists. She'd averaged three hours of sleep a night since the horrors she'd witnessed in the Plimsoll Club, and reliving it all again for the column her editor had leaned on her to write certainly hadn't helped much. In fact, it had resulted in her first visit to Sunday services in months, which had thrilled her mother no end, but left Marissa feeling a little desperate and weak.

But one thing was for sure; the teenager before her was in a lot more pain than she was, and she was willing to endure another few insults to find out why.

But had she *lied*?

It was an op-ed column, for Christ's sake. Teen suicides had been the focus, not the gory blow-by-blow of Marshall Ferriot's horrific and fatal jump. Not *her*. But maybe that was just it. Lies of omission were the worst kind, really, maybe because they were so damn prevalent. Was that what he was accusing her of? Some unpleasant words exchanged with the victim before his leap and suddenly she was, what? A part of the story?

Come on, girl. Don't act like you haven't thought it yourself over the past few nights, staring up at the ceiling, remembering the soullessness in his eyes when he hit that window. Wondering if maybe you'd tipped a crazy man over the edge with that cute little line about having dinner with snakes.

"I'm very sorry about what happened to your friend," she said.

"He wasn't my friend," the kid muttered. And something about this admission seemed to make him more present; he registered their audience inside the lobby and his eyes widened with embarrassment. And there was that wet sheen again, but he quickly blinked it away.

"Then what was he?" she asked.

"His mother, she was being rude. Asking you questions about your family. Your *people*. Some of the other people at the table, they thought it was racist."

Well, glad I wasn't the only one, Marissa thought.

The boy continued. "But then Marshall . . ." And Marissa saw for the first time that uttering the guy's name seemed to make her surprise visitor sick to his stomach. "Marshall . . . he asked you something about snakes . . ."

"Yes. He did . . ."

And it pained her to answer. It made her realize that yes, there was plenty of weirdness before Marshall's big leap, and she'd left it all out.

Maybe if she'd taken a deep breath while she was writing the damn thing. If she hadn't rushed through it and let her sleeplessness get the best of her. And maybe she'd left out those pesky details because she didn't want to be writing the damn column in the first place. The whole thing felt gruesome and invasive and she couldn't find the right words to describe that mind-bending night. Hell, she'd also left out the part about how Marshall's mother, a woman who had radiated contempt for Marissa just moments before, had somehow ended up sobbing in her arms, sobbing for a son who would be declared brain-dead when he was wheeled into Ochsner Medical Center an hour later, and for a husband who had died breaking their son's thirty-one-story fall.

"And you said something back," the kid said, only his voice had gone soft, and maybe that was because Marissa couldn't look him in the eye anymore.

"He asked me if I could recognize certain snakes in the wild and I said I was more worried about the snakes I might have to have dinner with." And as soon as the words left her mouth, she saw the soulless look in Marshall's eyes again, the lattice of cuts on the boy's face. And . . . *Oh my God. Holy mother. He'd* said *something! He actually said something and I plum forgot it with everything that—*

She didn't want her struggle to remember Marshall Ferriot's last words—*maybe* they'd be his last words; he wasn't technically dead yet—to show on her face, not with her tiny accuser still standing right there, looking calm and focused now that she'd been thrown off her game.

"You forgot, didn't you?" The boy said. "That he said something . . . before the window gave way . . ."

"I put . . . That was it. He said, *I put a* . . . And then. That was it. The window gave and he was gone. He and his father . . . just gone."

His slight nod told her she'd just given him what he'd really come for, that her sudden recollection matched what the other guests at

Table 10 had told him. And only then did she stop to consider how remarkable it was that this quaking teenager had managed to get to all of those people in just a few day's time. Her column had gone up on the website just the day before, and it wouldn't be in the print edition until Monday. So, either he'd done his investigative work in a day, or he'd been working this since it happened. Working it, or living it, she wasn't quite sure, given that the kid's connection to Marshall Ferriot still wasn't clear. Either way, holy crap! Who *was* this little guy?

"Is that why you went to church with your mother last Sunday? 'Cause you feel responsible for what happened to Marshall Ferriot?"

"That's stalking, son."

"Oh, but if I was you, it'd be journalism, right?"

"It'll *all* be semantics when my mother pulls the pepper spray."

"And you still won't have answered my question."

"I went to church because I haven't been sleeping well since it happened and I believe in *something,* so I thought it might help."

"Did it?"

"Yes. But so did wine."

"My mother drinks wine to go to sleep too."

"Yeah, well, if I had to deal with your mouth every day, I might need wine to get up in the morning."

"That's nice."

"I see. So *nice* was your objective here?"

"Well, if your objective is *not* to answer my question, then—"

"Tell you what. If one of those nice ladies over there steps in front of a truck by mistake later today, you gonna feel responsible because you shot off your mouth at them before they had time to digest their lunch?"

"It's not the same thing and you know it—"

"Don't tell me what I *know,* young man."

"He bashed out a plate-glass window with a metal folding chair and threw himself against it. He took a *running start,* for Christ's sake!"

"I know what he did. I was there. I saw it!"

"Yeah, but you didn't *write* it. No, you wrote all about teen suicides and mental health resources in high schools. Oh, and you took a bunch of pot shots at *my* high school because everybody who goes there is rich—"

"Rich *and*?"

"I didn't say that."

"The answer's no. I don't feel responsible. I think Marshall Ferriot was clearly unbalanced and it wasn't going to take much to tip him."

"I'll say," the kid growled under his breath.

"But you're asking the wrong question."

"How so?"

"You should ask me if I regret saying it."

He was regarding her for the first time without open hostility, and she felt the tension in her chest turn into a vague wash of heat that ran down into the pit of her stomach.

"Do I think he tried to jump out that window because of me? Hell, no. But what I said to him that night might be the last words he ever hears. And they were unkind and they were meant for his mother. So yes, I regret saying it. I do. But if you're after some kind of truth with me today, son, let me tell you the only thing I know to be true, one hundred percent. Nothing in life is under our control except how we treat people. Nothing."

It didn't look like she'd knocked the wind out of him, but those big, bloodshot eyes of his had wandered to some point just behind her, and she realized he had the look of someone reading off a script. And when he spoke again, she was startled to stillness by how devoid of emotion his voice was.

"Junior year we had a transfer student come to Cannon named Suzy Laborde. Her parents didn't have two pennies to rub together, but Suzy was a killer math student so she got a scholarship and she worked her ass off to stay there. She was from outside Thibodaux, so that was about a two-hour drive each way. Her mom would have to drop her off near school at six in the morning so she could get back to Houma in time for her first job. So Suzy would have to wander the neighborhood for a couple hours, maybe hang out at gas stations 'cause those were the only places open that time of day. Sometimes Mom and I would see her on the way in and we'd give her a ride. But most people just ignored her.

"She didn't care that barely anyone would give her the time of day. She didn't care that she couldn't afford the nice clothes the other girls wore. She didn't ask to be invited to anyone's parties and she sure as hell didn't expect to be Homecoming Queen. And I don't think she gave two shits when Marshall Ferriot started spreading rumors that he'd seen a roach crawl out of her shirt during assembly.

"Then she made a mistake, see. We were all in American History class and the teacher had put Marshall on the spot. I can't even remember what the question was but Marshall didn't know the answer and the teacher was letting him hang himself. And then Suzy jumped in and corrected him. And she was right. And I remember thinking, *Oh shit, Suzy. Now he's really going to come for you.*"

A sudden spike of emotion caused the kid to suck in a deep breath. Marissa watched, silently, as he gritted his teeth in an attempt to get his composure back.

"Cannon has this big courtyard in the middle of school. And there's a giant oak tree right in the center with these benches all around it. Suzy and one of the art teachers built this birdhouse for the doves that used to nest in the tree. It was like her thing. She was out there every morning and every afternoon, feeding the birds. Making sure the house was still in one piece.

"One morning, when everyone was in the courtyard before first period, Suzy went to check on the birdhouse and she saw someone had nailed a piece of wood over the opening. And there was a smell coming from inside it, a bad smell. So bad, nobody was sitting near the tree that day. So she ran and got some maintenance staff and they pulled the board off . . . and I just remember her screaming. Screaming so loud everyone in school could hear. See, there was a security light in the tree right over the birdhouse and whoever had nailed the birdhouse shut had replaced the bulb in it with a heat lamp. The doves had cooked to death overnight."

"And you think Marshall did it?" Marissa asked.

"I *know* he did it."

"How?"

"Because I went to every hardware store in Orleans *and* Jefferson Parish before I found the clerk who sold him the bulb. And I took what I found to Suzy and I told her we had to go to the upper-school principal. And she begged me not to because if her parents found out that anyone that *crazy* was threatening her at Cannon, they'd pull her out in a heartbeat. Because they were tired of driving her two hours every day, tired of her needing to be too good to wait tables like her mother. And that's the only reason Marshall got away with it."

"Because Suzy asked you not to do anything," Marissa said.

"All I'm saying, Miss Hopewell, is that maybe you should let yourself off the hook if you were *unkind* to Marshall Ferriot. Also, they say most coma patients can hear everything that's said in the room with them. So that comment you made to him in the Plimsoll Club. It's not like it'll be the last thing he hears. Not until he decides to die."

"Is that what you really believe?" she asked. "You think he's in some kind of limbo?"

"Well, if he's not in hell, I hope he's got a real good view."

The kid's jaw was quivering again, and the wet sheen in his eyes was back, and that's when Marissa realized why he'd looked vaguely familiar. His jaw was quivering the first time she ever laid eyes on him, on the WDSU nightly news, when he was one of scores of other well-dressed Uptown teenagers and their parents standing along the banks of Bayou Rabineaux and setting glowing Japanese lanterns adrift in the black waters that had swallowed the Delongpre family with one final, unforgiving gulp.

The Delongpres. Funny how the name itself had been scrubbed from her memory by the horrors she had witnessed at the Plimsoll Club.

"What's your name?"

But he was halfway down the block, and he was moving so fast down the grim little concrete canyon, the white soles of tennis shoes seemed to be winking at her.

10

"I want you back in school tomorrow," Peyton Broyard told her son when she found him slouching in front of his laptop. She'd only been home from the grocery store a minute or two when she abandoned her bags in the kitchen and came straight to Ben's room, and that meant the message she had to deliver was important *with a capital I, P, T and another T*, as she liked to say.

Ben's mother had stopped searching his face for evidence of teenage secrets a while ago, mostly because she wasn't any good at it. Too many alarmist news stories about teenagers and drugs had given her the false sense that her only child was a lot more predictable then he actually was. Three times last year she'd accused him of *recreational cough medicine abuse* when in each case he was just sluggish at breakfast because he'd been up most of the night downloading pirated gay porn.

Now, as she stood planted in his doorway like a miniature Beefeater with a festive scarf, Ben was reminded once again of how his mother would always look twice as masculine as him, even when she was decked out in J.Jill. They were almost the same height, but the gymnastics training she'd gone through as a young girl had left her brawny and bullish. Her Suze Orman haircut and sharp jawline didn't do much to soften her appearance either.

It had been a few hours since Ben's run-in with Marissa Hopewell and he'd spent the time since perusing Nikki's Myspace page, now plastered with heartfelt tributes from students who just couldn't go on with their lives in the wake of her disappearance even though they'd hardly said more than a few words to her in their lifetimes. But it wasn't the desire of his classmates to cast themselves as major stars in *The Great Delongpre Disappearance* that had left him dazed. And it wasn't his spat with Marissa Hopewell either. It was the dawning realization that he and Anthem probably wouldn't be doing any more flyering anytime soon, not after what had happened the day before.

"Mom, I have *two* classes tomorrow and I'm passing both of them."

"That's great. And I want you back in some kind of routine, so you're going to go to both. Even if you plan on getting a C in both."

"I've never made a C in my life."

The doorbell startled them. Theirs was a small shotgun cottage on a block of mansions, so it was just a few paces to the front door, down a short hallway wallpapered with the annual Jazz Fest posters his mother collected and had framed every spring.

In her youth, Peyton Broyard might have blanched at the sight of a strange black woman standing on her front porch, but Ben thought even that was growth considering his grandmother had once said to him of black people, *They're like dogs, Ben. You can't show them you're afraid of them.* But Peyton's widowhood had included several dalliances with black men. Also, after a second or two of awkward silence, it became clear to everyone that Marissa Hopewell wasn't a stranger to her at all.

"I read your columns!" his mother cried.

"Thank you."

"You're wrong most of the time, but I read you anyway."

"Well, good. That's what they're for."

"So why are you—" Peyton turned and gave her son a look. Then pivoted toward Marissa, one hand going up as if to ward off an offer of Girl Scout cookies. "Oh, no, no, no. No interviews. Nah uh. No way!"

"Uhm, actually, Mrs. Broyard, your son came to interview *me* earlier today."

"I see," Peyton said. "So we didn't do more flyering, did we?"

"I didn't say we did," Ben answered.

"You didn't say you didn't either."

"Hey. Can we do this all night?" Ben suggested. "It'll be awesome!"

To Marissa, Peyton said, "Are you here to sue us?"

"Well, your son is a very articulate young man. I'll say that much."

"My son is a verbal terrorist who doesn't believe in personal boundaries." Peyton's stage whisper must have been for effect because Ben heard every word.

"I see . . ." Marissa answered, searching Ben's face. The woman was probably trying to figure out if Ben had been wounded by his mother's description, or if the two of them always sparred like this. Ben rolled his eyes to let her know it was the latter. "You know what they say. One man's terrorist is another man's—"

"Journalist?" Ben finished for her.

"Who says that?" Peyton asked. "No one says that."

Then she saw the two of them smiling at each other and realized it was a joke. "All right, well, come on in. Since you seem to be friends and all. Just think twice before you give this one a *platform*, okay? He's loud enough already."

A few minutes later, Ben and Marissa were outside in the backyard, seated at a wrought-iron patio table blanketed by the deepening shadows cast by the oak tree overhead. The yard was sandbox size and it always felt to Ben like the oak was going to literally take it over one day. His mother had worked hard to cover the fences with walls of bougain-villea, and a moss-dappled cherub sat on a lone stone bench at the very rear of the garden.

Peyton brought them both glasses of iced tea. Then she departed with a bright smile, relieved that her son was someone else's worry, if only for the next few minutes or so.

"Were you pulling my leg when you said you went to every hard-ware store in Orleans Parish to find that bulb?" Marissa finally asked.

"Which bulb?"

"The one that killed those birds at your school."

"The one Marshall used to kill those birds? No. I wasn't pulling your leg."

"Jesus . . . Do you ever actually go to school?"

"I'm a second-semester senior and I was already accepted to Tulane. I don't really *need* to go to school."

"Well, there's always the whole *learning* aspect, especially if you want to go into journalism."

"Who said I wanted to go into journalism?"

"You did, when you went around acting like a reporter."

"I'm working on a novel."

"Don't bother. There're too many already and not enough people to read them."

"*Seriously?* You realize you said that out loud, right?"

Her arch smile told him she didn't care. She seemed utterly at ease in his presence despite their brief, tempestuous history together; when she took a sip of iced tea and brushed her free-form dread-locks back from her brow, she did so with hands that were still and controlled, unlike his own. He envied her stillness, her maturity. Her poise.

"You know," she said, "I recognized you today. From the news.

That's how I found out who you were. You're one of Niquette Delong-pre's friends. That's what the flyers are about, right?"

"We're done with the flyers."

"Why's that?"

"Something bad happened yesterday."

"Oh?"

"My mom said no interviews."

"And I haven't said the word once."

"We were in Ponchatoula and Anthem wanted to put some up in this sorry-ass little bar. I didn't think we should go inside but he wouldn't listen. So he just barged right in and started giving his little speech. Like about how our friend might be lost and she was in an accident so maybe she's disoriented and wandering around out in the swamp somewhere and doesn't even remember her name—" Saying the words now made him believe them even less, and remembering Anthem's pained desperation as he'd said them, studded with pathetic attempts at good cheer, made Ben want to cry. "The bartender went off on us 'cause he thought we were scaring off his customers. But Anthem didn't give a sh—damn. He just kept at it. So finally the guy ripped the flyer out of his hand and he read the date when they disappeared and said, 'Sorry, pal. Looks like your little slut walked out on you.' "

"That is unfortunate," Marissa said.

"Actually, the unfortunate part was when Anthem broke the guy's nose and knocked out two of his front teeth."

"Seriously?"

"Seriously."

"How old is this Anthem?"

"My age. But he's bigger. *A lot* bigger."

"Boyfriend?"

"Yeah . . ." Then he noticed she was studying him closely and he realized her words might have been some kind of trap. "*Her* boyfriend."

"I see," she said calmly. Apparently she would have had no problem hearing that Anthem was Ben's boyfriend. The idea was absurd, of course, but the fact that she would have accepted it so easily made Ben feel exhilarated and terrified at the same time.

For a while, they sat listening to the nearby fountain's gurgle and then the sustained wail of a train blowing its horn as it traveled the Mississippi's crescent.

"You can't blame me for thinking that if you're chewing me out over a column about Marshall Ferriot, you think there's some connection between what he did to himself and your friend's disappearance?"

"Remember how this isn't an interview?"

"I remember. But if you think there's a connection, I'd be curious to know why you wouldn't want it made public."

Ben looked away, ashamed by his inability to answer. All he could think of was the flask Anthem had brought him yesterday; silver, freshly polished, sloshing with bourbon. There'd been almost no time to savor their quick escape from that awful little bar before Anthem began to drink himself into a full-blown vomit fest.

Almost as bad as the sudden loss of his best friend was the dawning realization that his next-closest friend in the world was becoming completely unglued because of it and that in just a week's time, Anthem Landry had been sent the way of his bar-brawling, jail-visiting older brothers.

"Why are you here?" he asked her.

"You made an impression today."

"And you don't get a lot of chances to visit the Garden District?"

She flinched. It was slight, but he noticed it, and even though it wasn't much, it was more emotion than she'd shown him on the sidewalk that day, even when he was really laying in to her.

"That's offensive, Ben," she said quietly.

"I'm sorry."

She nodded but there was no awkward, placating smile, no real need for her to let him off the hook right away. She wasn't his teacher or his mother. And there was no denying it; he'd hurt her feelings. But he'd only been able to do that because she'd let her guard down. And if she'd let her guard down that meant her motives for being there were more pure than he'd imagined.

The idea that she might be genuinely concerned about him left him at a loss for words; worse, it threatened to undam a tide of emotions he'd held at bay for a good four or five hours now. He knew his mother loved him and cared about him, but as always she thought she could save him from his feelings by barking a bunch of sensible orders at him. And Anthem? Had Anthem once turned to him and asked him how *he* was handling everything? And for Christ's sake, he'd only been with Nikki for three years; Nikki had been Ben's closest friend in the world for fifteen.

He didn't want to go down that road. He really didn't. But he was so damn tired, and when he wasn't absorbed in some obsessive quest to find another person who had been sitting at Marshall's table that night, the inside of his head felt like a jar full of wasps.

"I think he caused the accident," Ben said.

It was the first time he'd said the words aloud, and their effect on Marissa was instantaneous. Her eyes widened and she leaned forward so far she had to place her fleshy elbows on the edge of the table. "Marshall Ferriot?"

"Yes."

"Start at the beginning."

"Nikki and Anthem broke up about a month ago because they had a big fight and this girl at our school claimed Anthem hooked up with her afterwards. The girl was lying. I got to her admit it. Then, when Marshall did his *thing,* the girl called and told me Marshall was the one who asked her to lie about it."

"Why'd she agree to lie?"

"The bottle of Vicodin Marshall lifted from his mother's medicine cabinet helped."

"Okay . . . Keep going."

"The night the Delongpres went missing, I went to the house before the cops got there. I knew where the key was. I didn't tear apart her room or anything. Mostly, I just wanted to see if any of her belongings were there. Like her cell phone or anything. There was *a* phone there, all right, but it was in her desk drawer and it wouldn't turn on, which was weird because it looked okay. But after a few minutes, I realized it had been soaked in water."

"Wait a minute. You think she came home *after* the accident and—"

Ben shook his head. "That's what I thought at the first. But the cops checked the records and saw the last call she'd made on it had been the week before. And I know she had another phone on her the night she went missing because I talked to her on it before Anthem and I left to go meet up with them at Elysium."

"So she replaced her phone, the week *before* she went missing?"

"Yep. Because it got soaked. Not wet. *Soaked*. And she didn't tell me where or how. And we told each other *everything*. But that wasn't all . . ."

"I'm listening."

"There was a card. It was on her desk. *Can't wait to see Elysium. XO, M.* I didn't make much of it at that time. There was going to be a party at Elysium that weekend, the weekend they . . . I mean, that's why we were all driving out there that night. But the more I thought about it, it just didn't seem right. And she only had one relative I know of whose names start with *M*, an uncle. And he died two years ago. Besides, the card had hearts all over it."

"But you've got no real proof the two of them went out there together."

"I've got the card."

"A card that says *M* on it."

"Marshall uses drug dealing and lies to try to break them up. Days after they get back together, her entire family disappears. A week later he throws himself out a thirty-one-story window and no one knows why. Remember his last words? The ones you couldn't remember until today? *I . . . put . . . a . . .*"

"I remember," Marissa said.

"I think he was trying to confess. I think he put something in their car. Maybe it was in the gas tank or the brakes, I don't know."

He could tell from the way she was staring openly at him, without any apparent regard for how her mouth was hanging open and her nostrils were flaring, that he almost had her. That she was more convinced by his theory than she would like to be. But all she said was: "Well, Mister Broyard, you are imaginative *and* articulate."

"Only when I have to be."

"Do you have to be?"

"You expect me not to find out the truth?"

"I think the truth is always good. And if that's what you're after, you'd be jumping at the chance to give me an interview. But you're not. Do the police know everything you just told me?"

"They know about the phone and the card."

"But not what Marshall did to try to break up your friends?"

Ben hoped it was dark enough that she couldn't make out his flaming cheeks.

"So you're keeping this all to yourself because you're afraid if your pal Anthem gets wind of it he'll yank Marshall Ferriot off life support."

"Marshall's in a coma, but he's not on life support."

"Still . . ."

"Something like that," Ben whispered.

"You really think Anthem's capable of that?"

"I didn't think he was capable of what he did to that bartender yesterday. But he did it. And I just stood there and watched him."

"It's not your job to keep that boy from blowin' sky high if that's what he needs to do about all this. Not if it costs you your mind."

"So you think I should go to the police?"

"I think you made up a theory because it gives you something to *solve,* and you think solving it will keep your Anthem from going off the deep end."

"That's not true."

"Maybe. *Maybe* it's not true. And *maybe* Marshall had something to do with what happened to your friend. And maybe he didn't. Either way, you're gonna have to start living your own life at some point."

"Is that why you're here? 'Cause you just wanted to give me a bunch of advice?"

"No. I'm here because you were right about one thing."

"Which thing?"

"My column was crap. What that boy did . . . it was one of the worst things I've ever seen in my life. And I just couldn't go there. So as a result, my column . . . well, it was crap. Also . . ."

"What?"

In the long silence that ensued, Marissa Hopewell seemed to be summoning her courage. For a crazy instant, Ben thought she was going to ask him out on a date. Finally, she said, "You *really* went to every hardware store in Orleans Parish to find that bulb?"

"Orleans *and* Jefferson Parish."

Peyton Broyard was on the front porch, sucking nervously on a Virginia Slim, when Marissa went to leave. "God damn you," Peyton whispered.

"Excuse me?"

"I'm sorry. I just . . ." She exhaled a long drag through pursed lips, angling the smoke stream in the opposite direction from where Marissa stood just outside the front door; it was an oddly polite gesture, given her angry greeting. "This whole Delongpre thing. It's awful, but I thought I might have a shot . . . I just listed the house. My sister, she lives in St. Louis. I'm going to move there as soon as it's sold."

"You were eavesdropping?"

"Once he has the diploma, I'll stop. Until then. My house, my surveillance rules. Okay?"

Marissa nodded and showed the woman her palms.

"You got kids?" Peyton asked.

"No."

"Pity. If you did, you might think twice about having Ben hang out at your office every day?"

"I think your son has some real investigative skill. He just needs to learn how to focus it." Peyton's laughter turned her next drag into a series of light coughs.

"A shot at what?" Marissa asked.

"Excuse me?"

"Just now. You said you thought you were going to have a shot at something. With Ben. What did you mean?"

"He's just like his father with this damn city. The two of them, they see . . . *promise* in it that I just don't see. You know he didn't apply *anywhere* besides Tulane? Oh, you should've been here for that. The fight, I mean I thought the neighbors were going to call the cops. And now . . . Now he's going to stay here and end up working for you, trying to take down the latest in an endless series of felons we keep electing to public office."

"It's a summer internship, Ms. Broyard. I wouldn't say we're deciding his fate here."

Peyton stamped out the cigarette in a tiny ashtray on the porch rail. The street around them was quiet and oak-shadowed, save for the pinpoint spotlights set within the manicured front lawns of the surrounding mansions. To Marissa, beholding the beauty of the Greek Revival façade was like taking a sip of champagne studded with broken glass; the Doric and Ionic columns and the soaring keyhole doors always appeared edged with the blood of field slaves.

"I keep having dreams," Peyton Broyard said, as she studied their beautiful surroundings with an expression that said she had come to regard them as threatening. "The same dream, really. About it all just getting washed away . . . But maybe that's just 'cause of what happened to them. The Delongpres, I mean."

"I didn't think we knew what happened to the Delongpres."

"Well, they had to have gone into the bayou, right? I mean . . ." She cut her eyes to the door to make sure no one was listening, then she whispered, "They had to have *drowned*, right?"

"A bayou has almost no currents to speak of. If they had drowned, the bodies probably would have turned up by now."

"So . . . what? What do you think happened?"

"I think no one knows."

I think they're on the run for something, something the father did. And I don't think all of them got to go along for the ride; Noah Delongpre probably decided who would be excess baggage and who wouldn't be.

"That won't be good enough for him," Peyton said.

"The only Press Club Award I've ever won was for a column about levee protection in St. Bernard Parish. They don't even like black folks in St. Bernard Parish."

"What are you saying?"

"I'm saying if your son's got any real knack for journalism, he'll have to learn what we all do. You do your best work when you're not working your own agenda." Marissa had never put it quite that succinctly before, and now that the words we're out of her mouth she wasn't quite sure she believed them. Peyton Broyard didn't look like she was all that sold on them either.

"I see . . . okay. Well, good luck, Ms. Hopewell."

"Good evening, Ms. Broyard."

"Drive safe now."

As she slid behind the wheel of her Prius, Marissa gave herself some credit for not firing off her mouth at Peyton Broyard over her recurring flood nightmare. As if anything could wash the Garden District away, perched as it was on the highest, safest ground in the city. If a deluge ever did come, it would be the poor black folks in her neighborhood who'd see their whole lives swept away in an instant.

But the woman was right; her nightmare probably had more to do with her own dark imaginings of what fate might have befallen the Delongpres. Although there had been a wire story just that afternoon. Apparently the Atlantic storm season that year was poised to produce some of the strongest hurricanes on record.

III

MARSHALL

11

ATLANTA
MAY 2013

The nurse who had saved Marshall Ferriot's life liked to take long walks in the morning. To the other joggers and bicyclists in Freedom Park, Arthelle Williams probably gave off the unhurried air of a retiree. But if you studied her the way Allen Shire had been hired to do, you could make out her stunned, thousand-yard stare and the white-knuckled grip with which she held her purse on her lap, even though there was no one within striking distance of her favorite bench and the halo of shifting shade offered by the elm branches overhead.

Movies had filled people's brains with stupid ideas about private detectives, so when Arthelle saw the short, balding man with knife-slashes for eyes and a broad, ungainly smile take a seat a few feet away from her, she didn't seem to pay him any notice. A good private detective was not a dapper, sharp-tongued fox; he was the type of guy who you wouldn't have second thoughts about inviting into your living room, or allowing to take a seat on your bench. Allen Shire was that guy—unattractive, unremarkable, quiet; that's why Cypress Bank & Trust gave him their most sensitive cases.

He kept his mouth shut, hoping the woman would get lost in her thoughts again so he could catch her off guard when he finally did speak. New town homes were sprouting up across the street, and beyond them, downtown's shiny skyline etched a clear blue sky. Something about Atlanta always got him a little; as if the city had become everything his hometown of New Orleans might have been if it was just a little less corrupt, a little more above sea level, a little less *easy*.

"You a cop?" Arthelle Williams asked him. Her gaze was focused on two young female joggers as they passed in a burst of excited chatter. "You been followin' me for four hours and you haven't shot at me yet, so you must be *somethin'*."

"I'm not a cop."

"Reporter?"

"Nope."

"You lookin' for somebody?"

"You've been on to me all day and you haven't called the police? Brave woman."

She shrugged, as if she wasn't brave because he wasn't all that scary.

"Figure this has got something to do with Marshall Ferriot, right?"

"That's correct," Shire answered.

"Well, if you're lookin' for the woman who tried to kill him, I'm not sure why you're botherin' the one who saved his life."

"I'm not looking for Emily Watkins. I know where she is."

"Jail, I hope."

When he didn't answer, she looked at him for the first time, adjusted her giant purse on her lap, craned her neck a little as if his silence had caused him to double in size. "*No*. Come on, now—"

"You sure hightailed it out of Lenox Hill fast, Ms. Williams."

"They didn't charge that girl with *anything*."

"There was no one around to."

"What are you— What do you *mean*?"

"I mean the person I'm looking for is Marshall Ferriot."

The confusion passed over the woman's deeply lined, jowly face, leaving behind a look of mild satisfied surprise. Then she laughed, the kind of bitter, sarcastic laugh people picked up from characters in movies. "Well, good for her, then."

"Good for who?"

"Marshall's sister. She took my advice, it looks like."

"And that was?"

"To get her brother the hell out of town before *another* crazy nurse tried to kill him."

"Mind control?" Danny Stevens asked for the third time since they'd started their phone call.

"I'm not trying to argue that it's a thing here, I'm just telling you what the woman told me today, okay? And she didn't believe it either. She thought the other nurses were all nuts, which is why she quit."

The two men had been frat brothers back at LSU, and Danny had been Shire's entrée into Cypress Bank & Trust back when Danny started his own one-man firm. But most of the jobs they'd worked on up until now had been extensive background checks on high-profile new hires. This was the first real headache they had ever suffered together.

Before she had died the year before, Heidi Ferriot, grande dame of Uptown society turned tragic widow and bitter, shut-in nursemaid, had drawn up a will that shuttled most of her estate into a fat trust fund intended to provide medical care for her son, who had, according to the file the bank had given Shire, made one of the stupidest suicide attempts known to man and landed in a permanent vegetative state.

Heidi Ferriot and her son had evacuated New Orleans during Katrina's approach, never to return. But as penance for abandoning the city that had made her family a small fortune, the woman had kept her money in one of the last locally owned banks in Louisiana. The only problem? Because her son had not spoken a word or responded to stimulus in almost eight years, the job of caring for him, and of receiving the hefty checks that came from the trust each month, had passed to his older sister, Elizabeth, a job the woman tended to only when she wasn't engaged in the dogged pursuit of other women's husbands and cocaine.

For most of the four days he'd been in Atlanta, Shire had been treated to a nonstop cavalcade of ugly stories from friends Elizabeth had stolen from, lied to or cheated on. And with each new sordid revelation, he and Danny Stevens had inched closer to the working theory that Princess Ferriot, as they'd come to call her, had saved up as much as she could from the disbursements and then hightailed it to a tropical island somewhere. As for her brother . . . well, every time they got close to discussing the awful possibility that she'd dropped him like deadweight, Shire would say it was time to alert law enforcement, and Danny would stall by saying Shire needed to interview more friends— as if the girl actually had any *friends*. And around and around they'd go while Shire lived it up at the Renaissance Concourse Airport Hotel, watching Delta Airlines jets take to the sky.

But now, in light of Arthelle Williams's revelation that morning, the narrative had shifted, as his political clients like to say.

"How long were you working this nurse angle?" Stevens asked.

"It just seemed weird to me."

"A bunch of nurses thinking an invalid is sending out . . . what? *Messages*? I mean, how does this mind control shit even work?"

"Look, if you want me to open up a file on the nurse who killed herself, I can, but I'm going to bill you for it. So let me just tell you now, for *free,* that everyone I talked to said Tammy Keene wasn't remotely unstable or intoxicated that day. But for some reason, she used a box cutter to gut herself like a catfish when she went inside the kid's room."

"Let's not get dramatic, Shire. Just curious how much of this you actually believe. That's all."

"I didn't say I believed any of it. I said it was weird, is all. And the only part that matters is . . . well, now we know someone at that facility told Elizabeth Ferriot to get her brother out of town or he was going to be killed. Which means no income for Princess."

"She won't get any income if she stays out of contact, Shire. Six of one, half dozen of the other, as they say."

"I know that."

"I'm just saying. We got two questions here. And you haven't answered 'em both. Not yet. So they're running from the nurses, fine. But why's she running from *us*?"

"Will it matter if I know where she went?"

The ferry landing was in a little town called Fernandina Beach, that sat just on the Florida side of the state's border with Georgia. Apparently, there was a historic district, but all Shire could see was a few blocks of two-story brick buildings painted various pastel shades. The tallest thing in the skyline was the plume of white smoke coming from the refinery at the water's edge.

Shire had expected at least a clutch of people at the harbor, but the blonde inside the ticket booth looked up from her copy of *Twilight* with a dazed expression that suggested he was the first person to ask something of her since she'd been hired. The harbor itself was tiny, just a few rows of slips around a pavilion-style restaurant that looked empty. Steel-colored clouds were knotted across the eastern horizon, draining the color from the expanse of tidal pools and rounded islands of marsh grass below.

Somewhere out there was Chamberland Island; he'd get there on the 3:00 ferry. He had Elizabeth Ferriot's former best friend to thank for bringing him to this humble little coastal village. During the tongue-lashing she'd been giving about her ex-roommate—hell hath no fury like a woman who discovered you borrowed her AmEx number without permission—Margery Blakely had made one of those invaluable offhand comments that doesn't mean anything until you look back at your notes and plug it into a search engine. *End of the day, all that skank wanted was some rich sugar daddy to buy her a place out on Chamberland Island.* He'd never heard of the place before that moment. Now he was doing his best to commit a map of the twenty-mile-long coastal island to memory. Large salt marshes made up its western shore, but the ocean-facing side was one of the longest stretches of undeveloped beach in the continental United States. Most of the island was national park, but nestled at the northern tip were a few private parcels wealthy residents had managed to hold on to when the parks service took control of the island in the early seventies. When he located the deeds, Shire recognized the name of only one of the owners, but it was a hell of a hit. Perry Walters, chief financial officer for Ferriot Exports from 1992 to 1999. His name had even been on a list of extended family and business contacts Danny Stevens had given him in case his investigation in Atlanta hit a dead end. Walters was pushing ninety now; it was doubtful he was making many visits to his family's old cottage. There was no bridge to the mainland, just ferry service that ended around dusk. Overnight camping was prohibited, which meant the only people allowed on the island after dark aside from residents were guests of the White Tail Inn, the historic bed-and-breakfast located at the island's southern tip. It was, in other words, the perfect place to hide out from a bunch of crazy nurses who were convinced your cash cow brother was responsible for the death of one of their own.

The ferry was small, with a half-open wheelhouse in the bow, an open deck in the middle, and a small seating area in back covered by a wind-jostled blue tarp. They hit rain almost as soon as they left the harbor,

and the ten passengers who had boarded along with Shire found themselves fighting for space under the tarp alongside their own luggage
and the boat's fat smokestack, which was so overheated that even the
insulation it had been wrapped in was hot to the touch. (More than
one passenger made the mistake of leaning against the padding, only
to recoil as if a snake had bitten them.) Only residents could use the
car ferry that ran to the island's northern end, otherwise Shire would
have taken it in a heartbeat. Anything would have been better than this
trembling, steaming junk heap.

The rain got so heavy you couldn't see more than a few feet in any
direction. A tense hush fell over the passengers. The two small children
who had been excited by the downpour just moments earlier seemed to
recognize the gravity of the situation and began pawing at their father's
pant legs. But Daddy Dearest was too busy staring at the spot where the
northeastern horizon had been, with a tense set to his simian jaw. Then
some protective urge roused him from his paralysis. He picked up his
little girl in one arm, forcing his young son to cling to his right leg.

At least the seas are calm, Shire thought. But you still couldn't see a
damn thing, and that seemed important, even if the island was probably to the east of them now, sheltering the surrounding waters from
the open sea. And he'd love it if the boat rocked and rolled, just a little
bit. Right now, the whole thing felt too heavy on the water, its determined course the product of that steely arrogance that comes with old
age. At any minute, it felt like water would close over the bow and the
whole thing would just start chugging straight for the sandy bottom as
if nothing were amiss.

The engine cut out. A dock appeared a few yards ahead, and just
beyond it, several SUVs waited to shuttle guests to the nearby bed-
and-breakfast, which Shire saw only in a glimpse of soaring Greek columns through the mist. Everyone disembarked except for Shire, the
father and his two munchkins. Fifteen minutes later, they arrived at an
isolated dock in the center of the island where a National Parks Ser-

vice sign reminded them that the last ferry was at 6:00 p.m. They had reached the last stop, the island's wild center.

Shire followed the father and his two kids up a dirt trail that led straight into a dense forest of gnarled live oak branches. Spiny palmetto leaves shot up out of the dense understory like claws. The island's central trail ran north to south, wide enough to accommodate two vehicles side by side; tire tracks and hoofprints, presumably from the wild horses that inhabited the island, marched the patchwork of gravel, loose rock and sandy soil.

When it was clear he wasn't going to follow them to the beach, the father appeared to recognize Shire for the first time; he offered a nod and a smile while his kids raced off into the expanse of low sand dunes, pursuing the sound of pounding surf. Then Shire was all alone, walking north under the constant canopy of interlocking oak branches, listening to the sounds of his own lonely footsteps, dodging the occasional palmetto leaf that reached out to snag his shirt.

After twenty minutes, he passed a sign that informed him he was leaving parks service property. Then he saw a large antebellum mansion sitting in the middle of an expansive clearing, shutters drawn, barn-style garage closed and locked. Yet to open for the summer season, he figured.

Ten minutes later, he spotted two brick columns marking the entrance to a gravel driveway. The Walters place; it had to be. The map had been right so far.

Without slowing his steps, Shire slid the right strap of his backpack off his shoulder so he could grip the whole thing in front of him like a papoose. Out came the hand-sized Sony digital camera, with the small telephoto lens attachment. He shifted the backpack to its previous position, and suddenly Shire was just a lone hiker, preparing to lift his camera at an interesting shot. Meanwhile, he held his finger down on the button, snapping a random, constant series of pictures of the Walters place while he held the camera against his thigh.

Once the house and driveway were out of sight, he stopped and examined his work.

The driveway was empty, but the gravel had fresh-looking tire tracks leading into the closed garage. The existing vegetation had been sculpted into a dense perimeter wall between the trail and the house, and the roof had two steeply sloped levels that intersected at a right angle; a trick to make the house look like it was two stories instead of one. It was a glorified cottage on a generous plot of land. And if the map continued to deliver, there was a narrower hiking trail that ran beside the property's western edge. He trudged through the mud and tree branches in search of it, scanning the ground for snakes as he went.

A few minutes later, he had a pretty decent view of the house's backside. He was crouching down in the brush, snapping photos of the house's dark windows, when the smell hit him; too sour to be the septic tank, too full of rot to be household trash. His eyes were watering, his nostrils dilating, and then there was movement behind him. His first instinct was to jump to his feet, but he didn't want to give away his location, crouched down in the dense brush, so he looked behind him over one shoulder.

The horse was nosing its way through the trail behind him. About seven feet tall from hooves to head, with a shiny coat the color of milk chocolate and a band of white hair around its neck, it didn't seem to notice him at all. Shire couldn't tell *what* the animal was doing, and he was less afraid of it than he was of having his cover blown.

Was the *horse* making that awful smell?

The damn things roamed wild on the island, didn't they? Or maybe it had been drawn to the smell. Maybe there was something big and dead somewhere in the leaves nearby and the horse was trying to sniff it out. But that was ridiculous. He didn't know much about any animals, but he knew horses weren't carrion eaters, for Christ's sake.

"Buzz off, pal," Shire whispered. "I got work to do."

The brush all around them erupted, and it took Allen Shire several minutes of clawing at branches and spitting leaves from his mouth to realize that he hadn't been shot at, that the horse had just lost its fucking marbles on him. It was bearing down on him, hooves flying up, trailing mud clumps, piano key–teeth bared, lips sputtering, flaring nostrils washing Shire in damp heat.

If something had frightened the damn thing, it had responded by bearing down on Shire with sudden, wild fury. And in a terrible instant, he realized he'd tumbled backward through slick palmetto leaves and into the house's backyard. The horse exploded through the brush after him. He tried to feign left and the monster mirrored him, still kicking and bucking like something from hell's rodeo.

Knees bent, arms at his side, Shire found himself taking long backward steps across the yard. Then his feet slid out from under him and he landed ass-first in a patch of mud that smeared his hands. Even though it would have been the perfect moment to do so, the horse didn't trample him. It closed the distance, then started pacing back and forth—*horses can pace?* Shire thought wildly—in case the man tried to run in either direction.

It's corralling me. Son of a bitch, the damn horse *is corralling me!*

His right heel hit something hard, and then his ass landed on the house's back steps with a hard thump, like a little boy who'd been cast into the nearest empty chair by the hand of an angry father.

The horse whined, an awful, piercing sound he didn't know a horse was capable of making. Then the creature's hind legs bent at the knees, and bile rose in Shire's throat as he realized the monster was about to lunge at him.

Then the horse's head exploded.

The animal's skull seemed to give way down the center, as if an invisible sledgehammer had struck it in just the right spot. The jawbone slipped free from the collapsing skull in a single piece. After it came the brain matter, a slick, corded tumble the color of mud laced with red wine. And even as it all hit the earth with wet smacking sounds, the horse remained standing, and Shire realized that explosion wasn't the right word for what he was witnessing. It was as if some congenital weakness inside the animal's skull had picked that exact moment to trigger a total collapse. And as the seconds passed, as the horse remained standing, it looked as if the animal had just offered up its brain matter to Shire as a welcome present.

Then the animal keeled over and landed on one side so hard its legs bounced, and Shire was left with his own desperate gasps, the same sounds his pal Bobby Hurwitz had made after they all hurled him into the shallow end of the Audubon Park pool when they were kids and he'd been hauled to the surface, goggle-eyed and wheezing, too stunned to gasp for a complete breath. That's what Allen Shire sounded like right now; a little boy who had been slammed into a wall of unforgiving concrete.

Then he took in the sight of the rest of the yard. It was not a patch of mud he had fallen into a few seconds earlier. He had, in essence, separated the remains of a deer's head even further from its lifeless body and the stains all over his pants and arms were too red to be pure mud. The yard was littered with them, animal carcasses; skunks, possums, a few bobcats and snakes, plenty of goddamn snakes, and all of them had suffered the same fate as the horse from hell; their heads had been reduced to molten-looking piles of snapped bones and dung-colored brain matter. He'd been too busy trying to get a peek through the house's windows to realize he was shooting pictures over a grotesque, open-air slaughterhouse.

Invisible hammer. Invisible hammer. These were the two words he couldn't get out of his head; he thought if he kept thinking them over and over again they would bring him to a logical, earthbound explanation for what he was witnessing. *No, it's not an invisible hammer that did in these poor little critters, you silly fool, it was actually a . . .* But his mind wasn't filling in the blank, and there was blood over his clothes and hands, and the smell was worse here, much worse than it had been on the other side of the yard.

He was on his feet suddenly, because now the only thing that mattered was getting the bloody mud off his hands. Not just off his hands. Off his *flesh*. He spun around and knocked into the glass door at the top of the steps. Inside there would be water. Inside there would be a sink and soap and paper towels and maybe some of that new white tea–scented soap that always put him in a good mood because it reminded him of the redhead in Biloxi who'd kept it in her bathroom, one of the only decent one-night stands he'd ever had in his life.

He closed one gore-smeared hand around the doorknob.

Marshall Ferriot stared back at him from the other side of the glass. The kid was sitting upright in a motorized wheelchair. And he was smiling at him, and the smile was growing, his chapped lips curling into a leer that seemed to take up his entire emaciated face.

Hello, there.

He had mouthed the words so clearly Shire could read his lips. Then he cocked his head to one side and his leer softened into a smile that was less eager, and more self-satisfied.

Shire was still wondering how the doorknob had managed to dissolve in his grip when suddenly the entire world was wiped away as if with one quick swipe of a giant hand.

12

The darkness gained texture. Fading sunlight glinted off the floorboards between his bloody sneakers and the foot of the bed across the room. For a few delirious seconds, Allen Shire thought it possible that the animal slaughterhouse and the stallion from hell had been the components of some terrible dream, and that he was really back in the Renaissance Concourse Hotel, watching flights to Paris, Los Angeles and—*oh, please, God, yes!*—New Orleans take to the air outside his window.

The blood on your sneakers is plenty real, jackass.

Nylon rope secured his legs to a dining table chair that was all cherrywood slats, but for some reason his hands were free. The chair wasn't that heavy. He could probably make a run for it if he hoisted the thing up onto his back and pumped his legs with all his might. But he wasn't alone. There was a woman sitting on the floor nearby, and she wasn't moving.

His eyes were still adjusting to the darkness, and he knew that if he looked away he would spare himself some soul-searing, unforgettable sight. But he couldn't. In the corner of the room, Elizabeth Ferriot leaned against the wall, legs splayed, head rolled forward on her neck so that her dirty blond tresses looked like frozen icicles framing her downturned face. The bloody meat cleaver she'd apparently gutted herself with rested precariously in one lifeless hand, and on the white wall above her head, part of a word had been smeared in blood—*her blood, her blood, her blood,* a shrill voice screamed inside Shire's head— across the wall: E L Y S

Every profanity he'd ever learned came hissing out of him in a wild rush of desperate whispers.

Across the room, a single paper trembled slightly in Marshall Ferriot's slender hand as he set it down on the tray table in front of him. The tray table was attached to his wheelchair, and his wheelchair was the high-backed kind designed to accommodate a patient capable of almost no upper body movement. The kid was fully conscious but barely capable of getting around on his own. So how in the name of God had Shire's file end up on his tray table?

"You've read this?" Marshall asked, holding up one page of the file in his trembling fingers. Shire nodded. "Fascinating," Marshall whispered. His voice was still raspy from years of disuse. "Do you believe what you read? You really think I was trying to kill myself that night?"

"I d-don't know . . . Really. I—"

"I mean, there are far easier ways to kill yourself, aren't there?"

"I guess . . . yeah . . ."

"I didn't, Mr. Shire. I didn't try to kill myself that night. What happened was something else altogether. The same thing that's happening to you."

"I don't under—"

"The bank sent you? Daniel J. Stevens—he's the trustee?"

Shire felt his lips moving, but there was nothing coming out. No sound, no breath. Marshall looked up from the papers in front of him, and maybe it was just a trick of the fading sunlight, but he looked surprisingly calm and patient for a man who had just returned to the world after eight years of darkness.

Shire nodded; it was the best he could do.

"And he sent you after us because she took me out of some place called Lenox Hill?"

Shire nodded again. His Adam's apple felt like a cue ball inside his throat.

"Why?" Marshall Ferriot asked.

"Wh-whad d'y do . . . you . . ."

"Why did she take me out of Lenox Hill, Mr. Shire?" he asked with what sounded like strained patience.

"One of the nurses, she tr-tried to k-kill you." This earned the young man's undivided, wide-eyed attention. "She thought you could . . . they th-thought you could m-*make* people do things."

"Smart girl."

"How—how long have you been . . . ?"

"Awake?" Marshall asked. "Is that really what you want to know?"

"I don't kn-know what you . . ."

"You want to know if it was an accident. Like the others. The nurse. You want to know if what I did to *her*"—he jerked his head in the direction of his sister's corpse—"is like what I did to them?"

"I don't know what—"

"Yes, you do, Mr. Shire. You know. They all told you. It's right here in your file. And *now,* you'd like to know if I was awake when I forced my sister to use the knife on herself and start painting."

Shire only realized he had started to cry when his image of Marshall Ferriot wobbled and split behind a fresh sheen of tears. Snot filled his nostrils, and several sharp intakes of breath weren't enough to clear them. And he longed desperately to be back on that sunlit bench in Freedom Park with Arthelle Williams. Or maybe walking along the shore with that father he'd ridden over with on the ferry, smiling contentedly as they watched the man's two small children blow the sand off seashells and speculate wildly about what might be swimming just offshore. Because now it felt like that same man's brusque nod of farewell had contained some sense of foreboding, some vague sense that horrors were waiting for Allen Shire just up the central trail of Chamberland Island. And he felt like a fool, a fool for having walked up here alone, all this way. But how could he have known? How could he have known that voodoo was real and that animals can explode before your eyes from blows struck by invisible hammers?

"To answer the question you are too afraid to ask, sir. I don't remember what happened to my sister, or the nurse."

"Tammy Keene," Shire said, so forcefully he startled himself. It felt as if some trapped bubble of determination and self-will had worked its way free and to the surface of his being. His captor might be a monster, but the nurse had a name, goddammit, before some phenomenon Shire couldn't understand had stolen it from her. "Tammy Keene. That was her name."

The young man in the wheelchair dismissed this with a distracted nod.

Outside the glass door were three metal trash cans Shire hadn't noticed before. He hadn't noticed them because they hadn't been there. And now they were lined up at the foot of the back steps, lids askew atop the animal carcasses stuffed inside. It started pouring all of a sudden, and the clouds of flies around each trash can departed like apparitions.

"Thank you for your help in the yard, Allen."

Shire screwed his eyes shut, as if he could will himself away from this dark bedroom with the same baffling, supernatural skill Marshall Ferriot had used to make him clean up all the carnage in the backyard.

"The animals are different, you see. They can't go for very long is the problem. Their little skulls, they just . . . *give way*. No better word for it. But with people . . . With people, everything is different. And now that *you're* here, I can find out how."

Shire was outside. He was holding a muddy shovel in his hands, his arms burning from exertion he couldn't remember.

The rain had soaked him from head to toe.

"Katrina, Shire."

He was standing in a five-foot-deep hole he couldn't remember digging. Marshall was parked in the open back door. He felt the same sense of lost time as when he'd come to after his wisdom teeth surgery.

"*Who* is Katrina? She's in your notes. It says, 'Marshall relocated before Katrina.'"

"We got hit," Shire answered. His lungs felt like they were seizing up as they struggled to perform deep, much-needed breaths he apparently hadn't been capable of while Marshall forced him to dig the hole. The trash cans towered over him. The rain had stopped, so the flies were back, and occasionally several of them would land on Marshall's blanket-draped legs.

"Hit . . ." Marshall said, with a furrowed brow and a searching, almost pleading look in his eyes.

"A hurricane," Shire answered, and it came out like a seagull's squawk. He struggled to get his breath back lest he risk the kid's impatience. "A big one. Almost as big as Camille. The eye, it hit Bay St. Louis, but the way it was moving, it drove water up all over the levees and into the city. Mid-City. Lakeview. Chalmette. St. Bernard . . . The Lower Ninth Ward. There was water all through 'em. People got trapped on their roofs, died in their attics. For days it went on. Days and days."

He was astonished to find that reciting the cold, clinical details of this cataclysm, which had shaped every nightmare he'd suffered since the summer of 2005, brought about a strange kind of stillness inside him, as if the only thing that could distract him from his present agony was the memory of a different, more distant, pain.

The kid's stare was vacant all of a sudden, dreamy almost, and it was impossible to tell how this news was affecting him. Shire couldn't even guess how the enormity of such a revelation about someone's hometown would have affected a normal person who had been asleep for almost a decade, let alone a sadistic fuck like Marshall Ferriot.

"But it's still there, right? New Orleans. It's still there, isn't it?"

"Yes. It's . . . different. But it's still there."

"Good. Then they'll still be there too, probably. Both of them."

Who was the kid talking about? Surely not his parents; their deaths were referenced in his file multiple times. Other family members? There were hardly any left except some second and third cousins who'd never been involved with the family business. The kid had no life waiting for him back in New Orleans. None that Shire had seen any evidence of. But there was no chance in hell Shire was going to point this out to him now.

"I'm so glad you're here, Mr. Shire. See, it's going to take me awhile to walk again, and I'll need plenty of help."

The smell. A wave of the awful smell hit him from the trash cans, and it occurred to him that he was digging a repository for all the animal carcasses he'd been forced to collect, and he was digging the thing just a few feet away from the back door of the house. *Marshall* was making him dig the thing just a few feet from the back of the house. And if that was the case, that meant this thing he had, this *power* he was using, it had range. And if it had range, then maybe he could make a run for—

He held the last tendrils of this thought to him as the darkness closed in around him with silent speed.

He was staring down into the pit now and the trash cans were empty, their contents emptied into the grave's muddy bottom in a tangle of stiff legs and blood-matted fur and desiccated scales. And because it truly was like lost time, the thought he'd gone under with was still right there with him, a whisper in his ear through the rain. *Range,* he thought. And in a flash of insight, it turned into another word. *Run!*

"Now let's—"

But before Marshall could finish the sentence, Shire hurled the shovel at him and took off running.

He heard the blade strike something with a metallic *thwang,* but he didn't look back. Just kept running like hell.

Then his right foot seemed to sink into open air and he pitched forward, and when the palmetto leaves didn't slap him in the face, he knew he had failed and his sob of despair was swallowed by a darkness without time or substance or even the comforting finality of death.

Now he couldn't move. The house towered over him and his entire body was wrapped in a cold, wet embrace. When he coughed, his chin struck mud.

The grave was closed and he was in it, buried up to his neck. Marshall hadn't moved an inch. His wheelchair was still parked in the open back door, and the shovel lay across his lap. If Shire had managed to strike him with it, there was no evidence of the blow on Marshall's face and neck. And there was no evidence of anger in the young man's contented expression.

"I'm so glad you came, Allen Shire. You see? I have so much to learn, and I'm going to learn it all from *you.*"

IV

ANTHEM

13

What the hell are you doing?" Marissa Hopewell shouted. Her voice sounded rain muffled through the iPhone's tiny speaker, and for a moment, Ben considered hanging up on her and blaming it on a lost connection.

He should have known better than to answer a call from his employer after what he'd just done. But it was instinct, and ever since Marissa had been promoted to editor in chief of *Kingfisher* a few months before, he had been determined not to take advantage of their long personal history. Still, he had no interest in involving her in the text message he'd received a few minutes earlier.

It was almost ten o'clock, and he was speeding down St. Charles Avenue in his Prius. He was most certainly not sitting in the upstairs balcony at Good Friends across from the complete bore Marissa had set him up with because they were two of the only gay men she knew.

"Well," he finally answered, "I'm driving and talking on the phone at the same time."

"Well, that's fascinating."

"You're right. It's big news for people who think blonds can't walk and chew gum."

"Uh huh. How's your *date* going, smart mouth?"

"You first, hot stuff."

"Seriously, Ben. Did you just walk out on Dobie after I—"

"No! Pardon me, I did not just walk out. I excused myself and explained that I had a— Wait, *Dobie*?"

"Explained that you had a *what* exactly?"

"His name's not Davey?"

"Oh my God, Ben."

"Maybe it's for the best then."

"*Ben!* Do you have any idea how difficult it was to get him to—"

"No, actually. I didn't realize I was that hard a sell. Jesus Christ!"

"Ben!"

"Should I switch colognes?"

"It was a hard sell because you work for a newspaper and you might have to cover his office one day. But honestly, I might fire you before that ever becomes an issue, so it's just as—"

"You'd really fire me over a blind date with a guy who admits to listening to One Direction?"

"*Where* are you going? Dobie says you hightailed it outta there like your pants were on fire."

"So he was thinking about my pants, huh? Doesn't sound like it was a total bust then, right?"

"*Where* are you—"

"Did he actually use those words? The ones about my pants being on—"

"No. He did not. He thanked me for wasting his time and asked me not to fix him up with anyone on my staff ever again."

"So he was lying when he agreed to a rain check?"

"He was being polite. Which you have never, *ever* been in your entire life apparently."

"Yeah, because that's what *Kingfisher* needs more of right now. *Polite* reporters."

"Watch your mouth, Uptown Girl."

"Speaking of which, how is *your* date—"

"You have thirty seconds to tell me where you're going right now."

"Well, that's good, 'cause I'm going to be there in fifteen."

It was a lie but he hung up on her anyway.

The author of the text messages that had sent Ben Broyard flying through Uptown New Orleans was one Luther Rendell, an NOPD patrol cop with the Second District whom Ben had been cultivating as a contact for years.

The first text had read: *Shots fired at Fat Harry's.*

The second, which came just a few seconds later read. *& they were fired at yr buddy w. the funny name*

St. Charles Avenue was a broad, oak-shaded thoroughfare that gently mirrored the Mississippi River's crescent path through the city. Along most of its length, it was lined with Greek Revival mansions so beautiful and well maintained that an Oregon native Ben had gone to Tulane with had once asked him if people actually lived in them or if they were all museums. Antique streetcars traversed the street's broad, grassy neutral ground, islands of segmented light that gave off great lazy rumbles as they traveled the shadowy avenue.

Ben usually avoided Uptown bars like Fat Harry's. They were too popular with his old high school classmates. Every now and then it was fun to see which former crushworthy varsity athlete and small-time bully had been knocked from his genetic pedestal by a constant diet of fried seafood and Dixie Beer. But an occasional burst of schadenfreude

wasn't worth the risk of an old Cannon student he barely knew dragging him into a conversation about those awful final months of senior
year. Anthem Landry felt the exact same way for the exact same reason,
which meant that if he'd set foot inside Fat Harry's at all that night, he'd
have been pretty sauced by the time he arrived.

Ben was jogging across the grassy neutral ground when the lights
atop the ambulance parked in front of Fat Harry's spun to life. It peeled
off into the night, sirens screaming, revealing the crowd of mostly
white college students gathered in front of the bar's awning and large
front windows. Ben had an insane urge to run after the thing, or at the
very least, dash back to his Prius so he could pursue. But then he saw
Luther Rendell, one of three uniformed cops standing at the edge of
the crowd, and when the guy waved him over, Ben stepped out from
the path of an approaching streetcar and crossed the street.

"Was that him?" Ben asked, breathless.

"No. That was the other guy," Rendell answered. He was bantam-
framed, with knots of gray hair that looked like steel wool, and as usual
he reeked of Camel Lights and gas station coffee.

"The other guy?"

"The one who fired the shots."

Rendell walked them away him from the crowd. "So apparently
your boy Landry—"

"He's not my boy, but continue."

"Your friend, 'scuse me. He and the guy with the revolver get into
it over the video poker machines and everyone's watching like it's not
going to go so well for the guy with the revolver. Because they don't
know the guy has a revolver. They just know he's got a big mouth and
your buddy Landry's about twice his size. About twice *everyone's* size,
to hear them tell it." Which meant A-Team was long gone, Ben noted,
otherwise Rendell would have seen for himself how tall Anthem actually was.

"Who ID'd Anthem?"

"Old classmate of his tending bar. Classmates of yours too, I guess. Said Landry kinda went off the deep end when his girlfriend went missing."

"The video poker machines?" Ben said, hoping the effort it took to ignore this reference didn't show on his face.

"Gunslinger wanted to try his luck apparently. Landry didn't seem interested in giving him a turn."

"And so?"

"Things got physical. Sounds like Landry knocked the guy on his ass, then when the guy got up, he had a gun all of a sudden."

"And he fired it, apparently."

"Yep. Into his own foot."

"*You're fired, Ben!*"

Ben was so startled by the voice of his boss, he spun away from this baffling detail.

Marissa Hopewell Powell was dressed in a plain V-neck T-shirt and hip-hugging blue jeans, and she was approaching with a relaxed gait and a casual smile that made Ben wonder if he had imagined her outburst. Once again, Ben was reminded of how much weight the woman had lost since they'd first met. True, the stress of losing her home in Katrina had forced her to shed a bunch of pounds in a very short time. But the rest of it she'd unloaded the old-fashioned way. A diet, brought on, in large part, by the publication of her first book, a critically acclaimed account of Katrina's terrible aftermath that included a searing retelling of the seventy-two hours she, Ben and a few other *Kingfisher* staff members had spent pulling people from their flooded homes in the Lower Ninth Ward.

But Marissa's scheduled date that night had not been some blind fix-up with a dull city accountant. More like dinner with a housing rights advocate and attorney who'd graduated from the same college she did. The guy was marriage material, and jeans and a T-shirt were not what Marissa wore to dinner with marriage material.

"Were you following me?" Ben asked.

"I live close by," she answered, giving Rendell a polite smile.

"You live in the Marigny."

"It's called a police scanner. We used to use 'em before Twitter."

"You knew I was coming here, and you were testing me, weren't you?"

"Yep," she said with a bright smile. "And you failed."

"Yeah, sure. How'd your date go?" Ben asked her.

"How's all *this* going?" Marissa asked.

Rendell gave Ben a searching look.

"Oh, I see," Marissa said. "So you two are best buds now. *I'm* actually the reason those guys who knocked over your mother's restaurant got caught, Luther."

"I helped," Ben offered meekly.

"*I* wrote the story," Marissa countered.

"Because I bugged you about it every day."

"I still wrote it."

"That's because I didn't have a desk yet, so I couldn't write the story, which is why I had to get *you* to—"

"Keep talking. It'll go well for you. I promise."

Rendell lifted his hands like an intervening parent, and to Ben's surprise, the gesture was enough to silence both him and Marissa instantly.

"Now, Lord knows, I am truly indebted to both of you fine, fine journalists for the piece you wrote about what happened to my momma. But if memory serves, I've bought you both a helluva a lot of beers to make up for it. So right now I'm gonna need to tend to a bunch of scared little white kids over there who aren't used to hearin' a gun go off, 'less they're duck huntin' with Daddy. So if y'all don't mind."

Rendell started off.

"Well, that wasn't racist," Ben muttered.

"Oh, please," Marissa groaned.

When Rendell stopped and turned to face them suddenly, Ben

thought the cop might have heard his comment. But the man formed one hand into a trigger finger and pointed it at his foot. "Ben. I forgot— it was *both* feet."

Ben just stared at him, so Rendell mimed shooting his right foot, reaiming, and shooting his left.

"Are you serious?" Ben called after him.

Rendell nodded.

"How is that even possible?"

"Ask them," Rendell called back, jerking one thumb at the crowd. "When I'm done with 'em, of course. Guy who actually did it wasn't any help at all. Said he doesn't remember even pulling his own gun. But if you find your buddy, tell him we'd love *his* opinion on the matter as well."

Ben turned to Marissa. "One foot after the other? How's that possible? The first bullet would knock him on his ass, right?"

"Well, you know what they say."

"Do I?"

"God watches over children and drunks. And Anthem Landry is a combination of both. So maybe he's got extra, *extra* good luck."

"Yeah, that last part is what *you* say, I think."

"So you off to find your buddy now?"

"You want to join me?"

"No. And don't ever hang up on me again."

"Promise, as long as you tell me how your date went."

"It didn't go anywhere."

"You canceled?"

"On the phone today he made some crack about how he couldn't be married to anyone with a dangerous job."

"And?"

"I told him I had to ask tough questions of dangerous people. And that I'd be doing it for as long as I could."

"You wouldn't reform your dangerous ways? Not even for an attorney?"

"Not even for Barack Obama."

"Aw, come on. You could cover the Garden District beat. You know, new flower shops, the occasional car theft. It'd give you more time to actually edit the paper."

"Yeah, 'cause that's what I want to do. Spend the rest of my life interviewing nice old white ladies who think they're going to have some kind of moment with me because they just read *The Help*."

"Whatever. It's not like we're war correspondents out here."

"You're just sayin' that 'cause we haven't had an oil rig blow up in the past few months."

"Suit yourself."

"It wasn't a match, all right?"

"All right. Fine. Makes sense, I guess."

"How's that?" Marissa asked.

"Well, you're the one who told me if I was ever going to have a boyfriend, I'd have to divorce trouble first."

"I wasn't talking about your job, Ben. I was talking about Anthem Landry."

His cheeks burned. He averted his eyes from hers before he could stop himself. He'd actually lain awake a few nights since she'd made the comment, wondering if the stresses of being promoted to editor in chief by *Kingfisher*'s new owners were starting to wear on her, wondering if his mentor had, in fact, been trying to warn him off the very career path she had shepherded him onto eight years prior. Apparently, he couldn't have been more wrong.

"So I guess you don't want to help me look for him then?" Ben asked.

"I need you in my office nine a.m. Monday morning. Don't come strolling in at ten thirty just 'cause we have history. It doesn't go over well. Trust me."

"With you?"

"With everyone."

She was a few feet away when Ben called after her. "So you really are firing me?"

"Don't hang up on me again," she said and kept walking.

"What's the meeting about?"

"A story," she said, without turning. "And it's yours. If you're up for it."

With that, she waved at him over one shoulder and stepped into the intersection.

Ben checked his phone to see if he had any messages from Anthem, then he just stood there for a while, wondering what kind of drug a man would have to be on to fire two clean gunshots through both of his feet, one right after the other.

14

It was almost midnight by the time Ben crossed Lake Pontchartrain. He hadn't conducted a search of Anthem's favorite bars, hadn't so much as placed a concerned phone call to any of the guy's brothers, all of whom were so high-strung, a concerned phone call would have been enough to send them into a tailspin of worry. Instead, Ben had returned to his apartment, kicked back in front of the rebroadcast of the WWL evening news and waited for the inevitable text message from his bullet-evading buddy. It came right on schedule: *Big trouble. Meet me @ my baby ... Bring sanity.*

What did drunks do before they had text messages to manipulate people with, Ben wondered? Kept pay phones in business, he guessed.

Now he was heading north on Highway 22, the same route he and Anthem had traveled the night Nikki disappeared. But his destination tonight was well short of Noah Delongpre's old compound in the swamp, which was a good thing, because there wasn't a timber of the old place left.

After Katrina's surge flooded Elysium, none of the Delongpre cousins had stepped up to repair the damage, and Ben could only bring himself to visit the place a couple of times over the years as it devolved into a swamp-eaten ruin. He had his own special private places where he went to remember Nikki in peace; Elysium wasn't one of them. How could it have been? He'd never so much as grazed his finger across the surface of the artesian-fed swimming pool. (Someone, he wasn't quite sure who, had drained the thing right after their disappearance.) And he never got the chance to spend a single night in the raised Acadian cottage that had at times seemed like Mr. Noah's life's work. The year before, the State of Louisiana had finally given official death declarations to all three members of the Delongpre family and, in accordance with Mr. Noah's will, Elysium's flooded remains passed to the park service that managed the adjacent swampland.

Once he crossed Madisonville's tiny drawbridge and bypassed the strip of restaurants sitting on the bank of the Tchefuncte River, Ben made a left turn onto Main Street and headed in the direction of the lake. Recently constructed suburban homes with the filigree ironwork and broad front porches of the Old South lined the blocks leading up to the Maritime Museum. Then the blink-and-you-miss-it town was gone and Main Street became an undulating two-lane road through tall, wind-tossed grass and long pools of muddy water.

At the lakeshore he came to a broad asphalt parking lot with a boat launch. But the launch was empty, the only car parked in the lot Anthem's cherry-red F-150 pickup truck. Here, the river emptied into the lake with that same silent, unhurried ease that moved all the bodies of water in Louisiana, and resting in the shallows next to a crumbling wooden dock was Anthem's *baby*.

She was an old river push boat that had been sitting in her current spot for about fifteen years: a three-story hulk of steel with a white-painted shell striated by rust bands. If she'd had a name, the elements had stripped all evidence of it from her hull years ago. The rumor was, some rich guy had hauled the boat to its current spot because he planned to break down its parts and use them as a breakwater for his fishing camp. But the guy had either lost his will or his money, because here the boat sat more than a decade later.

Her tall wheelhouse was accessed by an exterior ladder on either side, her bow given over to two matching triangles of steel that had once acted as bumpers against barges and boats in distress. The bottom deck would have been flush with the water's surface if the boat hadn't been keeling slightly in the shallows. Still, whenever Ben saw a push boat working along the Mississippi, the design of its bottom deck unnerved him. Too many of those *Jaws* movies when he was a kid, Anthem had once chided him. That was only sort of true. Ben knew there weren't any sharks in the river. It was the currents that frightened him; they were ferocious and just below the surface.

In broad daylight, Anthem Landry was a giant. But when he was wreathed in shadow, as he was now, he looked twice as tall. If you cracked a two-by-four across his massive upper back, the board would probably split before any of his bones did. He had the same prominent Roman nose he'd had since he was a teenager, and the rest of his face was a fortunate blend of features arising from the blend of Italian and French blood that made up so many New Orleans family lines: delicate pink lips on a long, expressive mouth and a light olive complexion that seemed to repel everything from razor burns to acne. He'd gone with Ben to the gay clubs on Bourbon and St. Ann a few times over the years, and Ben was always surprised when the lascivious stares of the other patrons landed not on Anthem's broad chest or statuesque facial features, but on his hands: they were massive, the kind Michelangelo might have carved, but perfectly proportional to the rest of his giant frame.

"We use to do it in the wheelhouse," Anthem said.

"You're kidding."

"She didn't tell you?"

"She didn't tell me every time you guys did it. Just the first time . . ."

"When she made me wear two condoms and pull out after five minutes?"

"Yeah. That time."

It was still pushing eighty degrees outside and Ben was wearing a short-sleeved polo shirt and linen slacks, but the sight of the push boat's glassless windows opening onto impenetrable darkness made him shiver.

"Remember Ares?" Anthem asked him.

"Your first kiss. How could I forget . . ."

Ben had watched it transpire from a few yards away, where he held to a lamppost to avoid being jostled off his feet by the crowd. To be reminded of it now was to remember the quiet terror that overcame him as he had watched his best friend fall into Anthem's arms. It wasn't envy; he had no desire for either of them. It was a sudden, frightening belief that Nikki Delongpre had, in a simple series of movements, taken her rightful place in the world, a place he could not take beside her because there was something inside him that was broken, something that would keep him forever out of step.

And yet, here he was—alive—while Nikki had been torn from them just a few years after that night.

"There's a spot . . ." Anthem started. But he lost his voice suddenly. He pulled his silver flask from his pants pocket, but instead of taking a sip, he turned it over in his hands. Ben didn't hear anything slosh inside. Was it actually empty? There was no way. The thing had never been empty since they were both eighteen years old. "It's the spot where we . . . up in the wheelhouse. Every year on her birthday, I take some pearls and beads that I caught at the Ares parade . . . I ju— I take them up there and I make a little . . ."

"An altar?" Ben asked. His vision had blurred, but his voice sounded steadier than Anthem's.

"Yeah," Anthem whispered.

Neither of them said anything for a few minutes. And with the hot flush of tears running through him, the temperature of the damp wind seemed to rise. The rustling of the tall grass hypnotized him. And then he was hearing the distant sounds of marching bands.

He was back on Third Street and St. Charles Avenue, where Mardi Gras flags banded with stripes of purple, green and gold flapped against the Ionic columns of the Greek Revival mansions all around him and the diesel fuel smell from the float trucks mingled with the scent of spilled beer to make an odor as acrid and overpowering and suggestive of sex as the one that blanketed the shores of Lake Pontchartrain.

Ben didn't trust memory. He respected its seductive power, but he didn't trust it. Early on, Marissa had hammered into him how unreliable eyewitness accounts could be, how many gaps people filled in with their imagination and their biases. Multiple accounts were the basis of solid journalism. So didn't it follow that all memories, the good ones and the bad ones, were just fanciful re-creations of what a person had either wished for or feared in a given moment? To be accurate, and to remain accurate over a period of years, a memory required its possessor to have an almost impossible degree of awareness of each passing second, each smell, each touch, each sound. Waking dreams: that was a better description of what people called memories. And he didn't care for them.

But a small, persistent voice kept urging him to question these intellectualizations. Why? Because they were always prompted by a flash, an echo, the tail edge of a nightmare about Niquette Delongpre. And he feared that the righteousness with which he had repudiated the efficacy of memory over the past few years was driven not by maturity, but by his contempt for his own grief. A man who doesn't trust his memories cannot be easily haunted.

"You'd tell me if you thought she was alive, right?"

"She's not alive, A-Team."

"Most days, I'm sure. But you . . . Every day you're sure. How the hell you manage that shit, Benny?"

"Because I know she loved you too much to walk away."

"You too, Benny. She loved you too."

"It was different."

"Different, maybe. But not . . . *less*."

It wasn't like Anthem to be this charitable, not when he'd danced with the bottle right into the path of law enforcement or firearms. He had maybe another night or two in the drunk tank before someone at the New Orleans–Baton Rouge Steamship Pilots Association decided to look past his family connections and ask whether or not it was a good idea to let him pilot giant ships full of dangerous chemicals up and down one of the most populated stretches of the Mississippi River.

But tonight, something was different, and Ben wasn't quite sure how. Anthem reached inside his pocket and pulled out a crumpled piece of paper. There wasn't much of a moon, so Ben took out his iPhone and used his flashlight app to read it by.

There were three words written on the paper in the draftsmanlike block-printing in which Anthem wrote most everything except his signature.

I AM DONE.

For a while Ben stared at the note, until a gust of hot wind made it almost impossible to hold on to, and Anthem plucked it from his grip to keep it from blowing away. Ben was no stranger to the man's drunken theatrics, but this one he couldn't figure out. For starters, Anthem didn't seem that drunk, and then there'd been the text message. What had his closing line been? *Bring sanity.*

"Guy took a shot at me at Fat Harry's 'cause I wouldn't give up the video poker machine," Anthem finally said.

"I heard. But he missed."

"Yep. Shot his own foot."

"*Both* his own feet."

"Yeah. Guess he was drunker than I was. So I left, my evening being ruined and all, and I remember getting home, remember popping a bottle of Crown Royal. A little 7-Up. Next thing I know, I'm staring at this"—he shook the note in one hand—"and every bottle of liquor in my house has been emptied out the sink and the bottles are all smashed up in a pile on my kitchen floor."

Don't say anything, Ben told himself. *If this is real, if this is going to be . . . an actual thing, just keep your mouth shut.*

"You believe in God, Benny?"

"A couple of 'em, yeah."

Anthem cackled, then he reached through the darkness, pinched one of Ben's cheeks and gave it a little slap. "You're so clever, Benny. You've always been so damn clever."

"Yeah, well, I try."

"You don't have to. It's in your blood. It's in your brain."

"Sure . . ."

Anthem seemed to forget him altogether suddenly, his attention fixed on the old push boat and the warren of shadows within. "Hand of God wrote that note, Benny." He turns his flask over in his hands. "Don't know how. Don't know why. But I'm gonna listen to it. I'm gonna be *done.*"

Without warning, he hurled the silver-plated flask into the air. It vanished into darkness, and then Ben was amazed to hear the thing impact the side of the push boat yards away with a resounding, metallic gong. The same flask Anthem had drunk from, to nauseating effect, as they'd driven the state eight years earlier, putting up flyers of the Delongpres. The same flask he'd snuck in his jacket pocket to both his high school and college graduations.

"That's okay," Anthem finally said. "I wouldn't believe me either."

Anthem turned and clapped a hand on Ben's shoulder, shaking him with enough force to jostle Ben's ankles where he stood. Then he took him into a full embrace and lifted his feet off the ground.

"Guess I'll just have to prove it to you, you little shit."

"No," Ben wheezed. "I believe you. I promise." And maybe his words, despite being squeezed out of him by Anthem's childish aggression, were more true than he'd realized; he was blinking back tears as he said them.

15

Do you believe him?" Marissa asked. It was the Monday after Anthem's alleged run-in with the hand of God, and Ben had arrived in Marissa's office at nine o'clock on the dot, just as she'd requested. He was well rested and well caffeinated, but he'd also been possessed by a strange, energizing optimism in the wake of Anthem's declaration. *Maybe Anthem's bottle-smashing God gave me a little nudge too. What can I give up? Worrying half to death?*

Leave it to Marissa to question his faith in his friend so bluntly. "I'm not sure I'd bet the house on it," Ben said. "But you know . . . fingers crossed."

"AA?"

"I doubt it. He's not exactly a team player."

"Yeah, well, speaking of his *team*. We're doing an investigation of the pilot's associations. All three of 'em. It's going to be a whopper. Months of investigation, probably across several issues. Huge exposure . . . if you take it, that is."

"You're only putting one reporter on it?"

"Yes. And I'm offering it to you."

"What sort of investigation?"

"The usual allegations. That the admissions process is driven by nepotism. That they've got too much lobbying power in Baton Rouge. That the pilots are overpaid and don't have—"

"They're not overpaid."

"Three hundred thousand dollars a year. A lot of people would beg to differ, Ben. Including me."

"They pilot tankers full of deadly chemicals through one of the most populated and dangerous stretches of river in the country. One wrong move and the foot of Canal Street is gone."

"Ben—"

"They're *not* overpaid, Marissa."

"Well, that's a point of view worth exploring if you take the story."

"I want Crowley first."

"I'm not talking about a trade, Ben."

"I've got a member of Judge Crowley's personal staff who says they can get me chains of title on the man's plane, on all his boats, and all the other shiny little gifts he gets from the oil industry before he makes a decision in their favor."

"You *think* he gets those gifts from the oil—"

"I would *know* for sure, and so would our readers, if you'd let me run with it."

"He's off-limits. Sorry."

"Why?"

"Orders from on high."

"I see. So our new owner, Peter Lane, told us to leave Crowley alone. Is that it?"

"*Hilda* Lane is our owner, not her husband. And if you haven't heard her say it a *thousand* times, she's a registered libertarian who claims to have no political agenda with this paper—"

"But her husband and the judge are both members of Metairie Country Club so Crowley's off-limits."

"Take a seat before your halo falls off, Ben."

"Please. Just tell me you didn't ask the Lanes for permission to—"

"I most certainly did not!" Marissa barked, and for just a second, Ben glimpsed the old, fiery, Marissa, the one who'd been more journalist than bureaucrat, the one who hadn't had the entire fate of the paper resting on her shoulders and its temperamental, wealthy new owners constantly nipping at her heels. "Crowley's about to rule on whether or not five miles of natural gas pipeline running through Ascension Parish is going to need to reduce its maximum operating pressure to fit with current standards."

"And he will rule that the pipeline was built before 1970 and therefore if they have operating information that dates back that far, the law says they can keep pumping as much money as they want through all those poor people."

"I understand that. But the plaintiffs have good lawyers arguing that if the information from before 1970 is incomplete, then Hodell Gas will have to reduce the pipeline's pressure—"

"And Crowley will rule in favor of Hodell Gas, Marissa. He's got a history."

"I'm aware that it's a distinct possibility. But I can't offer you a trade on this, Ben. Not right now. We're still . . . Everything's still *transitional* around here, all right? Let the Lanes get comfortable. Let *me* get comfortable, and then you can go back to taking all kinds of risks. But right now, this is the best I can do."

He bit his lip because it seemed less risky than biting his tongue. The office's expansive window offered a view of the beautifully restored brick buildings outside. When he'd started work with the paper as a lowly summer intern, they'd been crammed into a decrepit office building in the Central Business District, on one of the last remaining floors that hadn't yet been turned into a valet lot for the hotels on Canal Street. Now they were in a shiny new office building in the Warehouse

District with a high-end spa on the first floor and a chrome water feature in the lobby that hadn't broken once since they'd moved in. But all of it—the three new full-time copy editors, Marissa's mahogany desk, even the professionally framed blow-up of her book cover hanging on the wall next to him, were gifts from Peter and Hilda Lane. For that matter, so was Marissa's promotion to editor in chief, and a lot of the holdovers liked to grouse that the Lanes had vaulted Marissa over folks with more editorial experience because they were smitten by the rave review her book had received in *The New York Times*.

"Any idea why the Lanes put the pilots in their sights all of a sudden?" he asked.

"Peter Lane's father, probably. Rivalry between the oil companies and the pilots predates this building."

"That's all?"

Marissa took a deep breath and rested her hands against the edge of her shiny new desk. Ben thought she was going to ask him to leave. Instead, she said, "Hilda Lane's nephew's had an application in front of NOBRA for six months. No one's even looked at it. They think it's 'cause he doesn't have an *in*."

"Or they know his uncle was one of the most powerful men in Louisiana oil."

"If you take the story you can control it, Ben. Within limits, of course."

"You mean keep Anthem out of it."

"It's a valid concern, considering his DUI last year. And that he wasn't pulled from the pilot's rotation even once because of it. If I toss this to Leo Pigeon and he turns that up, it'll be his to roll with."

"Not if I get to Leo first."

"That's between you and Leo."

"All right. Well, I appreciate the offer, but—"

"Ben. Come on, now—"

"Don't give me another ultimatum. Please. I've honored the last one for eight years now—"

"Ben—"

"—I never bothered his family. I never followed him to Atlanta after Katrina. Christ, I haven't so much as typed his name into a goddamn search engine, 'cause I'm afraid you're gonna fire me if I do. Marshall Ferriot could be *dead* for all I know and—"

"*Ben!*"

His face felt so hot he suddenly wouldn't have been surprised if his cheeks had started to blister. Even though it was a good five minutes after Marissa had first ordered him to sit down, he forced himself into an empty chair.

His outburst had embarrassed him on a variety of levels, not the least of which was the fact that both he and Marissa knew full well why her ultimatum had been so easy for Ben to follow. Deep down, Ben knew that if he ever turned up significant evidence that Marshall had contributed to the disappearance of the Delongpres, Anthem would find out about it and murder the bastard in his hospital bed—that fact hadn't changed in eight years. *Not a fact,* Ben corrected himself. *A fear. Your fear.* And he also couldn't deny that once the initial burst of adolescent resourcefulness and outrage had subsided, once Katrina ripped the foundations out from under just about everything he held dear, Marshall's long, uninterrupted sleep and the destruction of Heidi Ferriot's life as she became his embittered, shut-in nursemaid seemed to Ben like adequate consolation prizes for having to leave the whole truth resting somewhere in the shadows off Highway 22. Especially if the cost of going deeper into those woods was losing Anthem Landry to his own rage.

"I scared you that bad, huh?" Marissa asked.

"I'm sorry . . . I shouldn't have raised my voice."

"It's fine. I just wish I had that kind of power over the Lanes, I guess." After a long silence, Marissa said, "Last time I checked, Marshall was in a long-term care facility in Atlanta. His mother died last year, and his condition was unchanged, so he probably won't live much longer either."

"Just for the record . . . I didn't ask. That's not what that was about."

"I know you didn't. But, Ben . . . please. The Lanes were the *only* offer we had. You didn't want to work for a blog for free, did you?"

"No, I didn't."

"All right, then. Go see what else you can drum up. I'm sure you'll find something. You always do."

She gestured for him to leave, but once he reached the door, she called out to him.

"Are you in love with him?" she asked.

"Anthem? You serious?"

She nodded.

"Nine times out of ten, I look at him, I don't see him. I see her."

Marissa nodded again as if she were considering his answer, but she'd averted her eyes. He would have preferred if she'd ask him something this personal outside the office, but it wasn't like she didn't have the right, not after what they'd been through together: Nikki's disappearance, her own mother's death, Katrina.

"If I lose him . . . Nikki's gone forever. That's how it feels, at least. I don't know. What do you think? Does that sound like love?"

Marissa shrugged, made a show of rifling through paper she didn't seem to be reading.

"Besides, I only date black guys."

"Go."

"Especially if they're related to you," he said as he left.

"*Go!*"

That night, the dream came back. It was Ben's only recurring dream, and in it, he was never alone. Anthem walked beside him and the land under their bare feet was dry, cracked and uneven. As always, Ben was dimly aware that they were traversing the long-submerged bedrock of Louisiana after it had been scorched dry by a nuclear sun. The blackened, tangled trees on every horizon always seemed to be the same vast distance away, tattered fringes of shadow against a cloudless, bloodred sky. Great swirls of paper defied the laws of gravity all around them; propelling themselves through the air like waterborne bacteria. And on every piece of paper the word MISSING screamed out at the wasteland in 36-point typeface. And on every piece of paper there was a photograph of Niquette Delongpre, smiling confidently in her fleecy pullover, a pair of Mardi Gras pearls around her neck.

And even though they were stark naked, their skin lacerated and oozing from a thousand lashes with origins unknown to him, Ben and Anthem kept walking through the swirls of desperate, pleading flyers. And with one hand held against the small of Anthem's naked, bloody back, Ben urged them both forward through this wasteland of long-ago fire and perpetual loss. Then at some point, the papers would start turning to cinders the second they touched the scorched earth, and Ben would become aware that the man next to him was muttering something. Not just words but lyrics.

> *The Texas sun beats down upon me*
> *Like the Devil's smile*
> *I'd rather be anywhere else but here*
> *Was it a blinding lack of subtlety or just a lack of style*
> *Responding to the ways and means of fear?*

And though it would feel to Ben like he had joined Anthem in song, he was never able to hear his own voice, just Anthem's, raspy and muffled, as if he were singing in his sleep, his mouth half buried in a pillow.

> *Take me back to New Orleans*
> *And drop me at my door*
> *'Cause I might love you, yeah*
> *But I love me mooooore . . .*

Ben woke from the dream as he always did, with a sense of certainty that comforted him and the lyrics of Anthem's favorite Cowboy Mouth song cycling through his brain. Sure, the dream was full of blood and apocalyptic set pieces, but its message was always the same comforting incantation. No matter what happened, all he and Anthem needed to be on any given day were just two boys walking, wounds and all, one foot in front of the other, the other ready to reach over and right the other should he stumble.

The clock on the nightstand said it was 12:30. But the longer Ben stared at the glowing green numerals, the more his sense of peace departed.

12:31. The change of minute roused him suddenly. And then he realized what had awakened him, because he heard the noise a second time: the creak of a floorboard nearby. His apartment was one half of an old town house; the warped hardwood floors were sensitive. But this noise was too close to his bed.

He sat up, planning his next moves. First he'd pull the gun from his nightstand drawer, then he'd turn on the light. But before he could do either, a wave of darkness passed over the entire room. His first thought was that a plane had flown low over the house, but there was no way a plane could have blocked out the streetlights; everything inside the room—every shadow, every dull glare from outside—was suddenly gone. It felt as if the darkness itself had claimed him from within.

And then it was over. And the streetlight's tree-branch laced halo on the floor near his bed seemed preternaturally vivid, the result of having been blotted out entirely for several impossible seconds by . . . he had no idea what.

He pulled the handgun Anthem had forced on him for his birthday one year, firing-range lessons included, from the nightstand drawer— *If you're gonna be gettin' up in people's faces, you're gonna need to protect yourself, Benny*—then he turned on the lamp and swung his feet to the floor, gun leveled on his yawning bathroom door. The worst part was drawing back the shower curtain, but there was nothing there except his enormous collection of body washes.

In the living room, he found the front door locked, the lock undamaged, every piece of unopened mail exactly where he'd left it on his desk. The kitchen sink's usual mountain of unwashed coffee cups hadn't been disturbed, and the window just above was still locked. No impressions in his humble collection of IKEA furniture.

His apartment was empty, the doors and windows locked, the only sound the slight, steady rattle of the AC vents overhead. But the conviction that he wasn't alone was like a second heartbeat inside his chest. And he knew there was only one way to be rid of the feeling, and it didn't come from inside a bottle. It came from his phone. Or at least that's where it started.

The app had become a punch line among almost every gay man he knew, but it was effective, and within a few seconds of settling down onto his sofa, Ben was paging through semigrainy photos of other gay men like himself, most of whom were only a few blocks away, doing exactly the same thing he was. He swiped through a few familiar faces and lots of bare chests. Camera phones had shown the world there was no end of dehumanizing poses the male form could be contorted into before a bathroom mirror.

After a few minutes of searching, he hit on a potential target. A broad-shouldered linebacker type with the right dusting of hair on his pecs. They chatted for barely five minutes, each individual exchange barely more than a few words in length. No niceties, no flirting; nothing other than the almost split-second joining of two compatible and wildly superficial fantasies.

A few minutes later, he'd managed a quick shower, changed his T-shirt and boxers and was standing just inside the front when there was a flash of headlights turning onto his street. He'd dimmed most of the lights so he could peer out at his visitor without being noticed. When the guy stepped under the porch light's bright halo, Ben was relieved to see the guy matched his profile pic; the same brawn, the same five o'clock shadow.

He'd executed his next moves countless times. Open the door, give the guy a slight smile, nothing too toothy or broad or effusive (or effeminate). Don't say too much; who knows what turn of phrase could ruin whatever fantasy the guy had cooked up in his head about who Ben was or who he wanted Ben to pretend to be for the next twenty minutes or so? He'd offer the guy a drink, let him work his way toward the bedroom and then they'd be good to go.

Ben was halfway through this script when he realized that something about the guy was off. He wasn't sweating or skittery like the tweakers Ben often had to turn away. Instead he was a blend of sullen and tightly wound that set off alarm bells in Ben's brain. Hand jammed in his jeans pockets, surveying their surroundings carefully, as if he were inventorying the room. And he was big. Anthem big. But when Ben asked him if he wanted a drink, the guy asked for a beer in a breathy, even tone of voice that didn't have a psychotic edge to it.

When Ben emerged from the kitchen, Corona in one hand, the guy was gone. The door to Ben's bedroom was open. It was the only place the guy could have gone, so Ben stepped into the darkness after him. And that's when the guy hit from behind with bone-rattling, breath-stealing force, sending Ben hurtling face-first onto the bed. The beer bottle flew from his hand and smashed to the floor. Before he could protest, the guy had driven his head into the pillow, one giant hand clamped on the back of his neck.

"Bite it, you little faggot," the guy growled. *"Bite it!"* The smoothness had left the man's voice, replaced by a tone as precise and taut as a piano wire. But none of this was what Ben had agreed to do during their chat. He was into quick, frenzied passion, not outright violence. When he yelled, *"Stop!"* the guy seized the back of his neck and slammed him face-first into the headboard. A ring of fire encircled Ben's skull, so fierce and brilliant he couldn't tell what exact part of his head had struck wood. He tasted blood and realized he'd bitten down on his tongue. Then he felt a strange pressure in his jaw and realized some kind of gag was being shoved into his mouth.

Mouth at Ben's ear, the man growled, "You shut your fuckin' mouth, you little faggot. You hear me? You shut your *goddamn—*" And then his grip on Ben's neck went slack. His weight lifted off him and the breath suddenly rushed back into Ben's lungs. The bastard hadn't finished fastening the ball bag to the band in back, so Ben was able to spit the thing out onto the pillow. He threw himself onto his back, grabbed for the nightstand drawer and pulled out the handgun he'd never drawn on another human being before that moment.

His attacker was now wide-eyed, slack-jawed and standing a few feet from the foot of the bed, as if he'd been drawn off of Ben by an invisible cord. But there was a dullness to his eyes, a vacantness there. Maybe it was a trick of the light streaming into the darkened bedroom from the living room, carving strange shapes on one side of the man's face. *The gun,* Ben finally realized. *He's not looking at the gun. I'm pointing a gun at him and he's not even looking at the damn thing.*

"You deserve better than this," the man said, his voice drained of all aggression. "You are beautiful and you deserve better than this."

"Get out! Now!"

"You are beautiful and you deser—"

"*Get out!*"

Ben's scream was loud enough to wake the neighbors, and in response, the man pivoted on one heel, walked toward the doorway, grabbed the edge of the door frame in both hands and brought his own forehead into the wood with a crack that turned Ben's stomach. Without flinching or hesitating, he did it a second time. Then a third time. Blood sprouted from his forehead, painting the bridge of his nose.

"*Get out! Now!*"

The man turned on one heel and headed into the living room. Ben shot to his feet, gun raised and sighted on the man's back as he headed for the front door, steps steady. Blood from the giant man's gashed forehead dribbled into a neat trail along the hardwood floor. He left the front door open behind him so Ben moved through it, gun raised.

His neighbor Elsa lived in the other side of the town house, which meant they shared a front porch. She was a surgical resident used to blood and long hours but she was still given pause by the sight of her tiny gay neighbor in boxers and a T-shirt, holding a shiny gun on a giant, bloody-faced man who was shuffling toward his pickup truck with the casual air of someone who'd left his cell phone inside it.

"Give him three minutes," Ben said, his voice shaking. "If he's not gone in three minutes, we call the cops."

"Three minutes," she responded.

"Three minutes," Ben repeated, only now it was a trembling whisper.

As soon as the man slid behind the wheel of his truck, he jerked as if he had awakened from an alcoholic blackout. Split personality disorder, Ben thought. It had to be. Whatever it was, Ben didn't give a shit. Whatever it was, it was dangerous and his skull was still singing and he'd fire at the fucker's kneecap if he made a run at the house.

The nearby streetlight threw enough dull light inside the truck's cab that Ben could see that the man's eyes were focused now, and full of wild hostility again. But there was confusion there too. And for the first time, he seemed to notice the gun in Ben's hands. Maybe that's because Ben was now standing only a few feet from the truck's driver-side window, gun raised, his hands finally steady.

With the careful enunciation of a kindergarten teacher, Ben said, "Get the fuck out of here. Right now."

The truck sped off, giving Ben a glimpse of the Confederate flag sticker and pissing Calvin on the rear window. Once the taillights vanished around the corner, Elsa joined him on the sidewalk, portable phone pressed to her breasts.

Ben lowered the gun.

"Jesus Christ," she whispered. "What did you do to— Whoa." Her fingers went to the bruises on his face, bruises he hadn't seen yet so he had no idea how bad they were.

"He did it—"

"No. The blood on his face—"

"I know. He did all of it. He threw me on the bed and then it was like he changed his mind. He smashed his head into the door frame."

"Ben . . ."

"I'm dead serious, Elsa."

"How'd you get him off you?"

"I didn't. He just . . . stopped. I don't know."

"Because of the gun?"

"No. Before I got the gun."

"Crazy," Elisa whispered again.

"Pretty much. Yeah."

"You got a permit for that thing?" she asked him.

"Yeah. Why?"

" 'Cause I'm calling the cops," she said, heading back toward their front steps.

"And what are you going to tell them?"

"His plate number. I wrote it down."

She was almost inside her front door when she said, "And Ben. This might not be the time, but maybe you could try meeting men the old-fashioned way."

"What's the old-fashioned way again?"

"I don't know. Dinner?"

"I wasn't in the mood for dinner," he said.

"Were you in the mood for *this*?"

He returned to his bedroom, turned on the lamp, put the gun back inside his nightstand. Then he shook for a few minutes

What *had* he been in the mood for? He'd never dated anyone for longer than a few months because that was how long it took him to feel the upsurge of desperate possessiveness within him that he knew would destroy any chance at a healthy relationship. So instead, he'd nuke the thing with the usual platitudes and clichés. He had his career to focus on. He wasn't all that big on gay bars or leaving the house when he wasn't working or blah blah blah. Some guys were pros at the Internet sex game and as far as he was concerned, more power to them. But he was different, always had been. For him, these quick, late-night assignations had become a grim compulsion that protected him from the terror of being abandoned again.

You are beautiful and you deserve better.

Insane that the guy had chosen those words. They must have been fueled by some kind of schizophrenic self-loathing; maybe the sick bastard saw himself as Ted Bundy one minute, Ted Haggard the next. It was a good thing Elsa has insisted on calling the police. At the very least, they had to give them the guy's plate number before he hurt somebody else.

You are beautiful and you deserve better.

There was a pad and pen in his nightstand. He wrote the words down exactly as he remembered the guy saying them. And as soon as he lifted the sheet of paper in his hands, a flood of adrenaline-fueled warmth coursed through him, causing his extremities to tingle and the hairs on the back of his neck to stand on end in pinprick formations. He could hear the sound of his own breathing.

Hand of God wrote that note, Benny. A few nights earlier he'd held a piece of paper similar to this one, and the phrase written on it had been just as brief and direct. Of course, his story wasn't the same as Anthem's. He hadn't come out of some blackout to find this note sitting on his desk, in his own handwriting. But the words themselves had come from somewhere else, they'd tumbled from the suddenly slack jaw of his attacker, who had just been seized up and off Ben's prone body as if by the . . . *hand of God.*

Belief. Faith. Maybe those were the only apt words to describe the sensations that were moving through him now, edging out the stark terror of his assault, replacing it with something softer and more malleable. He hadn't been lying when he told Anthem that he believed in more than one god. But his faith in some kind of higher power was an untested thing, more of a bet on fifty-fifty odds than the result of an actual spiritual experience of the kind Anthem had described to him the other night. And now, here he was, feeling as if events around him had been manipulated in some mysterious and unknowable way, but at a speed that was suddenly visible and obvious. Undeniable.

You are beautiful and you deserve better. Not the words of that deranged man who had just filled his bedroom with terror. The words that had come *through* that man.

A faith experience. Isn't that what they called this? The kind of bullshit you read about on those vaguely Christian pamphlets left behind in hospital waiting rooms, the kind with crude, brightly colored illustrations. And it had happened to him.

When Elsa stepped inside his front door to tell him what the police had said, she froze in her tracks and gave him a funny look, and that's when Ben realized he was smiling.

V

MARSHALL

16

Danny Stevens made it to the front porch just in time to see the taillights of his wife's Mercedes disappear around the wall of stately oak trees at the end of their driveway. He tried her cell, but there was no answer. Satellite radio, Kelly Clarkson, his wife's impatience: Danny blamed all three in equal measure.

"Metamucil," he said after the beep. "Orange-flavored. None of that pink lemonade crap . . . And sorry. You know, about . . ." What was he apologizing for? His irregularity or his forgetfulness? He wasn't sure, so he hung up.

Just a few minutes earlier, Sally had cornered him in the kitchen, armed with pad, pencil and her plainest pair of eyeglasses, the ones she only wore to Albertsons on the weekends. Danny had insisted up and down that they weren't out of anything, only to realize his omission once he was alone with his bloat. But that's not what was really bothering him. Lately, he'd been consumed by a burning need to issue some kind of apology to his wife whenever she entered the room. And he often did, usually a mumbled, halfhearted thing, as reflexive and irritating as a dry cough. Sometimes she would hear it and stop in the doorway to ask if something was the matter, and he'd do his best not to give her a guilty look. Because in the end, what did he have to feel guilty about?

Unlike most of the men he worked with at Cypress Bank & Trust, he'd never cheated. (Not on his wife, anyway.) And he was a damn good provider—that was for sure. The house was proof of that: two stories of French Regency perfection with immaculate limestone walls and second-floor windows adorned by slender, intricate iron railings. Just another year of bleeding the Ferriot trust and the damn thing would be paid off too. Because that's what good providers did; they made deals that had to be kept in the shadows.

It was a crisp autumn afternoon. The house wasn't right on the Tchefuncte River, but it was pretty close. Just a few yards of smooth, rolling lawns separated them from the glassy green waters and the boat dock they shared with their neighbor Lloyd Duchamp. Technically the oaks between the house and the water belonged entirely to Lloyd, but he'd allowed Sally to dress them up with string lights last Christmas, probably as penance for that awful hog of a motorcycle he'd bought after his wife left him.

Danny loved Beau Chêne. And no matter how bad things got at the bank, he'd fight like hell to stay within its grassy, wooded borders. The place had given his son a damn near perfect childhood, a childhood where Douglas and his friends could water ski in their own backyard and spend afternoons on the rope swing without fearing stray bullets. Nothing like his childhood, trapped in the Irish Channel with a mother who refused to let go of the old house on Constance Street even after the blacks moved in on all sides.

But things at the bank were bad, had been bad for a long time in fact. Like most of the other managers and officers at Cypress, Danny wore the fact that he was employed by the last locally owned bank in New Orleans as a badge of honor. But lately the whispers about a sale to one of the nationals had grown into a dull clamor, and even senior staff were starting to jump ship to JPMorgan Chase. Layoffs were imminent, he was sure of it. And if his situation were any different, Danny probably would have left by now.

But his situation wasn't different. There was one trust he just couldn't afford to leave.

His son had arrived for a visit the night before, but he'd only been home an hour or two before zipping across the causeway to meet up with some friends. They'd probably done a circuit of all the old Uptown bars they used to frequent in high school with their fake IDs, and now Douglas was probably sleeping it off at a buddy's house. Midway through his junior year at Chapel Hill, his son's connection to his hometown was still as strong as ever. *Good,* Danny thought as he made his way to the kitchen. *Too many of us leave. Too many of the good ones anyway.* As for the fact that Douglas had left his bags at the foot of the stairs? Everyone has room for improvement.

Home alone, for a half hour at least. Too fast for a quick wank to some of the new porn he'd downloaded the night before: naughty nurse stuff, a little spanking thrown in, predictable but efficient. (And the truth was, at fifty-five, a quick wank wasn't as easy to pull off as it had been a few years before.) The news was out too. More depressing footage off that awful pipeline explosion over in Ascension Parish; trailers turned to molten heaps, mothers weeping for the incinerated children. The whole place looked like Pompeii, and though Sally couldn't seem to pull her eyes away from the coverage, he'd had enough after twenty minutes.

So John Coltrane and a quick scotch would have to do, but as soon as Danny closed his hand around the bottle of Balvenie, he was swallowed by a wave of silent darkness.

His first thought when he came to was, *I'm having a stroke.* He was in the front parlor. It was still light out, the Audubon bird prints were still safely in their frames.

The last thing he could remember was holding the bottle of scotch. Had he downed the whole thing? Was this the end of some alcoholic blackout?

But there was no headache, no sour stomach even. No pain of any kind. And for some reason, that scared him more than anything else—the fact that this feeling of complete disorientation, this sense of having lost time completely, wasn't accompanied by any physical sensations at all.

It was like he'd literally been plucked out of time and moved to a different . . . second? Minute? Hour?

Some kind of weight was tugging against his right arm. When he looked down, he saw he was holding one of the massive candleholders his wife kept on the mantel. The thing was solid glass, the base a fat pillar, the platform still matted with the waffle-print residue of those high-end beeswax candles Sally loved.

A brain tumor? Wasn't this how it started with Jake Bensen? No, that wasn't it. The guy had tripped. One day he was walking across his bedroom and it was like his right foot wasn't quite attached to his ankle. MRI. Inoperable. Four months. Just four months from diagnosis to—

A car engine distracted him from this quickening panic. Then he heard another sound: someone breathing, someone standing a few feet away.

Before Danny could turn or scream—and he started to do both at the same exact second—the darkness returned. And this time it felt like great pincers rising up from under his feet, closing high above his head, sealing him inside an obsidian tomb.

His office. He was standing in the middle of his office and the flat-screen computer monitor was turned around so he could see it. He blinked and tried to focus.

The candleholder was in his right hand still. He dropped it and it hit the hardwood floor with a deep, fatal-sounding thud. His entire body was sore, the same kind of bone-deep ache he used to feel after the gym.

The glowing computer screen looked grainy. He took a step toward the screen, fearing for a second or two that his legs wouldn't respond to his commands. But they did. He was back inside his body, and whatever was on his screen wasn't part of the plain blue wallpaper he'd opted for in a quick, distracted moment.

It was blood splatter.

His desk chair had been turned to face the window so he couldn't see who was sitting in it, just the coil after coil of bloody nylon rope that had been used to tie them down.

Against his will, Danny Stevens reached for the back of his desk chair so he could turn it around and see who it was, because whoever it was, they weren't moving. He'd heard a car engine outside in those last few seconds before the darkness returned, so whoever was in his chair, they had to be—

"Don't do that yet," someone said.

Danny bellowed and landed ass-first on the floor.

Marshall Ferriot stepped forward from the band of shadow beside the double doors to the hallway. The last time Danny had laid eyes on the guy had been six months earlier, on the same computer screen that was now smeared with blood. The kid called the house one afternoon, right after they'd sent Allen Shire after him and his sister, and a dumbfounded Danny had refused to stay on the phone for more than a few seconds without some kind of proof the caller was who he claimed to be. Skype: that had been the kid's suggestion, the same thing he and Sally often used to talk to Douglas when he was up at school. And so, stunned and slack-jawed and wishing he could hide the emotions passing over his face, Danny had listened intently that day as Marshall Ferriot made his pitch.

He hadn't just listened. He had given in, completely.

And it had all gone perfectly since then. But now, Marshall was in his office and there was blood everywhere, so maybe it hadn't gone so well after all. The kid seemed to have no trouble moving around but he looked gaunt and ghostly. How long had it been since he'd come to? Six months. What had he said at that time? *I need time to get my bearings. And a fresh start. After what I've been through, I think I deserve a fresh start, don't you, Mr. Stevens?*

And so, as far as anyone at Cypress Bank & Trust knew, Marshall Ferriot was still a vegetable, still being cared for in seclusion by his dutiful sister. Danny had taken care of everything: submitting fake medical reports to the trust committee, setting up a new account to receive the disbursements, which he and Marshall could both access—Marshall under a new identity Danny had provided for him, Henry Lee. He'd been handling Allen Shire himself, so there weren't a lot of questions to answer on that front.

The split was a little more than fifty-fifty, weighted more generously in Danny's favor. That had been the kid's proposal, not Danny's. And he'd never taken out a penny more than he was supposed to. So why? Why was this happening? Why was there blood everywhere? Why was the kid *here* in his house?

When Danny tried to ask this question, he tasted blood on his lips. He rubbed at his mouth and the back of his hand came away dark red. Suddenly all he could do was wheeze and groan for a minute or two while Marshall studied him patiently.

"I did . . . I did everything you asked . . . Everything we ag-agreed to . . ."

"I know." But he didn't sound grateful.

Marshall crouched down next to him and Danny looked into his eyes for the first time in his life. He'd only seen them in photographs. At first, their large size made them oddly welcoming, but then he saw they were utterly expressionless; staring into them felt like being invited to dive headfirst into an empty swimming pool.

"Please," Danny wheezed. "Please . . . tell me . . ." He gestured toward the chair.

"Oh, I get it. You want to know who it is?" Marshall asked evenly. "Your wife, or your son?"

A sob exploded from Danny's chest.

"I know, I know. It's a real mind fuck, isn't it? No pun intended. But the whole thing—it kinda makes sense, don't you think? My gift, I mean. After the way my sister dragged me around like a rag doll just so she could keep getting her checks. It's gotta be some kind of poetic justice. . . . Hey, you know what's also interesting, Mr. Stevens? How you never asked about her."

"Wh-who?"

"My sister. I guess you assumed she just walked away? No trust, no checks. Nothing in it for her. Was that it?"

Danny nodded. It was total bullshit, but Danny nodded.

"Uh huh . . . okay. And the private detective that you sent to find us? Allen Shire?"

"Well, I never heard from him again. I figured he'd—"

"No one ever heard from him again."

"I don't know what you're—"

"Yes, you do, Mr. Stevens. You know exactly what I'm saying."

"I figured you paid . . . paid him off, I guess . . . Both of them . . . I th-thought—"

"Did you really? Or did you think I killed them?"

"Now I do."

Marshall cackled and clapped his hands together.

"Very good, Mr. Stevens," he said once he caught his breath. "Excellent. In all seriousness, though, Allen Shire was a big help. Huge. Thanks for sending him. Eight years without moving your legs, well, it takes you a long time to learn to walk again. And I needed someone with me every step of the way. So thank you. Thank you for not sending the cavalry after him and causing a big mess for everyone. 'Cause there were other things I needed to learn too, you see? And he was very, very helpful."

Marshall tapped the side of his head with one finger and smiled broadly, and that's when Danny realized there was something in the kid's head, something that defied everything Danny had believed to be true about the world, something that had covered his office in blood while it thrust Danny into some corner of darkness inside himself.

"But you can't . . . I mean, that doesn't . . ."

"Doesn't what?"

"Just 'cause . . . My family . . . Just 'cause of what you did to them, that doesn't make it right for you to hurt my family."

"Silly rabbit! I didn't hurt your family, Mr. Stevens. *You* did."

Marshall stepped behind the desk. A few keystrokes later, a surveillance image from the hidden camera Danny had installed in the office filled the screen. He'd put the camera in after he and Marshall came to terms, and for one purpose only: to make sure no one was accessing his computer without his knowledge. But Marshall had clearly put it to another use.

There was his desk, clean, well lit, unbloodied. There was his empty chair. There was his computer monitor. The only thing that looked off was the window shade; it had been pulled and Danny couldn't remember drawing it himself.

Then, in a flash of movement that blurred and pixelated the low-resolution image, he and Sally erupted into frame, a tangle of limbs. His wife's arms pinwheeling, the glass candleholder arcing through the air, striking her in the jaw so hard Danny thought her head might rip from her neck. And then, slowly, the realization, rising up within Danny on a hot tide of bile, that he was the one bludgeoning his wife. That he was the one hurling his wife's rag doll body into the desk chair, barely waiting for her to slide limply to the floor before he brought the candleholder down on her again and again and again. And he knew the only reason he couldn't see the blood lashing onto the desk was because it was a cheap camera. But it was there when he looked down, black and oily in the dull sunlight coming through the shade.

Marshall spun the chair around. Sally was beaten beyond recognition, the border between blood and bruising impossible to distinguish anywhere on her skin, the stained flaps of the gray hooded sweater she'd been wearing squeezed by coil after coil of nylon rope.

Danny screamed. Marshall's gloved hand closed around his mouth and gathered a clump of Danny's hair in his other fist, forcing the man to watch the monitor.

"Look what you did, Daniel J. Stevens."

In his mind's eye, which he had retreated to with a suddenness and entirety that froze his sob, Danny saw his son, Douglas, blowing past the entrance booths to the causeway in his Jeep, windows down, singing along with the radio.

"I told you it was a gift," Marshall said.

He wanted to sink his teeth into the bastard's gloved fingers, but he knew that would just bring the darkness back. Because that was how this thing worked; the darkness came and then you woke up in a hell of your own making, of Marshall's making.

"I'm sorry. I know you probably think it doesn't mean anything. But I am, Danny. I'm truly sorry. You see, some things, they're just bigger than you. Bigger than me. Bigger than everyone. And this is one of them. I didn't ask for this. It came on . . . well, almost like an infection. At least I think that's what happened . . . anyhoo . . . the point here, Danny, is that I have a lot I need to get done in a very short time. And it's gonna be easier for me if everyone thinks I'm dead. Now, before you think I'm a complete bastard let me be very clear about something. A bad thing *is* going to happen to your son tonight. But you get to decide just how bad it's gonna be, Danny. Are you with me?"

The knowledge that he couldn't run, that if he cried out for help or made a mad grab for something heavy, the darkness would return in an instant, filled Danny Stevens with a kind of drunken, floaty feeling, a sense of complete powerlessness and surrender. But images of Douglas walking through the front door, calling out to him, were like jagged chunks of glass underneath his splayed palms, spiking him back into his body, preventing him from floating away to join his wife in whatever heavenly place she'd just escaped to.

"Danny? Are you listening to me?"

Danny nodded.

"Good. Because I'm going to ask you a question, and I need you to answer honestly, okay? 'Cause if you do, the worst thing that's gonna happen to your son is that he's gonna come home to find his parents dead. Which is very sad, I know. But my parents are dead too. So, boo-hoo. Join the club."

A silence fell, and Danny could hear the sounds of his own heavy breathing as if from far away.

"Ask me what's going to happen if you don't tell me the truth, Danny."

"Wh-what's going to—"

"If you lie to me, the police will find Douglas chewing your neighbor's face off."

"I won't. I won't lie. I promise I won't oh God please—"

"Okay. Okay. Christ, easy. Enough already. Chill. Just chill out and listen, okay?"

Danny nodded.

"Does anyone else know about our little arrangement?"

"I didn't tell anyone. Just like I promised. I mean, Sally didn't even—" Just saying his wife's name aloud squeezed the breath from him. Marshall shot the woman's bloodied corpse a quick glance, like he thought he might have gone too far but would consider that possibility later, after a beer.

"All right, fine. You didn't tell anyone. But do they know? Does anyone suspect anything? Anyone. Take your time. Think about it. Because believe me, I don't want to come back for your son, but I will if I have to, Mr. Stevens. I will."

Several minutes later, after he had finished a litany of silent prayers asking for forgiveness from a God who now seemed more remote than ever, Danny Stevens spoke the person's full name. And after studying his face for a bit, Marshall thanked him, nodded politely, and brought the darkness back for the last time.

17

Ben had been looking for Marissa all morning, but he only checked the dive bar a few blocks from her house because he was getting desperate. He'd actually forgotten about the place altogether; there was no sign out front and if you drove past it too quickly, you could easily mistake it for just another one of the Faubourg Marigny's brightly painted shotgun houses.

They were a few blocks from the French Quarter's jolly chaos, but it was just past ten in the morning, so Marissa was one of only three customers inside, and the only one sitting at the bar. Her hands were resting palms down on either side of a sweating, half-empty rock glass—rum and Coke, Ben figured, her usual, but not so early in the day—as if she were trying to levitate it with her mind.

"Can you change the channel, please?" Ben asked the bartender as he took a seat.

"Do *not* change the channel," Marissa said.

"Enough already, Marissa. You're not—"

"Do *not* change the channel," Marissa repeated, with enough force in her voice to make the bartender set the remote back on top of the register.

And so they sat there for a while, watching the same loop of terrible images most of the city had been hypnotized by for twelve hours now: blackened trailers guttering flames in their shattered windows, a morbidly obese white woman, her uncombed hair like bales of straw, screaming bloody murder as sheriff's deputies shoved her back from the scene of a scorched home in which her young daughter had burned to death. Only now the woman's screams were silent, her excruciating display reduced to a visual backdrop for speculating news anchors. The gas leak had probably started in the middle of the night, they were explaining for the thousandth time, and that's why no one had called the emergency number posted on warning signs that ran the pipeline's length through Ascension Parish; because they hadn't been awake to smell the cloud of methane spreading over their homes, before something, probably infinitesimal, had ignited it: a pilot light, the small spark inside a light switch. Someone's furtive late-night smoke in the backyard.

"Remind me again what I said to you in my office that day," Marissa whispered.

"I'm not going to help you punish yourself for something you didn't do."

"*Remind* me, Ben."

"Or else what?"

"Marissa Hopewell Powell is not in a position to reprimand anyone on her staff today. So, if you can find it in your heart, just remind me what I—"

"You said it wasn't the right time for us to take risks. You said . . . we needed time to let the Lanes get comfortable, to let *you* get comfortable—"

"Comfortable," Marissa snarled, and when she lifted her glass to her lips, it trembled in her hand. "If I wanted to make people comfortable, I should have gone to work in a fucking mattress store," she growled. Then she drank.

"Marissa—"

"You came to me with a line on Judge Crowley weeks before he ruled the owner of that damn pipeline didn't have to reduce their operating pressure—"

"And no piece of mine would have forced him to rule another way, and you know it. It's gradual, what we do. It's cumulative, if it works at all. You get a silver-bullet hit piece maybe once in a lifetime. Anything else is movie crap. And come on, you know how this state is. It's just like Edwin Edwards use to say. Unless we catch 'em in bed with a live boy or a dead girl, then we've got nothing. It takes *time*—"

"We don't have time!"

Ben hadn't seen her come apart like this in years, not since their fifth hour of night rescues after Katrina, their fifth hour of listening to the anguished, pleading wails of Marissa's trapped and dying neighbors calling out to them from attics and rooftops. One minute she'd been ordering them in the direction of one house, the one flashing SOS at them with a flashlight, then she'd crawled to one corner of their aluminum boat, curled into a ball and started shaking all over until Ben curved an arm around her back and held her until she went still. Of course, she'd repaid the favor a few days later, when they'd finally arrived at the Ernest M. Morial Convention Center on foot, expecting the National Guard, food and water and finding only masses of the abandoned and the dying. That's when Ben fell to his knees and wept, and the proud, educated black woman who had once snapped at him that she would never be *his mammy*, collected him off the ground, took him in her arms and kissed him gently on the neck while whispering assurances that everything would be all right. On many nights in the years since, they'd called each other randomly and without explanation, sometimes in the hours just before dawn, because something about the other person's

voice served to remind them that the bloated corpse they had awakened to find in their bedroom, the one piled in the corner like several
sacks of sand, was in fact just an untethered memory that had taken on
the illusory weight of a nightmare.

Had those late-night calls—they were always mock-casual, as if
the other was just calling to chitchat, even though it was almost 3:00
a.m.—pushed those years too far into the past? Had they lost hold of
some fundamental piece of themselves that had been revealed during
those seventy-two hours in August of 2005? It was as if the city itself
had asked them a clear and direct question when the levees failed—
Will you fight for me?—and they answered with courage and a boat. But
ever since, the answer to that same question had been: *Get back to me.
I'm busy trying to get comfortable.*

He studied her wide-eyed, furious stare, and the way she was now
lifting one trembling hand as if to hold him back, even though he
hadn't moved an inch since her outburst. Maybe it was post-traumatic
stress syndrome, or maybe it was the old, uncompromised Marissa.
One thing was for sure, he was so desperate for the return of that
long-lost woman, he didn't mind if she broke the door down on her
way in.

"This city lost its margin of error twenty years ago," Marissa said.
"Somebody's supposed to tell the truth even when no one wants 'em
to. Goddamn *Times-Picayune* isn't even a daily paper anymore. And
while I was waiting for some spoiled white lady to give me permission to do my *real* job, sixteen people burned to death in their sleep."

The door to the bar was swept open as if by a gale-force wind, and
when Ben matched the strength of the person on the other side with
the height of the baseball cap–crowned shadow suddenly blocking out
the sun, an involuntary groan escaped from him.

"This is *not* the time, A-Team," Ben managed, sliding off his bar
stool.

But by then, Anthem Landry had slammed the latest issue of *King-*

fisher down on the bar so hard the row of beer mugs behind the register clinked together, and for a few stunned seconds Ben and Marissa just stared at the cover: "RIVER ROYALTY: How a Culture of Nepotism Is Putting Our City, and Our Lives, at Risk."

The graphic, which Ben had literally turned away from when it first went up on the art board at the office, was a giant, bloodred oil tanker enlarged to the point that it looked like its wheelhouse was about to tear out the bottom half of the Crescent City Connection bridge. Ben thought it was a cruel irony that he would have been less afraid of this confrontation if Anthem had still been drinking. But at six months of sobriety, he wasn't just a live wire; he was a curtain of them wrapped around leaner, more efficient muscles. Sure, his skin looked great, and there was an unmistakable twinkle in his eyes, but ever since he'd tossed his flask into Lake Pontchartrain, he had a tendency to bare his teeth during everyday conversations and shout at waiters if they brought him a Diet Pepsi instead of a Diet Coke.

Ben saw no good end to the collision before him, no good end at all.

"You followed me here?" Ben asked.

"You wouldn't tell me where she was yesterday, and I have something to say to this nice lady."

"No, you don't. Not today."

"Oh, let him talk," Marissa muttered.

"San Francisco Bay?" Anthem growled. "You had your reporter compare our pay scale to bar pilots on San Francisco Bay? May I just point out to you that San Francisco Bay is almost as big as San Francisco. They don't have anywhere near the currents or the proximity to population we deal with out there every day."

"She didn't write the piece, Anthem."

"Did *you?*"

"Did you see my name on it?" Ben asked.

"You could have at least given me a warning, goddammit!"

"I apologize. Next time when I have to practically bribe a colleague to keep your DUI out of my paper, I'll give you plenty of notice so you can give some thought to where you're gonna buy me dinner."

"You really did that?" Anthem asked. Then, to Marissa, he said, "Did he really do that?"

"We both did," she said quietly.

"So is that some kind of consolation prize?"

"You know what, buddy?" Ben started, stepping between his best friend and his boss. "We're kinda having a day here, and it's not about you right now. I know this may come as a shock, but it's not *always* about Anthem La–"

"You're right. It's not about me. It's about the men I work with up and down this river. And they all want to know the same thing."

"Which is?" Marissa asked him.

"What do you want? You want us all fired? Restructured? Because if that's the case, then it's my duty to explain what the alternative is. It's a bunch of outsourced South Americans who will be willing to launch a tanker full of crude in a fog so thick you can't see your hand in front of your face, all so they can make a delivery deadline on the other side of the world for British Fuckin' Petroleum.

"How safe do you think our river will be then? How will you all sleep at night knowing you got ships moving up and down out there, full of God knows what, being piloted by guys who've got no connection to anything on the other side of the floodwall? Guys who live and die by what the oil industry tells 'em to do. And pardon me, but if you don't think being bossed around by the oil and gas companies is a problem, allow me to direct your attention to Ascension Parish today."

Rather than wince right in Anthem's face over this deep cut, Ben stepped out from between his best friend and his boss, and turned his back on them both. The reaction must not have been lost on Anthem, because when he spoke again, his voice had lost its hard, furious edge.

"Every moment I'm out there, I'm thinking about my family. I'm thinking about the two of you. I'm thinking about how far away every-one I care about is from the bridge I'm piloting my ship under, in case something goes wrong. Now, I know I rode out Katrina in a condo on Pensacola Beach. But if I had known what was coming, I would have been here with you both. But you have to believe me. There's not a day when I round the bend in the river and see all those build-ings still standing there that I don't thank my lucky stars . . . *There's my girl.* I say it every damn time, whether I want to or not. Ask any captain who's done a turn with me. *There's my girl . . .* But this . . . *crap* made it sound like men like me would run a ship straight through the Riverwalk if we didn't get paid on time. And that is wrong. It's just flat-out *wrong.*"

When he saw her watching the images of fiery destruction on the TV above the bar, Ben figured Marissa had tuned out Anthem's lecture altogether.

"You think you can put all that in writing?" Marissa finally asked.

"Excuse me," Anthem whispered. Ben was just as startled as An-them appeared to be.

"I *said,* do you think you can put that in writing? That way, I can have one of our copy editors go over it and we can put it up on our website this evening."

"What . . . like a letter to the editor?"

"No. A rebuttal. Better placement. Your photo. The works. It'll even get its own comment thread if your pals want to chime in."

Slack-jawed, Anthem shook his head, eyes moving from Marissa to Ben. Once he had his old friend in his sights again, he barked, "You write it!"

"I'm flattered, really," Ben said. "But I have grout to clean."

"Come on. I can't write!"

"Well, you know how to spell and you know how to shoot off your mouth. Apparently, that's all you need to know these days."

"It's all *you* knew how to do when I took you on," Marissa said to Ben.

"I don't want to work at your paper," Anthem said.

"Well, that's good, son," Marissa said, rising from her bar stool. She pulled a business card and pen out of her pocket and wrote something on the back of the card. "'Cause I didn't offer you a job. This is a one-shot deal, and I'll need it by three o'clock. Email it to Sue LaSalle, she's our Web person."

"All right . . . But you can't blame me for being suspicious. You've never liked me very much."

"Well, *A-Team,* let's just say I'm a bigger fan of Anthem two-point-oh then I was of the old version. Still, nothing can change the fact that I do hate white people. Even the pretty ones." She chucked Anthem on the cheek, then she headed for the door. "Good-bye, y'all. I have booze at home."

Ben returned to his bar stool. Anthem took Marissa's spot and gestured for the bartender. When he saw Ben's startled look, he said, "I'm gettin' a Diet Coke." Then he repeated his order to the bartender with petulant emphasis.

Ben ordered a Corona.

"You mad at me?" Anthem asked.

"No. But I do wish that you would, you know, *maybe* shut the hell up every now and then."

"Well, that's the pot calling the kettle a pot. You know, you're never going to find a boyfriend, you keep spending all your weekends with her."

"Funny. She says the same thing about you."

"I don't want a damn boyfriend!"

"That's not what I meant, genius."

"Whatever. You *don't* spend all your weekends with me."

"I used to. I used to have to chase you all over town. Your mother would be calling me all night, half out of her mind."

"Well, then you spent the weekend with my momma and not me, all right? Anyway, that's not how it is anymore."

"Guess not." The bartender brought Ben's beer. He took a slug. "Does it bother you that I'm—"

Anthem hissed and waved one hand at him dismissively, but in the same instant, he turned away from the sight of the froth collecting inside the bottle's neck as if it were a picture of Nikki Delongpre.

"This isn't some kind of setup?" he finally asked. "What do you—I don't even know what you'd call it. An article? A *piece*?"

"Piece is good," Ben said.

"You don't think she's going to try to make me look like crap?"

"No. I don't. I think it's a good thing."

"For who?"

"For both of you."

Anthem studied him for a while, decided that he was telling the truth and drained his entire Diet Coke in three uninterrupted swallows. Then he slammed the glass back down to the bar as if it were a shot of tequila. "Good!" he declared. "Then help me write the thing."

"I can't. Not today."

"Benny, *come on*. I don't have the time. I—"

"You've got nothing but time this weekend. You're on call, which means you're going to be staying home, gardening, downloading porn, and trying not to drink, until you have to go out on a ship."

"You really think I can do this?" Anthem asked him.

Ben was disarmed by the hope in Anthem Landry's reluctant smile, by the brightness in his eyes and the blend of childlike nervousness and exuberance Marissa's offer had stirred in him so suddenly. For years now, sarcasm had been his most effective shield against Anthem's physical beauty and frequent moments of raw, boyish charm. But this wasn't the time. And so what if one unguarded smile from a handsome friend had him relieving himself later that night to a preposterous and vaguely incestuous fantasy? He was allowed one or two every now and then, as long as he kept it a fantasy. As long as it was only every now and then.

"I think you're going to knock it out of the park, A-Team."

Anthem picked up his empty glass, clinked it against the neck of Ben's beer bottle, and tousled Ben's hair with one massive hand so forcefully Ben was forced to bend over and shield himself. Then he barreled out of the bar and into the blinding sunlight outside, proving with each step that it was possible for a giant to move with a spring in his step.

18

From where he stood, just outside the window above her kitchen sink, Marshall Ferriot watched the woman inside drag a meat cleaver across her left wrist, and then her right, and wondered, just as he had with her boss, Danny Stevens, earlier that morning, if it would have consoled her to know how beautiful she looked in the final moments of her life.

As she cut herself, Janice Walker appeared in Marshall's gaze as a shimmering, colorless apparition, trailing little starbursts of quantum material that shifted through the air around her like ghostly impressions of herself, impressions that effervesced so brightly in Marshall's vision, they distracted him from the resulting arterial spray when Janice effortlessly dragged the knife's blade across her throat. It was the same experience he had every time he willed himself to open to his subjects and felt the velvety rush of their souls moving into his.

As with all of them, he'd experienced a brief flash of her soul when he'd first hooked her. He'd seen a woman he knew to be her mother walking a young Janice by the hand through the Audubon Zoo, and the monkeys in their cages turned to stare at them with humanlike approval and warmth, the product of young Janice's fanciful imagination. And then the vision passed, and it felt as if he were drinking her in as he forced her to shuffle toward the cutlery block so he could get to work.

It hadn't been Marshall's intention to re-create that long-ago fantasy of what he wanted to do to Nikki Delongpre after she'd betrayed him. But that's exactly what he'd done, in all its bloody splendor, albeit from a slight distance and with a much older and less attractive subject. The little tableau was so appropriate to the day's agenda, Marshall laughed gently as the woman slid down the blood-splattered wall with lifeless, unblinking eyes.

Effortless, easy. No need for chitchat, no need to go inside and risk contaminating the scene as he'd done with Danny Stevens. And it was a painless death he'd granted her, despite all the blood. As far as Janice's consciousness was concerned, she'd been rinsing dishes one second, headed off to the afterlife the next. No need to inform her that her ticket had been punched because her boss of seven years suspected she might have had some suspicions about how much he'd stolen from the Ferriot trust.

Now she was crumpled against the blood-splattered wall just inside the back door, her Pepto-pink bathrobe spilling open over her bloodstained pajamas, her eyes glazed and lifeless, but her slack jaw still drawing slight breaths. With impossible, steady determination, she rolled over onto all fours, lifted a hand to her gushing throat and began painting letters across the nearest wall with a splattered finger: S O R R Y M A R S H A

Marshall felt the sharp tug deep in his chest that told him the woman's death had arrived. He released her, and he was relieved when she didn't spasm with sudden agony or grasp desperately for her gushing throat.

He didn't want her to suffer. After all, what was she guilty of besides answering phones for a crook for several years? He'd had no choice but to position her alongside all the other pieces he'd left behind in a precise trail of blood and lies, pieces that included her missing boss and the evidence Marshall had left on his computer suggesting his wife had discovered evidence of his crime and that this discovery had resulted in her violent murder; pieces that included Allen Shire, dead by self-inflicted gunshot wound in the house on Chamberland Island, along with a suicide note nearby explaining how he'd conspired with Elizabeth and Danny Stevens to kill Marshall and milk the trust, and that when he and Elizabeth had quarreled over his share, he'd killed her in a fit of rage, only to be consumed by guilt.

Which body would be discovered first?

The curiosity made Marshall almost giddy. He'd done such a good job. The discovery of one body would immediately lead to the others, and then the world would be made aware of a murder plot that hadn't actually been executed, by three individuals who had barely known one another. Yet the evidence would be undeniable, indisputable.

But there was one person out there who wouldn't be convinced, of this Marshall was sure.

How long before she'd hear the story? Did she have some kind of news alert set for his name or the names of his family members? (He'd set up one for the names of everyone he'd killed over the past few weeks.) There was no telling. But Marshall was confident that by the end of the day at the latest, as the news media and cops shook their heads in bafflement over the extraordinary, impossible details of the diabolical plot that had cost Marshall his life, one woman would hear the story and be gripped by fear and certainty. She would know that yes, the story of Marshall Ferriot's murder was too impossible to be true, and that the real explanation was far from ordinary, and in that moment it would be as if Marshall's ghost had floated up out of his comatose body and whispered in Nikki's delicate little ear: *I'm coming for you, bitch. I know what you did to me and I'm coming for you. But first, I'm going to destroy everything you ever loved.*

He was walking briskly down the alleyway toward the street, reaching for the notecard in his front pocket on which he'd written Anthem Landry's address, when he noticed his ring was gone. Marshall retraced his steps, but the brush alongside the house was cut back, the dirt exposed and visible, and there was no tiny glint of gold anywhere he looked. The ring he'd lost wasn't some nondescript piece of generic jewelry either.

He'd purchased the little beauty on Chamberland Island, the same day he'd left Allen Shire's body to rot. He'd walked the length of the island before he'd reached the bed-and-breakfast at the other end. There, shadowed by oaks and just a stone's throw from the plantation house that played host to honeymooning couples, Marshall had come across a tiny shack that turned out to be a gift shop. It was owned by the daughter of the woman who ran the bed-and-breakfast, and the dusty glass cases were full of custom-made jewelry fashioned from found objects native to the island. And those objects had included the carcasses of water moccasins. The ring he'd purchased and worn faithfully ever since had been a gold-dipped rib from a cottonmouth. And now it was gone. In fact, he had no recollection of seeing it on his hand after leaving Beau Chêne that morning.

And that was bad. That was very, very bad. Because it wasn't just any ring. It was literally one of a kind. And if he'd left it behind at Beau Chêne . . . well, then, the invisible hand that assembled his perfect little imaginary murder plot wouldn't be so invisible after all.

Hovering just inside the alleyway, Marshall rested his hand against his pants pocket and the address inside. He stilled his panic by reminding himself of his power and of its great depth. As he decided what to do next, he assured himself that he was entitled to act with as much patience and wisdom as the God that had given him his incredible gift.

19

"Ben Broyard?"

He'd only been home a few minutes when his phone rang. He'd expected Anthem, with some desperate question about the basics of English-language composition. But the woman who'd just said his name didn't sound familiar, and her phone number hadn't looked familiar either when it flashed on his iPhone's screen. Except for the area code, 228, Bay St. Louis, a quaint coastal Mississippi town about an hour's drive from New Orleans, close to where Katrina's eye had made devastating landfall.

"Speaking."

"My name's Alison Cross. I . . . forgive me for calling on a Saturday."

"It's no problem at all, Ms. Cross. How can I help you today?"

What he heard was the nervousness of a woman with a good story to tell, a story that was tearing her apart, so he padded to his desk, grabbed a pen and put his earpiece in, all without missing more than a few syllables of the woman's stammers.

"It's my husband, you see— Oh, Christ. I sound like a woman in some movie. I just can't believe I— He's *missing*. He's been missing for almost a month now, and I just— Okay. Maybe I should start over."

"No. Please. Keep going."

"I still get the paper, you see. Your paper, I mean. Jeffrey and I—" *Jeffrey Cross*, Ben scratched onto his pad. Vaguely familiar, but only vaguely. "—we lived in New Orleans up till just a few years ago and so I still subscribe to *Kingfisher* because it makes me feel connected still, I guess. Anyway . . ."

"Your husband? Jeffrey?"

"Yes. When I saw your name . . . that article you wrote about the cold storage facility that got shut down in New Orleans East . . . Well, I just thought that maybe . . . Do you *remember* my husband?"

"Honestly, I don't, Mrs. Cross."

"Well, of course not, it was so long ago, and I feel terrible bringing it all up now. I certainly don't want to make my trouble yours. Not after all these years. But I just thought, what with the connection and all—"

"What connection would that be, Mrs. Cross?"

"I've told you he's missing, right? My husband."

"Yes. You have."

"You must hear stories like this all the time. Husband goes missing, wife insists he wouldn't leave her. I mean, you probably think I'm as crazy as the police. But maybe there's one . . ."

Truck brakes hissed out front, and a large shadow fell across his front drapes. He padded to the window as Alison Cross continued, keeping his footsteps as quiet as he could.

" . . . You see, I wasn't the love of his life. I mean, we were happy but I know Millie was the real . . . I mean, she was the one he—"

"Millie?"

When he pulled back the edge of the drape, he saw a giant pickup truck with a small motorboat attached to its tow hitch, and sitting behind the wheel was Marissa Hopewell Powell. She saw him peering out at her, and punched the horn lightly. Ben just stood there wondering why his boss, who had been on her way to a good drunk just a few hours earlier, when she'd left him in that dive bar with Anthem, was now sitting in front of his apartment in someone's else truck, towing someone else's boat.

"Millie Delongpre," said the woman on the other end of the line.

Ben was too stunned to respond at first. He let the drape fall back into place. Marissa punched the horn in protest.

"I'm sorry. Did you say—"

"Millie Delongpre. Yes. You see, she and my husband, they were together before she met Noah and, well, Jeffrey always carried a torch for her. He even talked to her in his sleep . . . Jesus . . ." For a few seconds, he wasn't sure if she was laughing or crying. "I'm throwing all of this at you at once."

"Your husband is missing." Outside, Marissa honked the horn. "And he used to be involved with Millie Delongpre."

"Yes, and I remembered how close you were with her daughter and I thought maybe there was a chance you would help me."

The horn honked again. Ben threw open his front door and lifted an index finger to request silence. In response, Marissa shouted, *"Hot tip, Uptown Girl. Get in!"*

"Mrs. Cross, are you saying you believe your husband made contact with Millie Delongpre?"

"No!" she gasped. "No, no, no. I just—I don't know *what* to believe, to be honest with you. The police are so dead set on convincing me that my husband *planned* to leave me, I just . . . I've been thinking of any explanation. I mean, isn't this how it works in the movies? They tell you you're crazy so many times eventually they drive you insane."

"Sometimes," Ben answered.

"It's just . . . what with the connection between you and the Delong-pres, well, it was something, you know? Something I could *try.*" Now the woman actually was crying. And Marissa was honking the horn like they were a half hour late for a Saints game.

"Mrs. Cross, I'm going to call you back, okay? And I mean that. I am. I'm just in the middle of something right now and I want to be able to give you my undivided attention."

"Sure," she whispered. "Of course. Do you need my number—"

"I have it on caller ID. Is this the number you'd like me to call?"

"Yes. Sure. That's great. Thank you. I really— I appreciate it."

"Of course."

He hung up on her, then bounded down his front steps. "What is wrong with you?" he cried.

"What, were you makin' a date? I got a hot tip. Let's go."

"You also got someone else's truck and someone else's boat. I'm confused. I thought you were drinking today."

"Yeah, well, you and the River King ruined that one."

"Doesn't smell like it."

"Fine. You drive. I'm not good with towin' anyway." Marissa hopped out from behind the driver's seat but she left the engine running and the keys in the ignition.

"What's happening right now?" Ben asked the surrounding houses as much as he asked his boss.

"I'll tell you on the way."

"On the way *where*?"

"Beau Chêne. You ever been to Beau Chêne? It's lovely."

Ben got behind the wheel and pulled the door shut. He wasn't in the habit of towing boats either, but the thing wasn't exactly a yacht, so as long as he took corners slowly . . . "It's my neighbor Clem's. He told me if there's a levee failure before we get it back, he's going to haunt my dreams. He just keeps it in his driveway. Thinks it's gonna scare hurricanes away."

"What the hot tip?"

"Looks like some banker killed his wife and then hit the road. It's a crime scene, Ben, and we're gonna crash it."

"I'm not sure if that's a good idea . . ."

"Not sure *what's* a good idea?"

"For you to come along."

"Oh, really?"

"Marissa, you smell like rum."

"I'm a child of the Caribbean. Leave me alone."

"What's happening?"

Marissa threw up her hand as if preparing some big lecture, but instead her chest heaved and her breaths sputtered out of her and for a few minutes, they just sat there, the tinny voices of WWL News Radio playing faintly in the background. "Let's just say Hilda Lane picked the wrong morning to warn me off another story."

"Oh dear."

"Banker's name is Daniel J. Stevens. Son came home a few hours ago, found his mother beaten to death. TV hasn't gotten wind of it, but Hilda's friends with the family and she said she doesn't want us digging into it."

"So you dug into it?"

"Yep. Got an off-the-record source with St. Tammany Sheriff says they found something open on the computer, something about Mr. Stevens stealing from one of the trusts he managed. They think the wife saw it too, and that's why she's dead."

"I still don't think it's a good idea for you to go with me."

"Well, I'm not sure it's a good idea for you to go at all, given the man manages a trust that belongs to Marshall Ferriot." She let Ben absorb the impact of this body blow for a few seconds. Then, with a leering smile, she added, "Who knows? Maybe it was the one he was stealing from . . . That's right. How 'bout you thank me instead of acting like my daddy?"

"I hear he was a lot taller. Okay. The boat?"

"Gated community, but the Tchefuncte runs right through it and it's not gated."

"I see . . ."

"I'm going, Uptown Girl. You can do the driving. But I'm going."

"Why?"

"'Cause it might be the last story we work on together for a while."

"Oh, Jesus. What did you say to Hilda?"

"I told her if she didn't like the way journalism worked, maybe she should get her husband to buy her a store so she could sell shiny things to other white ladies and leave me to do my goddamn job."

"You might be able to recover from that one."

"Yeah . . . not the part about how I held her personally responsible for all those deaths out in Ascension Parish. That one's gonna stick, I think."

Ben was speechless, suddenly imagining a future at *Kingfisher* without his mentor, if such a thing was even possible.

"Come on, Ben. Time's a wastin'. We don't want WDSU catchin' this thing before we do."

Ben took the truck out of park and placed his foot on the gas.

"What was that phone call about?" Marissa asked, once they'd gone a few blocks and the shock of her revelation seemed further away.

"I'm not sure yet."

"Well, it's a day for that, isn't it?"

"You got that right," Ben whispered. "Marissa, if they fire you, I'll—"

"Don't. Not yet. We'll talk about it later. Just drive."

A few minutes later, Ben's phone let out a small chime that told him he had a new email. The message was from Alison Cross, and the attachment was a photograph of her and her missing husband, standing on a windswept beach in the light of dusk. She was a plump, fading beauty with flame-red hair, and he was a foot taller than her, with thick, ink-black eyebrows and a deeply recessed brow that looked poised to swallow his pinprick eyes.

Ben had seen the man before, in an old photograph the Delongpres used to keep on the living room wall. It had been taken on the night Nikki's father had proposed to her mother, back when Elysium was just a muddy acreage with two trailers parked a few yards from each other and string lights running through the low-hanging branches, all of it powered by a gas generator. In it, the happy couple and several of their close friends were crowded around a lounge chair as a young Millie Delongpre extended her ring finger toward the camera. Jeffrey Cross has been one of the friends featured in that photo. But that was the extent of his contact with the man—a picture on the wall of a friend's house, a friend who had been declared legally dead a few years before. And he was too distracted by the strong scent of booze coming off his boss to spend his afternoon wandering down the darkest part of memory lane.

Ben was glad they weren't the only boat launching from Madisonville that day. It meant the police hadn't closed off the Tchefuncte farther upriver. As he did his best to obey the no-wake rule posted on buoys that bobbed in the dark green water on either side of the tiny boat, Marissa fussed with her iPhone, cupping one hand over the screen to shield it from the sun while she tapped it with the other. The boat had a tiny tarp that only covered the captain's chair.

"Any idea how far into Beau Chêne we have to go?" Ben shouted over the motor.

"I'm workin' on it."

"Is that a no?"

"We're workin' to beat the clock here. I didn't exactly have time to pull out my swamp atlas, all right?"

She had a point, and to her credit, she'd tried ceaselessly on the ride there to get her phone to connect to Google Maps, only to have her signal drop every few minutes or so.

After just a little while on the water, walls of cypress rose on either side of the river, and it was easy to believe they were in the middle of a vast unending swamp. But the palatial homes of Beau Chêne would rise on the eastern bank in just another few minutes. They had only about another hour before dark and the setting sun laced the rippling green water with elongated tree shadows and great blades of orange.

"We could go it on our own," Ben said.

"Ben—"

"We could. Seriously. The whole online advertising thing's a whole 'nother ball game. We'd figure it out . . . eventually."

"Let's not get ahead of ourselves. Okay, now, I'm guessing we get two bends in the river before we hit the Stevens place. So why don't you—"

"I'm not staying without you."

"Ben. Focus."

"I'm not, Marissa. It'll just be a matter of time before I mouth off to that bitch too. Especially if she fires you—"

"We got houses up ahead, Ben."

She was right. A few yards down the suddenly manicured riverbank, a giant boat dock, big enough to house a spiral water slide, jutted out into the water, and beyond it, sunlight filtered through oak branches onto green lawns and redbrick McMansions. Ben saw no sign of the St. Tammany Sheriff's Department. Or of any of the residents, for that matter. Maybe the prospect of a wife-killing banker on the loose had them inside behind locked doors.

"Okay. There's one bend," he said.

"I think we got two more."

Ben throttled the motor and the tiny boat picked up speed. "How far from shore is the house?" he asked.

"Not sure. He's not listed."

"You didn't ask your source?"

"I was kinda drunk."

"Anastasis."

"What?"

"That'll be the name of our new website. It's Greek for resurrection. What do you think?"

"I hope you got a long list of those."

"You don't like it?"

"You're not going down with me, Ben. You're too damn talented, and you don't owe me that."

"I *do*—"

"You *don't*, Ben!"

The force of her anger startled both of them silent, and for a minute or two, there was just the whine of the boat's engine and the river's water whooshing past the fiberglass hull.

"No matter what happens with me and Hilda, I'm not leaving your life. Not now, not ever. And you won't have to chase me from bar to bar to keep me in it, either. I owe you that much 'cause you're my friend, and you're a good one. And I promise you, the only time you'll have to say good-bye to me is when one of us is leaving this great earth. Got it?"

He was grateful for his sunglasses because they hid tears so sudden and forceful, a few quick blinks were enough to keep them at bay.

"And Ben?"

"Yes."

"Looks like it was one bend, not two. Sorry."

The cops were suddenly everywhere along the bank up ahead, uniformed deputies, walking the perimeter, and as soon as one of them saw the boat approaching, he held up one palm in the universal signal of "Don't move another damn inch, son." Ben cursed up a storm under his breath while he yanked back on the throttle until they were almost drifting. The engine sputtered as the propeller slowed, the deputies clotting together on the bank to meet their approach.

"Goddammit," Marissa whispered. "I fucked up. Sorry."

"So I guess we have to keep going or else we'll—"

Just then the boat's propeller made a sound like a motorcycle slamming into a brick wall. The jolt was so strong it knocked Marissa forward into the back of the captain's chair. Ben's chest hit the wheel as the entire boat rose and fell beneath them; it felt like a whale had passed underneath the thing. But the terrible scream was coming from the propeller blades in back.

"Kill it! Kill it!"

Ben followed Marissa's instructions and in the silence that fell, he heard one of the deputies cry out, "You folks just stay right where you are!"

"Well, that should be easy," Marissa called back. "Looks like something just ate our propeller."

Ben scooted past her toward the back of the boat. He saw it right away, the bright loops of steel wrapped around the blades like the tentacles of an octopus, and as Ben used both hands to free it, Marissa started backing up, probably because she was stricken by the same thought as Ben. The chain wasn't some rusted, filthy river-bottom relic they had stirred to the surface by mistake. It looked brand new. And if it was new, that meant—

The corpse exploded to the surface a few yards away.

"Ho, mother," Marissa groaned.

Ben did his best not to look away. The body bobbed in the green water like a cork: greasy blue lips, brown hair plastered to one side in a style that would have been adorable on a little kid bursting from a swimming pool; but on this bloated, grown man it looked obscene. Two loops of chain crossed the man's naked, bruised shoulders, and a shiny padlock secured the four loops of chain at the center of his chest.

"Daniel Stevens?" The question was intended for his boss, but he'd directed it at the corpse floating a few feet away from him. When Marissa didn't answer him, he turned and saw that all the life seemed to have drained from her eyes, and from her body itself; her arms hung limply at her sides and he couldn't tell if she was pouting or if she'd lost all feeling in her lower jaw. Shock. It had to be shock.

"Marissa?"

She lunged at him, and before he could cry out, she'd shoved him headfirst into the water. He was choking, arms flailing, bumping up

against the corpse, pawing at its slick chest as he tried to get his bearings, kicking to get his head above water. Then he felt the chain he'd
loosened from the propeller tighten suddenly around his waist. She
was dragging him toward the boat, and for a second, he thought she
was helping him, that she was about to pull him out of the water. Then
the chain tightened suddenly and viciously around his neck. His head
slammed into something hard. The chain tightened again. His head
was wedged between two of the propeller's scored, mangled blades.
And when he tried to scream Marissa's name, what came out instead
was a frenzied chorus of high-pitched keening sounds that sounded
more animal than human.

And over them, he could hear the sound of Marissa's footsteps padding across the floor of the boat, heading in the direction of the captain's chair, the throttle and the ignition.

Lloyd Duchamp came to on the floor of his kitchen. He figured it was
the high-pitched screams coming from the river that had roused him.
But what had they roused him from? Yes, he'd allowed himself a beer
after the police had finished questioning him a few hours before. But
that was all. Just one beer. Surely not enough to trigger a full-on-black-
out, and that's exactly what this felt like.

And it wasn't like anyone would blame him for knocking back a
single Heineken either. It had been a helluva day, what with Danny Stevens going full psycho on everyone. Lloyd was basically a prisoner in
his own home until the cops were finished securing the scene, as they'd
put it. And in this case, the scene was the bloody murder house next
door.

His house sat right on the bank of the Tchefuncte, and from his
kitchen window, he could see a tiny motorboat floating in the river.
That's where the screams were coming from. A couple cops were running along the bank, shouting things across the water to the black

woman in the boat. But it looked like she was ignoring them. She certainly wasn't the one screaming, he could tell that much. And she didn't look like she cared much who was. Actually, it looked she was getting ready to start up the motor and get the hell out of there, which to be frank, is just what he wanted to do.

Crazy. This whole place has gone full-on crazy.

In a single instant, he smelled the gas and heard the sharp crack outside. He turned in time to see the black woman go down, saw the deputy on the bank who'd fired the shot still frozen, gun raised. A sudden, stunned silence washed over the entire scene; all heads had turned toward the river now and its lone floating boat.

Lloyd Duchamp would have stood at his kitchen window forever watching the scene unfold if it hadn't been for the gas. The smell was overpowering him now.

He threw open the cabinet doors under the sink. When the wave of gas hit him, his eyes started to water and he had to blink madly before he saw that the gas line snaking out from behind the oven had been completely unscrewed. It hadn't popped off or slipped out of joint. It was unscrewed, and that meant someone—

Then Lloyd Duchamp's vision seemed to slide sideways, losing resolution as it went, as if his entire world were being wiped away by a giant, invisible hand.

The gunshot turned Ben's panic into clear, focused action.

He drove himself straight down under the water. It turned out to be the magic direction. His neck jerked loose from the chain and when he surfaced, he was several feet away from the mangled propeller Marissa has lassoed his head to. *An accident. It had to be. An accident. She panicked* . . . But there was no sign of her, and that's when he realized they'd shot her.

One of the deputies on the bank was beckoning him toward the shore with both hands, and Ben focused on the man's stoic expression as if it were a goalpost. *Impossible. Impossible.* The word kept repeating itself in his brain, then, when he tasted rank water, he realized he was rasping it to himself even as he swam. Only now he could feel how deeply the water had gone into his lungs. His neck stung in a dozen different places from where the scored propeller had sliced into flesh as he'd struggled to free himself. But the deputy kept beckoning and Ben kept swimming.

And then, some strange sense of foreboding stirred inside him, and something behind the deputy caught his eye. At first, Ben thought he was hallucinating the clouds of splintered wood and glass hurtling through the air toward the assemblage of cops a few yards in front of him. Then everything seemed to arrive out of sequence: the belt of orange flames that exploded from the center of the redbrick house just down the riverbank, the uniformed deputies toppling like rag dolls, the explosion's deafening pop that seemed to come like an afterthought to the blaze of lights and flying debris.

He forced himself under the water again just as flaming timbers splashed down on all sides of him, praying that when he surfaced again, this deranged, impossible nightmare would suddenly be over.

20

"*Can you walk?*"

From the expression on the man's face, it looked like the sheriff's deputy crouching down over Ben had screamed these words at the top of the lungs. But to Ben they sounded distant and distorted; he was still partially deafened by the explosion, a *whomp* so deep and powerful it had rattled his teeth and kicked bile into the back of his throat.

Before the blast, it had been an orderly crime scene lined with uniformed deputies walking grid patterns. Now it was a war zone of flaming debris and crumpled bodies. The redbrick house a few yards away was geysering flames from its first-floor windows. And the fire had spread to the roof of the house next door, a stone French Regency affair Ben assumed to be the Stevens place. *Gas. It had to be,* he thought, because now it looked like the fire's only fuel was the interior of the redbrick house where it had started.

"Was it the gunshot?" the deputy screamed. "What was it? Did you see?"

Ben was startled by the question, then by the brief rain of flaming leaves that fell from the burning oak branches overhead. The deputy shoved them both out of the way. And that's when Ben realized the cop next to him hadn't witnessed the surfacing corpse, Ben's near beheading and the shooting.

The bodies along the bank lay facedown, motionless. Ben blinked a few times and saw that the bright red stains in their khaki uniforms had dimension and depth. They weren't stains; pieces of the men had been torn away from them by the explosion. One of those deputies had shot Marissa, and all three of them had witnessed the crazy thing she'd done to him with the chain.

And there was the boat, undamaged, still drifting a few yards from shore, Marissa a dark shadow across the floor next to the captain's chair.

No witnesses. None that were conscious anyway. Maybe not even alive.

"What the hell happened?" the deputy screamed at him.

"I don't know!" Ben shouted back, his voice sounding louder inside his own head than the nearby screams and approaching sirens. And the answer was partly true. He didn't have a damn clue what had started the fire. All he knew was that as soon as Stevens's body had shot to the surface of the river, his boss, one of his closest friends for eight years, had almost torn his head off. But it was all so quick, so confusing. Maybe she really had been trying to help him . . . *Then why did the deputy shoot her?* Ben thought, before he could stop himself. *If she wasn't about to kill you, why did the deputy shoot her where she stood?*

He didn't use the word casually, but this was honest-to-God *chaos.* The bloody scene all around them, the deranged events that had created it in the blink of an eye. There was no other word for it. He'd interviewed enough soldiers and surgeons to know they were trained to take quick, decisive action in the midst of chaos, but he was not a solider or a surgeon; his training told him to gather evidence, assess each piece, assemble a bigger picture once he'd managed to take a breath and get a pen in hand.

Had some kind of trip wire been attached to the corpse? Had Marissa somehow realized the explosion was imminent, panicked and gone to start the boat without realizing she was about to tear his head off in the propeller?

"*Why* did they *shoot* her?" the deputy shouted, with a kindergarten teacher's careful emphasis.

I'm not leaving your life. Not now, not ever. And you won't have to chase me from bar to bar to keep me in it, either. She'd said these words to him just minutes before everything had gone to hell. How could she have gone from those words to trying to kill him? How was it possible? It wasn't possible. That had to be it. It *wasn't.*

"It was an accident!" Ben shouted. "We're reporters. And Stevens— he's in the water. It looks like he was weighted down, but our propeller caught on him, and I fell overboard. And they must have thought—I mean, they must have thought she was going to hurt me because she couldn't hear them and she was going to start the boat. I don't know. She needs help. Now!"

The deputy shook off his own skepticism; neither of them had time for an interrogation. "There's a new perimeter just beyond that Mercedes. Go there and wait for the ambulance. You need . . ." He gestured absently at Ben's neck, then ran back toward the riverbank he'd been steadily guiding Ben away from as they'd yelled at each other.

Ben was almost as far as the new perimeter the deputy had directed him to when his legs went out from under him, and another set of hands was on him, another deputy, this one a woman. And charging toward them around the bend in the oak-lined street was an ambulance, lights flashing against the falling dark, the first of several.

Marissa was in surgery.

That was the best information he could get. In separate ambulances they'd both been taken to Lakeview Regional Medical Center, a short drive from Beau Chêne, and when they'd found him wandering the hallways after being treated in the ER for his minor cuts, the plain-clothes homicide detectives from the sheriff's department expressed surprise that Ben had decided to wait around so they could take his statement.

He didn't correct their mistaken impression. If you were going to lie to the police, it was important to look cooperative. And he'd fine-tuned his lies by then, even though he wasn't sure who he was buying time for, himself or the friend who had almost torn him to pieces.

There'd been such confusion after the corpse of Daniel Stevens had scared them all half to death, well, those poor deputies on the bank (the homicide detectives refused to disclose any details of their respective conditions despite the number of times Ben referred to them as *those poor deputies*) must have thought Marissa was trying to hurt him when really she was as confused as everyone else.

The gunshot? Simple. Ben had seen the deputy draw his gun on Marissa, but it must have gone off when the house blew. Maybe the force of the blast had caused him to fire by mistake?

Maybe. Perhaps. I'm not sure. Every statement he gave them was peppered with these qualifying phrases; he knew he'd have to back out of them eventually if any of the deputies recovered. But for now, the detectives had little to say in return; Ben hoped that was a sign that the Stevens murder was still their focus, that they knew more about the explosion than they were letting on. But he knew better than to ask, and when one of them firmly instructed him not to go anywhere, he nodded gravely and assured them he would camp out in the waiting room.

It was only then that he realized he'd been wearing wet clothes for almost two hours. They weren't soaked anymore, but they weren't exactly dry either. He tried to turn his iPhone on but it was fried. He'd asked a drowsy-looking woman sitting nearby if he could use her cell phone before he'd planned what he was going to say to Anthem if he answered. Only once he heard the ringing on the other end did he realize he couldn't ask Anthem to drive all the way across the lake. Not tonight. For one, he was on call, and secondly, he didn't want to tell anymore lies that night.

This thought speared him in the gut. Maybe it had been the mention of Marshall Ferriot's trust earlier that night, or maybe it was just fatigue and shock combining into a kind of nervous delirium, but the extent to which he had lied to Anthem over the years overwhelmed him suddenly. Eight years and he'd never said one word to the man about his suspicions of Marshall Ferriot. How many years did it take before a lie of omission that big became an all-out betrayal?

The waiting room was filling up, mostly with frantic women who stormed in as they talked on cell phones, detailing everything they didn't know yet about their loved ones to the person on the other end. The wives of the injured deputies from Beau Chêne; they had to be. He walked a safe distance away from the woman whose phone he'd borrowed. Then, before he thought twice about it, he pressed his nose to a plate-glass window that reflected the harshly lit interior of the room behind him.

"Hello?" Anthem finally answered.

"I'm okay."

"Ben! You're . . . Why? What happened?"

"There was an accident, on the North Shore."

"Beau Chêne! You were there?"

"Me and Marissa. Were we on the news?"

"No." *Good. More time,* Ben thought. "But it's crazy. That goddamn pipeline and now this. My brothers all called me 'cause they think the whole state's about to blow up."

"Listen, if we *do* show up on the news, call me, okay? Then call my mother in St. Louis and tell her I'm fine. My phone's fried and she won't be able to get me."

"I'll call her right now if you want me to."

"No. No. I don't need her freaking out before she absolutely has to."

"Is Marissa, okay? . . . Ben?"

"She's fine. Just . . . She's fine."

"You need me to come?"

"You can't drive all the way to Covington. You're on call."

"Oh, for Christ's sake, I'll get *off* call if I need to."

Anthem 2.0, indeed, Ben thought, when he heard the man's eagerness to put someone else's needs ahead of his own for once. But remembering Marissa's utterance of this flattering term earlier that day only reminded him of her lifeless expression as she lunged at him like a snake and shoved him overboard, of the scored propeller blades biting into his neck.

Ben's eyes watered.

"Ben?"

"I'm good. A- Team. But I appreciate it."

"All right then. Well . . . Hey, when you see Marissa, thank her for me."

"For what?"

"My piece. It's up. Sixty comments already. Some of them think I'm a shithead, but the rest of 'em . . . they're callin' me a hero, Benny."

"Yeah, well . . ."

The words he'd meant to say next were *You are a hero,* but a great, silent wave of darkness seemed to course through his entire body before it robbed him of his vision, and then his hearing a few seconds later. Ben expected to feel the floor rising up to meet him. Instead he felt nothing at all.

"Ben?"

A few more tries, and then Anthem Landry was answered by a dial tone, and once again he was alone with his glowing computer screen, filled with the big headline they'd given his article, "The River's Response," and the smart-looking photo he'd emailed them earlier that day. Ben had probably been called away or the call itself had dropped and he'd ring again in a second. Whatever the case, there was no sense in standing there like an idiot listening to a mocking dial tone.

Of course, that wasn't really what he was doing, now that he thought about it. It was the computer he couldn't tear himself away from. Every few minutes or so, more comments were posted. Hell, if the whole state could stop catching fire for an hour or two, his first piece of journalism just might make the evening news. But the suddenly dropped call had made it feel too quiet all of a sudden, and that's when Anthem realized that something else was missing, a comforting and familiar sound he usually took for granted.

His apartment was on the second floor of an old corner grocery store on Tchoupitoulas, directly across the street from the concrete Mississippi River floodwall and the wharves just behind it. The constant hum of idling container ships drove most of his neighbors insane, but he loved it. It made him feel connected to his lifeblood, especially on nights like this, when he was giddy with anticipation about going out on a ship. That's why he'd left open the door to the exterior staircase's second-floor landing. So he could hear the pulse and the throb of the river's constant call as he went about finding various ways to kill time until the phone rang.

Beignet. His dog. That was it. The little slobberbox had been snoring up a storm on the porch just outside. And now he was gone.

The building had a side yard shared by both the upstairs and downstairs apartment, but it was Anthem who had turned it into a veritable jungle. And he'd done most of the work on those first early nights of trying to stay sober while he was on call, when he had no choice but to avoid friends who hadn't taken his pledge seriously, and women who liked to knock back a beer after a hookup, and his brothers, who were the absolute worst. Those guys spun through the nearest drive-through daiquiri shop on their way home from just about anywhere.

First he'd planted the banana trees, then he'd started work on the birdhouses and then he'd gone about laying the flagstones for a circuitous path from the tall wooden back gate, through the dense leaves and to the foot of the exterior wooden staircase that climbed the side of the building. His neighbor, an overworked paralegal, had once remarked to him when he'd caught him working on the pathway, "You realize we don't own any of this, right?" As if Anthem hadn't known, as if he'd been doing it for any other reason than to keep his hands busy and his head filled with something other than the terrible fear that he wasn't going to make it through another night sober.

Now he stood on the second-floor landing, staring down at a million places where his pet might be hiding. But Beignet was an English bulldog, which meant he wheezed like a runner in the Crescent City Classic wherever he went; if the little guy was down there somewhere, Anthem would be able to hear him. But he couldn't hear him. Just the rustle of the banana leaves in the humid breezes off the river.

When he noticed the shadow in the garden below, Anthem's mouth opened, but nothing came out and then it appeared to him as if the shadow itself had turned into a column of darkness, shot upward and swallowed him whole.

21

The darkness cleared and Ben found himself lying facedown on a twin bed, lips parted against a chemical, institutional taste he couldn't quite identify. He braced himself for the agonizing throb of some head injury, or the stomach-twisting aftermath of Goldschläger shots. But all he could feel was a clean and quick release from a previously impenetrable darkness, and the same sense of lost time he'd experienced during hernia surgery as a child, after they placed the mask over his face.

He had to have passed out in the waiting room. Some kind of delayed reaction probably; shock or, God forbid, some injury he'd sustained during the blast.

He opened his eyes and saw the retro starburst comforter his face had been pressed to; the distant familiarity of the design made him recoil off the bed so quickly his back knocked into a wall of cabinetry just a few feet away.

The trailer he found himself inside of was all 1970s but everything about it had a new sparkle. The place was homey, but fake, no personal items anywhere he could see. He'd visited a few movie sets since New Orleans had turned into Hollywood South, and he felt like he was on one now. Nobody lived here. This trailer was some kind of re-creation. As soon as this word strobed through his mind, as soon as he found himself staring down at the comforter that had frightened him so badly, he realized where he'd seen it all before.

Elysium. Before Noah Delongpre had tried to turn it into a compound, when it was just two trailers parked together like lovers on an acreage of mud beside a serpentine bayou.

The door was barred from the outside, and he was on the verge of crying out when he saw the leather-bound journal sitting by itself on the immaculate kitchen table. READ ME, read the notecard sitting atop the scored leather cover.

Ben flipped the cover back. The sight of Nikki Delongpre's handwriting, still familiar to him after all these years from the labels of the mix CDs she used to make for him at least once every few months, forced a sound from him that was something between a gasp and a yelp. And soon Ben was sinking into the tiny booth that served as the trailer's pathetic dining area.

But even as he read, he told himself not to surrender to hope, told himself that this could be some kind of fake. Most of all, everything he was reading could have been written before that terrible night—the day Anthem had transferred to their school, some disjointed thoughts about Elysium and the well her father had dug, none of which Ben could quite put together in his race to find proof that this journal had been written after her disappearance

Then he saw the word *Katrina,* and he was forced to blink madly to keep the tears from spilling down his face. But then the swell of emotion hardened as he kept reading, like a charging ocean wave suddenly saddled with an iceberg.

My name is Niquette Delongpre and on the night before her 47th birthday I killed my mother . . .

VI

THE HEAVENS RISE

22

Patience, Marshall told himself.

He'd lost his cool in Beau Chêne and the resulting conflagration had made clear the one, unavoidable limit to his power—he could control only one person at a time. And while it was doubtful the police would find his lost ring after what he'd done to the crime scene, Marshall couldn't afford two mistakes in one night. He had to remind himself that Ben Broyard had never been target numero uno; that title belonged to the giant shadow now standing frozen and ramrod straight, one story above Marshall's head. Still, when the little fucker had literally floated into the middle of the crime scene, the opportunity had seemed too good for Marshall to pass up. But by giving into temptation, he'd come close to scorching himself to death and losing his shot at Anthem altogether.

Now he was here, and the connection had been made, but the visions coursing through him—the raw, unedited flashes of Anthem's very soul—were far more vivid than anything thrown off by the other souls he'd violated over the past few weeks. Compared to Stevens, his secretary and Allen Shire, this stuff felt like a fire hose blast that might knock him into the banana leaves. The burst, as he'd nicknamed it, was usually one or two brief pulses of hallucination that gave way to silvery, distorted vision (and the power to do whatever he wanted with the person in question). But this was movie quality.

Nikki Delongpre was embracing him (embracing Anthem), and he could feel the fleece of her pullover, could smell the chemical odor coming off the Mardi Gras pearls around her neck. All around them, a press of bodies, the familiar raucousness of an Uptown parade, a dance of flambeau fire and shadow beneath a ceiling of interlocking oak branches. Bloodred plastic beads smashed to the asphalt; Marshall recognized the spear-shaped logo of the Krewe of Ares parade. And pulsing beneath every sight and smell was the endowed knowledge that he was being flooded by the happiest moment of Anthem Landry's life. And even though Nikki was smiling at him—not just smiling, *beaming*—he could hear her voice in his head (in Anthem's head): *My hero, my God, my angel.* A soft, intimate whisper that didn't match the jubilant expression on her face, an expression that seemed to hold and hold and hold until it took on the appearance of a mask.

Jesus Christ, Marshall thought, *is that how they really spoke to each other? In those kinds of stupid clichés? Or were these supposed words of Nikki's more dream than memory?* Then he saw that the giant figure atop the Mardi Gras float rattling past them wasn't the typical shuddering papier-mâché rendering of some third-tier pagan god. It was a statue of Anthem Landry as Michelangelo might have realized him, impossibly flawless muscles, skin some shade between marble and flesh, and when the beautiful giant's eyes opened and stared right at Marshall, as if sensing the presence of a spiritual interloper in the midst of this hallucinated crowd of shadows, Marshall cried out, and the great, sickening burst was over. Now it was just him and Anthem, separated by the long exterior staircase. Everything in Marshall's vision fluoresced in the way it normally did once a hook had been established, but the pulse of it was stronger. Everything about this was different.

Stop, and it was his voice he heard now, not Nikki's. *Stop. He's different.*

But how could that be? How could Anthem Landry be the only anomaly after weeks of exercising his power on others without incident? The injustice of it was almost too much for him to bear. And the connection had been forged, hadn't it? He could force the guy to leap from the porch right now and break his neck. But he couldn't settle for that. A fall? That wouldn't do at all. Not after all the work Marshall had done to get to this point. That would be a downright cheat.

Besides, this wasn't the last game he planned to play; if there was something different about Anthem Landry, he had to find out what it was, even if it meant being forced to dispatch Anthem in some less than impressive way.

"Patience," Anthem Landry said quietly, giving voice to Marshall's thoughts, and the steadiness of his voice reflected the new steadiness in Marshall's mind.

"Indeed," Marshall answered himself.

And just like that, the leaping shadow was gone and Anthem Landry found himself still standing at the railing, the garden below him still rustling in the breeze. His heart was racing but that was probably just the result of whatever strange trick of light had convinced him a ghost was rocketing toward him from the foliage below. A train's locomotive blared, which wasn't a shock, given the tracks were just on the other side of the floodwall. But usually he heard the trains approaching before they got this close. Not this time, apparently. And there was someone down there in the garden, and Beignet was at the guy's feet.

"Hello?" Anthem barked.

And when the guy stepped forward into the security light's halo across the bottom few steps, Anthem gripped the railing in front of him to make sure he was still standing upright.

"Holy crap. You're . . ."

"Alive?" the man said.

"Yeah. Something like that."

"Well, it's been interesting, to say the least."

"Jesus Christ. I can't even remember the last time I saw you—" Anthem started descending the steps, quickly, as if he thought the ghost of Marshall Ferriot might vanish before he reached the bottom. But Marshall kept talking, his voice sounding fairly earthbound, if Anthem said so himself.

"PE. Senior year, first semester. Neither one of us played football, so we weren't exempt. You convinced Coach Clary to let us do badminton 'cause everyone thought it would be a breeze. And he agreed, so you were this big hero. Then he showed up the next day with an eighty-page packet on the history of badminton and told us there's going to be a test the next week. Suddenly you weren't such a hero anymore."

"Right! Shit, man. Good memory." Once they were face-to-face, Anthem clapped one of Marshall's hands in both of his. But after a few pumps, he realized the guy seemed a little thin and weak, so he let up.

"Yeah, well, for me, it's like it all just happened yesterday."

"Marshall Fuckin' Ferriot. Pardon my French, but welcome back to the land of the living, my friend!"

Anthem didn't know the guy's whole story; they'd never said more than a few words to each other back at Cannon. (There'd been too much other shit going on that summer for Anthem to keep tabs on some suicidal classmate-turned-vegetable.) But he knew the highlight reel; the coma, the father killed by the fall, the move to Atlanta. Kinda odd that Ben had never talked about any of it to him; he was usually all over that kind of scandal.

"You look good, man," Anthem said.

"Do I?"

"Yeah . . ."

"I'm sorry about Nikki." Anthem must have flinched, because when Marshall spoke again, he dropped his voice to almost a whisper. "I know it was a long time ago, but I just found out recently, given my . . . situation . . . My memory of the days before the accident, it's not really that good. The doctors say it should improve. But it'll take time, I guess. I just wanted to say—"

"Right. Yeah. Thanks."

"So the police . . . they never found anything?"

"Some pieces of the car. That's it."

Marshall winced and shook his head. "Sorry, man," he whispered.

"Is that why you—" Anthem looked around, as if it might be possible Marshall Ferriot was meeting someone else at this late hour, across the street from Anthem's apartment. "You just wanted to give your condolences? Or are you here to see Tim?"

"Tim?"

"My neighbor. Lives downstairs. I don't think he's home though."

"Oh, no. I'm here to see you."

"Yeah?"

Marshall struggled with his next words, hands wedged deep in his pockets, shoulders slumped, staring at the bricks under Anthem's feet. "I saw something," he said finally, slowly and deliberately. "When I was under . . ."

"Under? You mean, like, in a coma?"

"Yes. I don't know what it was, exactly. But it involved you and I felt like it would be irresponsible of me not to tell you about it."

"You mean, like, a vision or something?"

Marshall straightened and looked him in the eye. "A message," he whispered.

Anthem felt like he'd been doused in cold water, and it must have shown on his face because Marshall winced and looked away suddenly.

"This is ridiculous. I'm sorry. I shouldn't have come. It's late, and you don't need me . . . I mean, it was years ago and it was . . . I'll just . . ."

As Anthem watched the guy hurry toward the back gate, he found himself struggling to remember exactly how many days had separated Nikki's disappearance and Marshall's flying leap? A crazy, Hollywood-inspired image blazed bright and big in his too-sober mind: Nikki's soul zipping past Marshall's in some realm beyond this one, like those bright pulses of light at the beginning of *It's a Wonderful Life*.

Angels, he remembered. *Talking angels is what they were.*

"Hey!" Anthem shouted.

Marshall stopped walking.

"Look, uh, we're a dry house. But maybe I can offer you a Dr Pepper? How's that sound?"

"Dry?"

"Yeah, I gave up the hard stuff a while back."

"I see . . ."

"So what do you say, huh?"

"I think that sounds great."

23

No Dr Pepper," Anthem said. "Sorry. False advertising. How 'bout a Coke?"

"Water's fine," Marshall answered, distracted by a stack of papers sitting on Anthem's kitchen counter.

"It *is* the source of life, after all," Anthem said.

"You can say that again," Marshall muttered before he thought better of it. "The River's Response," proclaimed the headline atop the first page. "What's this?" he asked.

Anthem waited for Marshall to take the bottle. "Aw, *Kingfisher* published this article that had all kinds of bullshit in it about the pilots association. But they let me post a response on their website a few hours ago."

"That's nice of them." Marshall could not have cared less about the article itself. It was the comments that got to him. Anthem had printed out every last one. (Well, one hundred as of 2:30 that afternoon, according to the time stamp on the last one. Who knew how many there were now?) With a few outraged exceptions, they all said pretty much the same thing: Anthem Landry was a bona fide hometown hero, sticking up for local workers. Sticking up for *New Orleans.*

My hero, my God, my angel.

The thought of anyone calling Anthem Landry a hero tempted Marshall to force the man in question to yank a meat cleaver from the block of knives right next to him and drive it once through each eye; two quick stabs just like the ones their housekeeper used to inflict on the plastic wrap around the cases of water bottles that were delivered to the house.

How does one destroy a hero? Let's see. Let me count the ways . . . There were so many possibilities they all overwhelmed him. So many sharp edges, so many sudden drops, so many cars, so many flammable substances. Hell, the entire apartment itself was laced with one of the best weapons of all: electricity. But while all of those deaths might make for a delightfully hideous scene when the police arrived (or someone from Anthem's family, if Marshall arranged it properly), were they a fitting fall for a hero?

"A hundred comments," Marshall said, but he was setting the papers down on the counter as if he'd just realized they had shit stains on them.

"Pretty cool, huh?" Anthem said. Then he tapped his Diet Coke can against Marshall's water bottle in a quick, perfunctory toast before he took a slug. "Never fancied myself much of a writer. That was always Ben's beat. You remember Ben Broyard, right?"

"Kinda."

The apartment wasn't quite the pigsty Marshall had expected, or hoped for, but it was certainly threadbare. The whole building looked like it had once been a corner store, and the ceilings inside the apartment were about twelve feet high. No shades on the soaring windows, just frilly lace curtains that covered only the bottom half of each one. (Some girlfriend had probably hung them for him.) And the top half of each window offered a bleak industrial view of the loading cranes visible above the floodwall across the street.

The TV caught him off guard, just as every TV had since he'd come out of his coma. Out of all the things that looked different after eight years in purgatory, televisions had undergone the most dramatic transformation. They were flat as boards now, and hung all over like electrified paintings. The rest of the walls were mostly bare, except for a poster from the Krewe of Ares parade from 1999. It featured an expressionist rendering of the parade's lead float, a towering plaster statue of the god of war himself, multiplated armor sitting astride his insanely large muscles, giant head covered by a massive Spartan helmet replete with the typical Mohawk and plunging cheek guards that revealed a glimpse of his apelike jaw. It wasn't the dreamlike statue that had rattled through the perpetual Mardi Gras parade in Anthem's soul, but the resemblance was close enough that Marshall had to look away quickly to avert a twinge of nausea.

"How long you on call for?" Marshall asked.

"Till nine a.m."

"Do you love it?"

"Being a pilot?" Anthem asked.

Marshall nodded, trying to hide the fact that he was studying Anthem's every move. The way he was tapping the edge of the Diet Coke against the counter ever so slightly, shifting his weight back and forth between each foot. *A dry house, indeed. Maybe giving up the hard stuff had been harder than he let on.*

"There's usually a moment . . ." Anthem said, straightening. "So I'll pick up a ship anywhere from Baton Rouge to Chalmette. But my favorite route's southbound in the morning. Especially when I hit Audubon Park and it's sunny and the oak trees are all spread out, and you can just see Holy Name Cathedral above the tree line, watchin' over it all. It's like . . . I feel connected to the past."

"Awesome," Marshall said. "I've always wanted to go out on the river. Can you see Cannon?"

"Nah. It's not tall enough. Most of what you can see of Uptown's just trees."

"And the Fly, right? You used to hang out at the Fly a lot."

Don't lie to me, shithead. I followed you and Nikki there after you got back together. I watched you kissing on the stairs of rocks that lead down to the water's edge. If I'd known what I was capable of then, I would have made you drown her.

"Some," he said. "Who didn't, right? A few Coronas. A little weed, maybe. Blast some Cowboy Mouth. Same shit I'd do today if I didn't have a job."

Anthem gave him a big toothy grin, and Marshall tried to return it.

"The morning sun beats down upon me like the Devil's smile," he said slowly and quietly.

"I'd rather be anywhere else but here," Anthem sang back at him, straightened, eyes brightening. "Was it a blinding lack of subtlety or just a lack of *styyyyle*, responding to the ways and means of *fear*?" With that, Anthem skipped past Marshall toward the stereo. "Take me back to New Orleans, and drop me at my door. 'Cause I might love you—" He yanked his iPod from its charging cradle. "I've got it here, just a sec."

"The message . . ."

Anthem slumped over his stereo suddenly, and when he went to set the iPod back in its cradle his movements were sluggish and unfocused.

"Yeah . . . listen, man, I'm not sure I really—" But before he could finish his own sentence, he flounced down onto the sofa as if he'd been placed in time-out. The sofa was too small for the living room and it was too small for *him*; the cushion crumpled so much under his weight, Marshall wouldn't have been surprised if it spit out from under him like an inner tube on a water slide.

"So you think Nikki gave you some kind of message?" he finally asked.

"Not Nikki. Her mother."

Anthem Landry's eyes were saucer-wide, his lips pursed, his giant frame preternaturally still as he braced himself for a blow from another dimension of existence. He'd stopped nervously rubbing his thighs and now his hands gripped both kneecaps as if they'd been glued to them.

The connection between them was as pure as the one Marshall had forged just moments earlier by using his power, only this had come from quick thinking. Quick thinking, patience and the time-honored tradition of turning a disadvantage into an opportunity. Yes, Anthem's soul had seemed different, more vivid and overpowering, but it also given Marshall plenty he could use.

"It started as a vision, really." Marshall let his focus shift to the hardwood floor between them. "A Mardi Gras parade. I think it was Ares, the one that used to roll on Friday." Anthem flinched and glanced back in the direction of the poster hanging on his nearby wall. "I didn't know her all that well, but I kept seeing Nikki. She had a pair of Mardi Gras pearls around her neck and she was wearing this fleecy pullover and she was beaming and she had her arms around a man. And after a while, I realized that man was you. And she was whispering the same words to you, over and over again . . ."

Anthem's lips had parted and his chest was rising and falling and when he went to close his eyes, several tears slipped from them; rather than wipe them away with one hand, he chewed his lower lip and let out a desperate wheeze.

"Are you sure you want me to—"

"Keep going."

"I mean, it gets kind of—"

"*Keep going.*"

"My hero, my God, my angel. That's what she kept whispering."

It was as if the giant's strings has been cut, and six words alone had done it. Had they been a private incantation Nikki had whispered only while in the throes of passion, or the creation of Anthem's own longing and grief? Either way, they were the key. He slouched back against the sofa, his face twisting with the first contortion of a sob. Then his giant hands went to his face, forming a protective shield, and Marshall advanced several steps toward him, trying his best to prevent the sound of the sexual excitement flickering within his belly from lighting up his voice. "Then I saw her mother. I didn't know who she was at first, 'cause I'd never met her. But she told me who she was, and she told me who you were. And she said if I ever came back, if I ever joined the living again, I would have to set you free. I would have to tell you the truth about what happened that night so that you could move on."

Anthem dropped his hands from his face, which was now a snotty, tear-streaked mess. "Wh—what ha—"

"She was driving that night. Nikki. She was the one behind the wheel, but she had been drinking and she didn't tell her parents and they got into an accident . . ."

"An accident? Did she—"

"Millie was killed, and Nikki and her father, they covered it up. And they ran."

Marshall could see the disbelief fighting a losing battle inside the man a few feet away from him, and he wondered if he'd chosen the right tack. He'd thought of adding in some bullshit detail about Nikki drinking that night because she'd found out Anthem had knocked her up. But it was too far.

"You need to go, dude."

"She told me you had to know the truth so that you could finally let her go. So that you could stop drinking so much . . ."

Anthem was on his feet, pointing toward the door. "All right, man. That's enough. I've got a long night ahead of me and this is just a little— I mean, for *fuck's sake*, you're asking me to believe—"

"I'm not asking you to believe anything. It was just . . . I felt like it was my duty to tell you."

"She just *walked* away? Is that it? From all of us? She just walked away. All these years and not one word because she was *drunk*? Because she *killed* her own—"

"It could be a metaphor, for all I know."

"A metaphor *for what*?"

Marshall gave the man his best grimace, shook his head as if the very idea of metaphors in general filled him with despair. The more he tried to deny that his supposed vision had been the truth, the more the stupid Neanderthal across from him believed that it was.

"I appreciate you comin' and I don't mean to be rude. But I need to—"

Anthem rushed into his bedroom, but he was in such a desperate hurry that he didn't bother to shut the door behind him, so Marshall followed.

Anthem found it on the top shelf of his bedroom closet, just where he'd left it months ago. Silver-plated, gleaming in the harsh light from the overhead bulb, looking as new and full of untapped promise as it had the day his brother Merit gave it to him as a graduation present. He'd stashed it there because of the words of an old girlfriend from college, who'd assured him the only way she'd been able to quit smoking was by carrying an unopened pack of Marlboro Lights with her everywhere she went. *I needed to feel like my little friends had left me completely,* she'd told him.

He uncapped it and drank. There was no burn. Just a warm rush of inevitability, and already the rationalizations were tumbling through him right behind the firewater. Sometimes he didn't get called at all. Some guys would go whole shifts without getting called up once.

Floorboards creaked behind him, and there was Marshall Ferriot, standing in his bedroom door, and Anthem in the closet with a flask like some desperate gutter trash.

"Are you okay?" he asked.

"Seriously, dude. I need you to—"

"You shouldn't be alone right now, Anthem."

The phone rang, and Marshall seemed more startled by it than Anthem was. Anthem brushed past him and yanked the portable from its cradle next to the bed. The woman on the other end had already started speaking to him by the time Anthem realized he was still holding the flask in his left hand. From the weight of it, it felt like he'd downed half the thing in thirty seconds.

"Hey, Landry. Driver's gonna be at your place in about thirty. We got a grain ship hatched a leak in one of its dry bulk containers and they're turnin' it around and sending it to Houston for repairs."

"Don't send the driver," Anthem responded, the smell of the bourbon on his breath dilating his nostrils as he spoke.

"You're pickin' up this baby in Destrehan, A-Team. You gonna drive yourself?"

"Just . . . I'm good. I'll get myself there."

"All right. Suit yourself. These guys want to turn this ship around yesterday. Sounds like they're losing a fortune by the hour."

He hung up on the dispatcher before he might slip up and allow her to hear any intensifying slur in his speech. Some base instinct drove him to put the flask to his mouth and empty the rest of it down his throat. Then he hurled it at the wall so hard it sounded like the thing had dented before it clunked to the floor.

And there was Marshall Ferriot, studying him with a piteous expression.

"It was almost empty. I . . . I couldn't just let it go waste. Had to finish the . . ." Anthem sank down onto the foot of his bed. Six months gone in an instant because of, what? One sick kid's deranged coma dream, brought on by medications and brain injuries and God knows what else? Six months, down the drain. Down his throat.

My hero, my God, my angel. The very words she used to whisper into his ear after he'd finished bringing her to the edge of pure bliss out at the old push boat in Madisonville. Same damn words he'd hear every time he went there to add beads to the little altar he kept for her in the pilothouse. No one knew those words.

"Do you still want me to go?" Marshall asked.

"No. No, I don't."

"Okay . . ."

"Can you drive me to Destrehan? Aw, fuck that. I need you to stay with me. Make sure I don't do anything stupid. Half the fucking Russian captains pop open a bottle of vodka to welcome me onto their damn ship, and I'll— I just need you to watch me. Okay. Make sure I don't do anything stupid now that I've . . ."

"You want me to come on the ship with you?"

"Well, it's only fair, right? Now that you've done your duty and shared your little message with me, it's only fair you stick around for the consequences, isn't it?" His voice was boiling with anger, and when he saw the wounded expression on Marshall's face, he felt a stab of regret. Then he felt the bourbon, sloshing in his stomach, fiery and potent and poised to unleash its black magic into his veins.

"I'm sorry," Anthem muttered.

"Don't be," Marshall whispered, but he looked crestfallen, and he was studying the floor between them. "Of course I'll go with. The way I told you, it was all wrong—"

"Enough about that. I'm sure you saw all kinds of things while you were under"— *my hero, my God, my angel*—"and if it'd been me, I don't know, I probably woulda wanted to tell people too. So just . . ." His face flushed, but he couldn't tell if it was the booze or the threat of new tears. He gestured to the closet. "Pick out a jacket. It's gonna be cold out there. Then we gotta hit the road."

FROM THE JOURNALS
OF NIQUETTE DELONGPRE

For days now, I have watched the horrors that have befallen the city of my birth. And while I must admit, they pale in comparison to the perversions of natural laws that sent me into exile from the very city the world now weeps for, they have inspired me. Inspired me with such force I'm reminded that no matter how much I have been changed on a cellular level, I am still human. Still a teenage girl who will always consider New Orleans her home.

There are masses of starving and dehydrated and dying black people gathered outside the Convention Center without help or any sign of it. I have seen the cries for rescue painted on the rooftops sticking up out of the ebony floodwaters. I have tried to stare at all of it without turning away, and for the most part, I have succeeded.

In the hours after Katrina apparently bypassed the city by a hair, I watched the first reporters stumble out of their hotels and onto Canal Street and into the milky light of a post-storm dawn. They walked dry streets, surveyed a few tree limbs and, because the power was out, they made superficial assessments of their immediate surroundings and declared that the savagery Katrina had been expected to visit on my hometown had not come to pass. Sure, part of the Superdome's shell seemed to have been torn loose and a bunch of shattered windows in the Central Business District. But aside from that ...

And I knew they were wrong. They didn't know my city like I did. They didn't know the fingers of water that bisected most of its neighborhoods, the streets upon streets of tiny, one-story houses sitting in the shadows of levees and passing ships that often sat higher in the water than the midpoints of the levees themselves. I knew as soon as they put helicopters in the air, as soon as the first reports from outlying areas started pouring in, that the devastation would become clear.

And I was right.

I'm ashamed to admit this, but at first, there was a part of me that was relieved. I knew the body blow of this awful storm would knock my family's disappearance out of the city's collective memory. For a while, at least. And that would give me time, more time to consider what lay ahead for me.

I had a nightmare last night. I know I will have it again. I hope I do. It will remind me of my newfound mission.

Apparently Sid-Mar's, a Bucktown restaurant Anthem's family used to always drag us to, has been destroyed by the surge. Last night, I dreamed of its flooded interior. The gray water's inexorable tug peeled Mardi Gras posters off its walls and the overturned tables drifted through the swirl of debris like the skeletons of porpoises. There were no people in this dream; just a slow ballet of ruin.

But it's the first vivid dream I've had since what happened on Highway 22 that night, and it reminded me that I am not dead, that my life is not a nightmare on pause. But I'm going to need a reminder every day, and that's what this journal is about. I've gone days without speaking, and I probably will again, but if I talk to these pages, maybe all of those days won't end with the same lost, hollowed-out feeling. It's either that, or start cutting myself.

I am alive. I am real. I still dream, and I still wake up.

My name is Niquette Delongpre and on the night before her 47th birthday I killed my mother.

24

DESTREHAN

The crew boat pulled up out of the darkness, spitting a trail of bright froth. The black river behind it was a thicket of tug boats and idling container ships. Presiding over this scene was the monolithic Luling–Destrehan Bridge, with matching tuning fork–shaped towers of steel that rose into the night sky, crowned with blinking red lights.

"Hey," Marshall whispered.

Anthem gave him a steady look. He was still a bit glassy-eyed but a couple cans of Diet Coke had given him some edge. *Not his blood, though,* Marshall thought. *The alcohol level in his blood is still plenty high, and that's all that will matter once this ride is over with.*

"Do me a favor and don't throw my name around out there," Marshall said. "There's just some bullshit with the estate, now that I'm alive again and all. And you know, it's a small town and I don't want people to—"

"Yeah, yeah. Sure," Anthem answered. "Who should I say you are?"

"Cousin?"

"Sure. I got plenty of cousins."

Once they were standing together on the open back deck of the crew boat, charging across the obsidian vein of the Mississippi toward the towering black hulk that was their destination, Anthem shouted, "She's a grain ship. A Panamax, the largest they have. But she's empty so she's running real fast on the water. She was supposed to load up north of here but the crew found a leak inside one of her dry bulk containers right after she passed under the Luling–Destrehan Bridge. Other pilot and those tugs got her turned around. Now it's my job to get her as far as Chalmette, so they can send her to Houston for repairs. Greek crew. Registry, Singapore. Do you even care about this shit or should I just let you—"

"No, no. I care!" Marshall shouted back over the wind. The railing he held was attached to a narrow metal staircase that went up ten steps to a platform atop the crew boat's wheelhouse. The entire boat was rolling so much in the chop that Marshall was forced to hold on with both hands. And he was praying the gun tucked inside the waistband of his jeans didn't fly out into the river. That would really screw everything up.

But the worst part was how the giant ship had almost no definition at all as they barreled toward it. It gave Marshall the nauseating sense that they were heading straight for a looming black void, a realm of hallucinatory nightmares ready to swallow them both. But the grain ship wasn't all ghostly darkness. Floating a hundred feet above the water, the bridge was a bright halo of light tucked at the very back of the vessel: electrified, human, *real.*

"All right, look," Anthem said, voice raised over the wind. "I'm not gonna lie to you. This part is dangerous, okay? But it's quick and you're gonna have people helping you. How's your movement?"

"My *movement*?"

"Your muscle coordination. Your reflexes. You were out for a long time so I'm—"

"I'm good. I can *move.*"

"Good. Okay, so ship's crew's gonna throw down a ladder. It's short and you just go straight up. I'll help you from behind, and some crew'll pull you up from on deck. Sound good?"

Marshall nodded. The crew boat pulled parallel to the grain ship's enormous black hull, and about fifteen feet overhead, a hatch popped open, piercing a rectangle of bright fluorescent light in the ship's flank. An unfamiliar, stinging heat speared up through his chest, raking the back of his throat. *Fear.* He hadn't felt much of it since he'd awakened six months ago, not since almost killing himself at Beau Chêne that afternoon. Now, here it was again, as fresh and overwhelming, as full of hot pulsating life as it had been when he was a pimply teenager.

One of Anthem's powerful hands came down on Marshall's shoulder and gave him a tight, paternal squeeze.

"Steady and ready, podnah. That's what my dad said to me first time I ever did this. When we're done, we'll put it on a T-shirt for yah. How's that sound?"

"Why's it so dangerous?"

"'Cause neither boat's gonna stop moving. Also, the river's so high now they had to ballast down the stern so we can get under the Huey P., which means the ship's gonna be angled . . . kinda."

"Kinda?"

So we'll fall in the water. What's so bad about that?

Well, you could get crushed in between both boats on your way down. Or you could make it to the water alive and then get torn apart by one of the giant propellers right below the surface.

Of course Anthem didn't mention any of these facts specifically. Because he was such a gentleman. *A hero.*

This was too ambitious, braving the elements with Anthem like this. He could have done something to the guy on dry land, for Christ's sake, something that would have disgraced him as effectively as what he was planning out here. It was people he could control; not ships, not currents. And he still hadn't figured out why Anthem's frequencies seemed to all resonate at Mach 10 when he'd tried to hook him. But maybe he was reading too much into that to begin with. Maybe it was just performance anxiety, this whole need to murder Anthem Landry in the most spectacularly perfect way.

He'd been provided with a wonderful opportunity the minute the phone had rung in Anthem's apartment. How ungrateful it would have been for him to turn it down.

"You don't have to do this, man!" Anthem shouted.

High above them, two crew members tossed a rope ladder out of the open hatch. The rungs were metal, heavy enough to keep the ladder weighted and to the side of the ship. "I can have the crew boat take you back and we can meet—"

"No, no, no!" Marshall shouted back. "It's fine, it's fine. Really."

"You sure?"

Why don't you go first, you patronizing piece of shit? You go first, then I'll make sure you slip and fall and turn into mincemeat in the muddy Missusip?

But he couldn't have that. An *accident* would never do. Yes, it might be enough to bring Nikki out of hiding, but from the moment he read all those groveling comments in response to Anthem's missive, Marshall knew disgrace was the only option. And for that he needed the river. And for that he needed to stop being such a goddamn pussy and climb the fucking ladder.

It was over in a few minutes.

The worst part was mounting the platform on the crew boat, those few nauseating minutes of being trapped on a tiny platform swaying with the vessel's every movement ten feet above the churning river. But the climb was mercifully brief, only a second or two of weightlessness between the moment when Anthem couldn't push anymore and the crew members overhead started pulling on his shoulders. Then his feet were planted on a solid metal floor and a sickly, sweet stench plugged his nose and throat. Empty or fully loaded, the grain smell was still overwhelming, like loaves of bread that had been left in the sun for days.

Behind him, the crew members hoisted Anthem through the hatch. And the guy had a shit-eating grin on his face even before his feet came to rest on steel. Pride. He was proud of Marshall. Genuinely, stupidly proud of his new friend. Marshall managed his best sheepish grin in return, but he had to look away because all he could think of was that Anthem had probably smiled that way when he was fucking Nikki. And she'd probably given him plenty of reason to.

A stout bearded white guy in a baseball cap and a vest jacket was hovering behind the tiny, dark-skinned crew members. "Who's this, A-Team? One of your journalist friends?"

Anthem cackled, but immediately looked away from his fellow pilot, probably to avoid breathing on the guy. "Naw, man. Just a cousin of mine from out of town. Careful on the way down there, Favreaux. Wouldn't want to have to comfort your wife in that nice Jacuzzi of yours."

"Only comfort you're ever gonna give a lady is a child support check, *Landry*."

And then the pilot disappeared down the ladder, and Anthem gave Marshall a conspiratorial grin, as if they had just accomplished something momentous together. Then the two crewmen—Asians, Marshall could see now, probably Thai or Malay or some other for-shit country where the only thing to do was leave—led them down the long metal-walled corridor.

Anthem had been so concerned with remembering the walkie-talkie he'd need to communicate with other vessels on the river, he'd forgotten Marshall was carrying his cell phone, and he didn't notice when Marshall fell back and hurled the thing through an open porthole.

25

She would drain the pool as soon as she got there. That was her plan.

The execution of it was another matter entirely, and that's what Nikki Delongpre was plotting as her family trundled along Highway 22 in her father's massive Lexus SUV, a car so big and cosseted, her mother claimed it could double as an insane asylum cell for a wealthy heiress. And her mom would know; whenever they took long drives together as a family, Millie Delongpre would stretch out across the length of the backseat with her favorite pillow, several strands of platinum-blond hair draping her slack mouth as she dozed. Tonight was no exception. Her father was driving, as always, and he was caffeinated but silent, probably running through party preparations in his head.

While Nikki kept her head turned to the window so she could chew her fingernails without fear of parental disapproval, her father gently tapped his fingers atop the steering wheel, keeping time to Louis Arm-

strong's "A Kiss to Build a Dream On." It was the official song of her
parent's epic, enduring love affair, the song her father had played on a
cheap old stereo the night Millie had accepted his marriage proposal
in a shadowy cathedral of cypress and string lights. The song of Elysium, and the song of their lavish wedding, still spoken of in ecstatic
terms by the close friends who'd been in attendance. But Nikki always
found Satchmo's voice to be haunting and mournful, and this piece of
music relegated her to the sidelines of a mythic romance she feared
she'd never be able to live up to in her own life.

She kept telling herself she should be grateful for how quickly things
had worked out, and part of her was: Ben's detective work, the confession from Brittany Lowe, all of it was miraculous, really, and now
Anthem, the only man she'd ever loved, had been returned to her after
days of darkness and grief and worst of all, *uncertainty*, days of having
her carefully crafted life plans blown to the winds like dust from her
palms. But there was one loose end, and it was a big one.

The pool.

It hadn't been touched since her terrible night with Marshall Ferriot, and odds were it was still swarming with those awful little name-
less things. They'd been all over her skin as she'd run for her 4-Runner
and she was willing to bet the little creepy-crawlies were the cause of
the terrible headaches she'd suffered for days after. They weren't excruciating; it was the brief, distortions of her vision that had frightened
her the most. A pressure would start in her temples, and then for a
few seconds, everything was grayscale, and a little twinkly around the
edges, like she was looking at the world through a fish tank stained with
ash. But she hadn't said a word about them to anyone. How could she?

Any mention of the headaches or the stuff in the pool and suddenly
one question from her father was sure to turn into two and then her
mother would get involved, her mother who could never keep a secret,
and then they'd both be demanding to know why she'd gone all the
way out to Elysium without telling anyone, and swimming? Had she

really gone *swimming* out there by herself?... Time. That was what she wanted. Just a little time to let everything settle, to let the reconciliation between her and Anthem become a solid, reliable thing before she had to answer any questions about Marshall Goddamn Ferriot.

But she didn't have time.

Ben, Anthem, her own parents; she had no right to let them become victims of her secret. She couldn't let them get anywhere near that stuff, whatever it was. Tons of Google searches had given her all kinds of images of bacteria and parasites and microbes but none that matched what she'd seen floating through the flashlight's beam that night. So a nickname had come to her unbidden, and she couldn't manage to shake it no matter how hard she tried. *Swamp sperm!* And the real reason she couldn't get the words out of her mind was obvious; they were part of her not-so-subconscious belief that the headaches were divine punishment for what she's done—what she'd *almost* done. Even though she'd read tons of pamphlets on domestic violence, even though she'd rolled her eyes at plenty of TV shows where battered women blamed themselves for the abuse heaped on them by their lovers, her thoughts about what Marshall had done to her always reset at the blame game.

If you hadn't kept it a secret. If you hadn't been so quick to believe Brittany Lowe's story about Anthem. You knew something was wrong with Marshall. You've always known. But you ignored it because he was so handsome and because he made you feel special and valuable and worth going to North Carolina for if it ever came to that.

A better person than her would have gone back to Elysium on her own and drained the pool before now. But she'd barely gone anywhere alone after Marshall had slammed her into the side of the pool; she'd never been subjected to that kind of violence before, had never even been threatened with it. It left her feeling so timid, broken down. And yes, a little privileged not to have known that kind of fear before, but still terribly ashamed at how badly it had sidelined her. Of course, she had gone to replace her water-ruined cell phone on her own, but that had been a real struggle. As she was standing in line at the Sprint store, her hand had traveled reflexively to the welt on the back of her head, and as soon as her fingers grazed the enduring soreness there, she found herself in a panic, looking over both shoulders, convinced that Marshall was about to come barreling into the store, a semiautomatic pointed at her head.

Just point. Divine inspiration. This is what she'd been looking for ever since they'd pulled away from the house. *First thing, walk to the pool, turn on the light and point and say, "What the hell is that stuff?" You'll have warned everyone, no one will get exposed without their knowledge. And it won't be a lie because fact is, you still don't know what that crap actually is.*

It was perfect. She'd been overthinking everything. What else was new?

Just point.

She was on the verge of laughing aloud at this simple revelation when a pickup truck flew past them going in the opposite direction, and in the rearview mirror, Nikki saw the truck's headlights illuminate the large black snake sliding across her mother's chest.

Darkness descended. She told herself it was a trick of the eye. But she could hear its scales rustling against her mother's blouse.

Her lips parted; she heard herself wheeze. She went to reach for her father's arm and saw the speedometer. They were hurtling down the highway at seventy-five miles per hour. And so she froze. She froze because the snake she'd seen had been huge, body almost as thick as her wrist, scales the color of smoke. A water moccasin, it had to be. And yes, yes, yes, snakes only attack when their territory is threatened, but this bastard had been removed from his territory and placed in hers and so there were no rules. There were no rules and oh my God it was huge and her mother couldn't wake up because she'd scream and if she screamed, what would she—

"Dad," Nikki whispered.

The head. She needed to see the head. Her father had taught her everything about snakes when she was a little girl. Too many things, in fact. He'd scared her so badly that she'd never after ventured farther than a few yards from the trailers at Elysium without Ben right beside her. She had to see the head. If it was rounded, they were okay. They would be fine. But if it was flat and pointed, then—

Millie Delongpre stirred, let out a soft grunt, the same kind of sound she made when she took an unexpected bite of cilantro. She hated cilantro. Then, her eyes still closed, she lifted one hand toward her chest and that's when Nikki screamed, "*Mom! Don't!*"

Ear-piercing screams. Her father shouting "*Hey hey hey what?*" And suddenly her mother was a dancing silhouette in the backseat, arms pinwheeling, the snake lost to shadow, no way to tell if she'd been struck. Dancing up and over the backseat, onto the bench seat behind it, still screaming, still oblivious to her daughter's cries.

Then Nikki saw it. The snake was coiling up on the floor of the backseat, all five feet of it, poised to strike. And her mother was still screaming and screaming. All three of them were now. A deranged blend of pure fear and desperate cries for calm.

Then they hit the guardrail.

There was a deafening pop that was louder than the rest of the chaos and it felt as if Nikki's wrists had caught fire; she'd thrown her hands out in front of her just as the air bags had exploded. Shards of glass skated across her cheeks and nose. Her father was thrown backward against his seat, tongue jutting lewdly from between his teeth, eyes slits. Then came the water, a great, dark green curtain of it that turned milky in the plunging headlights before slamming into the spiderwebbed windshield. Everything shifted underneath her; the tail of the giant SUV was spinning outward from the bank, and they were floating. Floating under the highway bridge, the nose of the Lexus dipping further below the surface, floating past dark banks of knotted cypress branches and nothing else, no boathouses, no lights in the dark. And in a deranged instant, Nikki felt as if the shattering glass, the exploding air bags, her broken wrists all amounted to a blessed thing, because they had all brought an end to her mother's terrible screams.

Her father was out cold, slumped forward against his seat belt in the space left by the rapidly deflating air bag. Lukewarm water rose over her ankles as it poured in through the door frame. Behind her, the snake was swimming in frenzied circles in the flooding backseat. But when she went to reach for her seat belt, her broken wrist sent rings of fire up her arms and she cried out in agony. The pain triggered something else; a headache, just like the one she'd suffered for days after her awful night with Marshall. Only this one was stronger, much stronger, and for a few seconds, she feared she'd broken part of her skull along with her wrists.

Then Nikki Delongpre lifted her eyes to the rearview mirror, and that's when she saw that the world had changed.

It was worse than the brief, grayscale distortions the headaches had brought on previously. The world itself had gone silvery and luminescent, and where her mother was crouched and frozen in the very back seat, her form seemed to be shedding tendrils of bioluminescence. It was as if the intense pressure inside her skull had given way, and left her seeing invisible threads of . . . she didn't know what, so the words that danced through her brain next were *stroke, aneurysm, cerebral hemorrhage.* But there was another feeling, and it was in her chest, and it was pure pleasure. A sense that she was taking in great, greedy gulps of the purest oxygen she'd ever inhaled, and it was cleansing her, dousing the pain in her broken wrists, numbing her to slick swamp water crawling up her legs.

And then she heard her mother say, "Stroke. Aneurysm. Cerebral hemorrhage." But Nikki was allowed only a second or two of realizing that her mother had just spoken her thoughts aloud before it felt as if she was thrown from her body. Suddenly, she had only the vaguest sense of her back resting against the wet leather seat. Up and down had become relative terms, and the hallucinations that gripped her were more than vivid, they were multidimensional and she wasn't sure if they were passing through her or she was passing through *them*. Cypress branches and string lights and the voice of Louis Armstrong coming from everywhere and nowhere at once, and then her father down on one knee before her, crying, extending a ring in one hand. But her father's face was so intricate, so vivid, so *real*, that Nikki knew this couldn't be the product of her own mind—she had never known her father's face that well when he was so young. No, some fundamental piece of her mother's memory, of her mother's very *soul*, was passing through her. And then when her young father leapt to his feet, screaming, and the tall grass all around them began shifting from the motion of a hundred approaching serpents, Nikki realized that her mother's soul had been irreparably damaged by what had just happened in the concrete world. That what was pushing through Nikki was a terrible hybrid of her mother's greatest joy and her greatest terror.

And then the hallucination was over, but the delicious, unzipped feeling was still in her chest, the world still swimming in silvery luminescence that both mirrored and danced gracefully with all the solid elements of the ordinary world.

Nikki imagined the fish-skinning tools she'd seen her father load into the back of the SUV, and her mother turned, pulled the case out from between two suitcases.

Nikki envisioned one of the curved steel blades and her mother, who was miraculously and entirely under Nikki's control, unzipped the set and withdrew the tube skinner.

Then, before she could think twice, Nikki drove her mother to reach down and seize the snake by the neck, and because she had been drained of all life, Millie Delongpre did so without a moment's fear or hesitation.

She lifted the snake from the rising water, its body whipping like a horse's tail. Then she slammed it against the back of the seat in one hand, plunged the tube skinner into the center of its fat body and dragged the blade down its length. The snake's breaking ribs made a sound like glass crunching under a boot heel. Once it was filleted, Nikki forced her mother to cast the limp, scaled body into the cargo bay and crawl forward over the backseat, through the water, then over the armrest, until her breasts were resting on Nikki's lap and her legs resting across her father's.

There was a gun in the glove compartment, but there was no way Nikki could manage it with her broken wrists, not without possibly killing one of them. She drove her mother to stretch across her lap, and as her hands struggled with the latch, her eyes were wide but vacant, her face betrayed no frustration. The door wouldn't budge. The window was closed and intact and the pressure of the water was holding the door shut from the other side.

There was no other choice. Still shrouded in silvery, shifting halos, her mother opened the glove compartment and removed the black pistol inside, unsnapping it from its holster, raising it and pressing its barrel directly against the glass; all of which Nikki commanded her to do with a series of simple visual images she had placed in her own mind.

Then she forced her mother to fire. While the world had been visually altered in ways previously unknown to her, the sound of the gunshot was deafening and vicious. Her father jerked awake next to her. And it was only then that Nikki realized she'd never heard a real gunshot before, and certainly never so close. The muzzle flare blinded her, seemed to scald her face with flecks of white-hot powder. When she screamed, so did her mother, only Millie's sounded like a mute's pantomime.

Then it felt as Nikki's entire rib cage had been pulled on by a giant hand. The impossible connection she'd forged with her mother had been disrupted in the blink of an eye, and she could feel it being yanked away from her now. Her instinct was to pull back, but when she followed it, there were searing flashes of pain inside her skull, and after a white flare that wiped her vision, the normal, shadowed world and all its gory, wet darkness returned.

Water was pouring in through the fresh gunshot in the passenger-side window. The SUV was tipping nose forward. Her father was scrambling out of the pitching, sinking vehicle. But her mother had rolled onto her back in Nikki's lap. And even though her eyes were wide, she still looked lifeless and hollowed out; she didn't react as the water rose over her face. That's when Nikki realized that her mother was shuddering, teeth knocking together, arms jerking and splashing in the water.

You did this to her. You had a connection with her, some kind of impossible connection, and then the gunshot scared you and it all went wrong. And now . . . And now . . .

The SUV tipped forward, the windshield suddenly flat with the bayou's surface. More water gushed through the gunshot window, but before it rose to cover Millie Delongpre's face, Nikki saw the woman's eyes collapse until her pupils were great yawning black holes, spreading outward to devour her forehead. And her mouth; her mouth opened as if she were about to scream, but the teeth inside folded in on themselves and blackened, and before the bayou filled the interior of the car, Nikki realized that whatever she'd just done to her mother, it was turning her body into something formless and primordial, something in which flesh and bone were being reduced to the same fluid consistency.

And then the water claimed them both, and suddenly Nikki Delongpre was kicking and struggling, the pain in her wrists causing her to scream, causing her to swallow water which set fire to lungs that just seconds earlier had been blessed by oxygen so pure it seemed to come from heaven.

Something was grabbing her. And it had tendrils. Snakes? *More* snakes? She kicked at them and batted them away, before she realized that whatever it was, it was changing shape in the water around her. It was grasping at her. And she could hear the sound of metal being rent all around her. Whatever was clawing at her, it was clawing at the car too, with greater success. And it was getting bigger.

She was yanked upward, suitcases knocking into her, pulled up through the darkness by some tremendous force. At first, she thought it was just air pressure forcing her out of the car as it sank nose-first toward the bottom of the bayou. But she was rising too quickly, and when she exploded through the punched-out rear window of the SUV, lungs aflame, she kept rising up into the air, until her legs were dangling. And that's when she felt a massive pressure against her chest.

The creature that stood perched on the sinking, upended tail of the Lexus, water sluicing down its scaled body, was at least seven feet tall, and it had her mother's eyes. They were shaped like inverted teardrops, the largest features on a conical head, but they were Millie's and they were huge and they were blinking madly with newfound life. The rest of its face and humanoid body were covered in giant versions of the smoke-colored scales of a water moccasin. The monster's mouth was a long, lipless leer, and on its back, three thick, scaled tentacles danced through the air behind it, meeting in a knotted amalgam of muscle and tendon against its upper back, a grotesque knapsack that made its lithe, slender body look like that of a butterfly. The tentacles flexed and coiled, a constant roil of serpentine energy, assuming a graceful pose one minute, a predatory stance the next.

It was a living nightmare. Her mother's living nightmare, and whatever Nikki had done to her, it had turned her mother into this thing that now held her in two claws, high above the rippling water. The creature's mouth opened, revealing row upon row of jagged teeth shaped like snake fangs. Then there was a loud pop and the creature's right eye exploded, shedding ocher-colored gelatin across Nikki's chest. Then another, then another, as her father, standing on the nearby bank, emptied the pistol from the glove compartment into the creature's head before it could speak its first words. By the third shot, the creature released Nikki from its claws, and the water closed over her once again, just as she glimpsed the monster her mother had become tumble sideways off the tail of the Lexus with deadweight.

FROM THE JOURNALS
OF NIQUETTE DELONGPRE

I'm not lying when I say I only remember scraps of what came afterwards. My father carrying me deep into the cypresses. The floor of the abandoned boathouse we took refuge in. The sound of my father stealing the tiny skiff. I remember helping him haul the monster into the back of the boat and then breaking down into something between sobs and screams when I realized what I was doing.

Actually, a couple months later, right before I was drifting off to sleep one night, I remembered what set me off. It was the sight of one of my mother's hideously enlarged hazel eyes rolling up to meet mine in that scaled . . . thing's face.

Dad told me later that the place where we hid out was a fishing camp that had belonged to a patient of his who had died of pneumonia during recovery; his widow had confided in my father that she couldn't bring herself to clear the place out and sell it.

But for me, it's all a jumble. I didn't think I'd wake up and be told it was a dream. But part of me hoped the sparkling world I had seen with my altered vision as I had controlled my mother like a puppet would return to embrace me and carry me away. That the monster my mother had become, and the sounds of my father's deranged sobs, were just the unfortunate side effects of having been returned to a solid, ordinary world I no longer belonged to.

My first clear and simple memory is of wandering through the swamp, summoning that blissful unzipped feeling and using it on the animals in my vicinity. There was no burst of having looked into someone's soul, but I was able to place a few birds under my control for a dazzling five to ten minutes. And then their heads exploded and they tumbled to the ground, tiny masses of gore. They didn't change shape or form, aside from this gruesome split-second death I triggered.

I can use my ability without creating monsters. And I can use it for an almost limitless amount of time on strangers in ordinary settings. God knows, I used it plenty to get us out of the city without being detected. But it's not just a reaction to a sudden shock or trauma that will pervert the connection; it's any swell of deep emotion within me. I've had a few close calls this past year, and they weren't all the result of being frightened or distracted. In every one, the person I'd hooked bore some physical similarity to someone out of my past; a tense set to their brow that reminded me of Anthem, a full, generous mouth that reminded me of Ben, a perfume that reminded me of my mother. And when these qualities distracted me, when they stirred memories that began with a seed of nostalgia and then flowered into blossoms of grief and loss, that's when things almost went full nightmare again. There's only a few seconds in which I can break the connection before my instincts take over and I pull back against that horrible tug on my rib cage. But it's a tiny window, and if I'm a second off . . .

That's why total strangers are the most easily controlled. No emotional connection. Their bursts of soul that rush through me are brief, nothing like the overpowering sensations of my mother's soul flooding through me. And that's the terrible tragedy I live with every day. It was my love for her, my connection to her, my inability to detach from her as I manipulated her like a doll that caused her own nightmares to consume her physical form.

There's still so much we don't know about what I can do. The samples haven't told us much. He calls it the Elysium parasite and it seems to have stuck with both of us; so much for the nickname I came up with—swamp sperm. And that's just fine, I guess. My MRI didn't tell us much either. There's swelling in some areas where there shouldn't be and his working theory is that they're still in there. The parasite. His working theory is that they've altered fundamental, nonvisible light waves in me that make up my soul, thereby allowing me to suck on and take in the nonvisible light waves that make up the soul of someone else.

In his view, I am a parasite governed by human will and emotion. Why I can only control one person at a time, he's not exactly sure. Whether or not the little buggers are still inside me—he's not sure of that either. Maybe they aren't. Maybe I pissed them away. But one thing's for sure: they're the cause of everything.

As for the other guy who was exposed?

Well, to be honest, after what I did to him at the Plimsoll Club, I don't think he'll be waking up anytime soon. I might have been able to force a confession from his lips but as my hatred for him swelled, I realized what was about to happen.

So it's love and hate, isn't it? It's just kind of hitting me now as I write this.

My love . . . my hate . . . their nightmares.

Anyway, maybe if I'd let him transform into some kind of beast before everyone in that ballroom, his father would have been too afraid to run toward him and the poor man would have been alive today. Meanwhile, I could have watched from the safety of the elevator lobby, concealed in the velvet cape and Mardi Gras mask I'd stolen from a costume shop so I could blend in with the waitstaff. Maybe if I'd let the process unfold, Marshall's dad would be alive.

It's ridiculous, I know. I couldn't let it happen. But his father . . . I didn't want that. I didn't want that at all.

But I didn't want any of this, now, did I?

I lie awake nights remembering the view into his soul my gift afforded me. We were writhing together in the grass, a few yards from the pool at Elysium, and he was holding me by my neck while he drew a short knife with a sharply curved blade up the length of my sternum. And I wasn't screaming or crying out for help or even gasping for breath. I was accepting this evisceration with serenity and calm. And I could feel his pride, his sense of triumph, at my silence.

Can you blame me for what I did to him?

Have you ever looked into the soul of someone who craves your evisceration? Can you see why I changed my mind at the last minute and decided to go for more than a confession? "I put a snake in their car" . . .

It's been a year now. I'm sure they medevaced him out of New Orleans before Katrina. But with each passing day, his chances of waking up again diminish. I've read up on what happens to patients in a persistent vegetative state. I hope all of it happens to him.

Yes, I've thought about finishing the job on many occasions. My father was so horrified by what I'd done, he made us leave New Orleans before I could try. But how would I do it? I can't use my ability on a person who isn't technically conscious. (Trust me. I've tried, just to satisfy my curiosity on this front.) And I'm not going to make an innocent person do my dirty work.

And then there's the whole not knowing. There's what I heard him say at the table that night, about knowing the difference between a venomous snake and a nonvenomous one.

The water moccasin and the diamond-backed water snake are easily confused, you see. Both grow to lengths of six feet, both have smoke-colored scales and bodies as thick as a person's wrist. Only the diamond-backed water snake isn't venomous at all. Was it just a prank? And was he just a boy who didn't know any better? (Am I just a girl???)

As for the peek I got into his soul? Maybe there are similar visions of violence inside the souls of men who have never lifted a hand to harm anyone in their lives. But he did harm us. And so . . . yes, there is a little regret.

Just enough to keep me from driving a knife through his heart with my own two hands.

I like to believe that with each day, with each hour, death has pulled Marshall Ferriot a little closer to the gates of hell; some souls are just heavier than others.

But I wonder if as he lies there, some part of his brain is replaying that image of me, gutted like a catfish, over and over again. And when those thoughts become too much for me to bear, I tell myself that a father for a mother is a fair enough trade. For now.

26

B en Broyard threw himself against the door so hard that the journal he'd just finished reading went spinning off the table and clattered to the floor beside him. There was no response from outside.

Then he was standing in mud, his shoulder still aching from the blow.

String lights sparkled in the low, shadowy branches overhead. The trailer was several yards behind him. Once again, time had been excised from his consciousness with a surgeon's precision. And as he turned in place, he realized there were two trailers parked in the mud a few yards away, not just the one in which he'd been confined. The other was a bright silver Airstream that had the same stage-set newness and shine as the tiny prison in which he'd been forced to read a chronicle of monsters and magic.

He was standing amid a re-creation of Elysium as it appeared more than two decades ago, in that photo of her newly engaged parents Nikki had described in her journal. (It had to be a re-creation. The land on which the original Elysium had stood was now a wash of untamed swamp.) Everything seemed perfectly arranged except for the small tangles of shredded plastic lying close to the trailers. The closer Ben got, the more he could see that they were pieces of the original lounger Noah and Millie Delongpre had been reclining on as she'd extended her ring hand toward the camera. But just pieces. Something had torn both lounge chairs to pieces.

A snake's scales. Claws. The eyes of a lost woman.

Just then, approaching footsteps squished in the mud and when he turned, Ben saw a stooped figure hobbling toward him with the support of a cane. There was some vitality underneath the man's strained movements, and Ben sensed that his contorted walk was not the result of age, but of some recent and serious injury.

Once they were a few feet apart, the pale glow from the string lights above illuminated the man's face. Ben felt his vision narrow and a weight on his chest that made him gasp.

The last time Ben had laid eyes on Noah Delongpre had been eight years ago; the man had been home early after doing his rounds at the hospital and rifling through mail in the kitchen as he pretended not to eavesdrop on the conversation Nikki and Ben were having in the other room; another whispered, frantic how-can-I-ever-forgive-Anthem session Ben felt overwhelmed by and powerless to bring to a satisfying close. Noah's eyes had briefly met Ben's through the doorway, and for the first time he'd seen real concern for Nikki in them. The sight of it had so startled him in that moment, he'd stammered through his next few sentences to his best friend.

Noah Delongpre had always struck Ben as a wildly self-centered man, and his only real joy in the world seemed to be his love for his wife, a love he saw his only daughter as a distraction from. Perhaps if Nikki had been less self-possessed, more in need of his constant guidance, he could have treated her like a patient. Or a case. Maybe that's exactly what he'd done following the madness recorded in the journal he'd just read.

But now, here he was, looking as if he had aged two decades instead of one. Gone was his military-grade buzz cut; it had been replaced by a thick salt-and-pepper mane he'd tied into a ponytail and threaded through the back of his gnawed baseball cap. He had the same angular features, with small, deeply set eyes, dwarfed by his boat's prow of a nose. But Ben couldn't tell if the tightness in his expression was the result of controlled fury or a great, interior strain.

"If you're going to waste our time with protests, do it now, by all means," Noah Delongpre said. "But allow me to remind you that there was a time when the mere notion of there being a chemical inside of plants that essentially metabolized sunlight itself would have seemed like an insanity to most men. Maybe it still does . . ."

"You exposed yourself to it too?" *Insane,* Ben thought, even as he spoke. *All of this is insane.* But it felt as if some long-buried set of instincts inside him had taken over and was answering for him, some primitive yet essential ability to believe in the impossible. He didn't dare call it faith. Not yet, anyway. To do so would imply that the hell of which he'd just read had something of the divine within it.

"So you believe what you read?" Noah asked.

"Whatever you can do, whatever *she* can do, you've done it to me twice. So I'm not sure I really have a choice."

"You were hoping it was her, no doubt. When you opened the door."

"No. I knew it wasn't her."

"How?"

"Because she would never treat me like this."

"It's been almost a decade, Ben. You have no idea what she's capable of doing to you or anyone—" His anger caused him to straighten a bit, and just this small movement stoked the fires of whatever injury he was struggling against. "That's the only reason I drove you again—"

"*Drove* me?"

"That's the term we came up with for it. Her power. He's got his own name for it too, I bet. Marshall Ferriot, that is. But I warn you, don't become lost in the language of the thing. Terms, labels—they'll do nothing to blunt its reality." When he noticed the expression on Ben's face, his eyebrows lifted and he recoiled, both hands balanced atop the head of his cane. "Oh my. You are upset with me, aren't you?"

"If Marshall Ferriot is out there . . . if he can do what you can do, why did you bring me *here*?"

"You would rather I leave you unguarded?"

"*Anthem* is out there!"

"If it's Marshall's intention to hurt Anthem Landry, then Anthem is either already dead by his own hand or he's been changed into something you will never want to lay eyes on!" This eruption sent Noah into a coughing fit, and when he lifted one fist to his mouth, Ben saw that that the space from his index finger to his thumb was a mass of red welts and fresh scar tissue.

"How would you know?" Ben asked.

"What do you mean, how—"

"If he's . . . if he's been *changed*. The thing you described . . . Miss Millie . . . You killed it right away. How can you know what it really was, or if it was—"

"If it was still *her*, you mean?"

Ben nodded.

"There were others," Noah said. "Many others. And we made it a point to keep them alive for as long as we could just so we could answer that very question. And if you think I harbor one scrap of guilt for shooting that *thing* my wife turned into exactly when I did, then you are a worse listener than I thought."

"Others . . ."

"You don't think I've been *here* for eight years, do you? What? You think we just vanished into the swamp to live like rats? No, that part came later. First, we had to learn. First I had to play mad scientist, and she had to play test subject. You see, when I was in med school I did an exchange program in Thailand, so I knew the country fairly well. I also knew what we could get away with once we arrived. That's where we conducted our experiments."

"Experiments? On . . . *people*? You experimented on people?"

"On men who became sexually aroused by burning children with cigarettes and penetrating them with the legs of furniture. Trust me. We put them to a far, far better use. And no one will miss them. Least of all the children they traveled halfway across the world to abuse."

"And what did your experiments prove?"

"Most of our initial conclusions were confirmed, just as she wrote them in her journal. The parasite resides in the brain and it allows the host to consume and metabolize frequencies of light which are not visible in this dimension of existence. On any equipment I could get my hands on anyway. But the pupils of both Nikki and her subjects dilated to twice their normal size during a drive, as we called it. Leading us to the conclusion that the eyes truly are the windows to the soul."

"You consume . . . a person's soul?"

"Close. You absorb part of it. It flows through you on a kind of conduit which we can't see. The person completely loses all consciousness as a result. So forget what you've seen in the movies. This is not possession. You can't see the world through *their* eyes. The mind-control aspect . . . well, it's just a by-product, you see. A by-product of the fact that you can draw the person's fundamental quantum material into your body by metabolizing part of it."

"And the monsters?"

"Ah, see, that was the interesting part. Sometimes I would tell her what a subject was guilty of. This one, for instance, enjoys tying up young girls and applying abrasive chemicals to their bare flesh. Nikki would be able to drive that unsavory subject for as long as she wanted, and no monster. Unfortunately. But if, on the other hand, I spritzed the man with a little bit of Anthem Landry's favorite cologne—Ralph Lauren Polo, is it? Well, then . . . showtime."

"And what were they? The monsters?"

"They were from the mouth of hell is what they were. They were malformed hybrids of that person and one of their worst nightmares or some element of a past trauma. Just as it happened with Millie. Don't worry. We did our due diligence. We confirmed what their worst nightmares were beforehand just to be sure we weren't off the mark. The interviews were not my favorite part. She mostly handled those, well-spoken girl that she is. I can show you some photographs, if you'd like."

"What I would *like* is to make sure Anthem Landry is okay so I can—"

"*Anthem Fucking Landry,*" Noah bellowed. "It all gets back to Anthem Landry. You've both tried so hard to save him—"

"What do you mean we both—"

"Oh, don't you see it? *Don't you?* She suffered a crisis of conscience in Bangkok, you see. She couldn't go on with the experiments and she abandoned me. She *left* me there. But I knew exactly where she was going. Exactly. It's the only reason I exposed myself, as you so eloquently put it. You see, I had taken samples from the pool before I capped the well. When she left me, I had no choice but to expose myself. But the problem? Well, the samples weren't enough. It's a funny creature, you see, our Elysium parasite. A drip and drab of it here and there has no real effect. In the wild, on its own, floating free through the swamp, it's as inconsequential as a drop of water. But in concentration, it's another thing entirely. If you capture it the way we did in that pool, if you get it to *flock,* then immerse someone in it, the change takes effect. So I came home as well to get—"

"As well?" Ben cried. "What do you mean *as well*?"

"Oh, come on, Ben. You're smarter than this. You've always been smarter than this. A big brute you meet on the Internet walks into your apartment late at night, gets violent with you and suddenly just walks away."

It took Ben a few minutes of gape-mouthed silence to remember what Noah was talking about. "I . . . I pulled a gun on the guy . . . I—"

"Is that why he smashed his head into your door frame three times in a row, the exact same number of times he smashed your head into the headboard?"

"How do you know all—"

"Or better yet, Anthem Landry, in an *alleged* blackout, smashes every bottle of liquor in his apartment and writes himself a note that says he's done drinking forever. She was here for years, Ben, working on your lives from the shadows. But then she got scared. You see, she ignored my warnings all together, and she flat-out ignored what we had discovered in Bangkok. Which is that it isn't contempt or anger that makes the monsters rise. It's *connection*. It's true love and true hate. Not the kind of petty, childish hate that gets bandied about on the Internet as some petty device against strangers. I'm taking about true hatred, the kind where you're convinced the other person has been taking from you year after year after year and you're powerless to stop them. *That* kind of hatred, Ben. The kind of hatred you feel for Marshall Ferriot."

"How?" Ben said. "How could she . . . Did she not feel a connection to *us*? How could she have been using her power on us and not turned us into—"

"She wasn't using it on you! She was using it on the people *around* you. The people who threatened you on the way home from the bar, the people who were standing in your way at work. She was your guardian angel, Ben. And it was going so well, she started to get careless. I had found her by then and I warned her. She went too far with Anthem that night. The bottles, the note. She knew I was right. So she went back to your apartment to remove all the surveillance software she'd installed on your computer so she could track your movements and whatever stories you were working on. That's when your angry visitor showed up and she was forced to take action to keep you from becoming a hate crime. After that . . . Well, I haven't seen her since."

"That was six months ago. She has to know," Ben whispered. "Just like you, she has to know after everything that's happened today that Marshall's awake. That he's here. She *has* to know."

"Maybe she does. I don't know how far away she is. And you're so desperate to leave. Do you really have the time to wait for her?"

"What does that— What do you mean?"

"I have more of it, Ben. I went to the source and I took as much as I could ever need."

"It looks like you took too much," Ben whispered.

Noah lifted his scarred hand from the top of the cane. "Nice try," he muttered. "But this is from something else altogether."

Noah's smile was wobbly. "You always hid behind your sarcasm, Ben. Always. When you weren't hiding behind Anthem and Nikki. You're still hiding behind him, by the way. Standing here, at the threshold of one of the greatest miracles ever to be visited upon mankind, wondering how that vulgar, self-obsessed drunk will fare by the time the night is over."

"I haven't heard anything that sounds like a miracle," Ben whispered.

"Then you haven't been listening!" Noah roared.

"Why didn't you stop him yourself?" Ben fired back. "Why go to all this trouble and waste all this time?"

"So time spent on *you* is wasted?"

"Stop fucking around with me!"

"There is no shield against what Marshall Ferriot has. There is no antidote. And if he gets you in his sights and he gets close enough, there's no running. I am going to give you what you need to stop him,

Ben. But first it was my responsibility to tell you our story so you would know the risks. So you would know how this works."

"You've told me *nothing*," Ben said. "I've got one journal entry from eight years ago, and nothing about what came afterwards except for your word. Which I don't believe, by the way."

"How could you deny what I can do after every—"

"I'm denying your *story*. You were the only person she had left in the world. She wouldn't have left you in Bangkok unless she had a damn good reason."

Noah lowered his eyes as if he were disappointed, and this time, Ben felt the darkness come like an insect darting through the air behind him before coming in for a landing on the back of his neck.

He came to on his knees, just outside a weak halo of light thrown by a Coleman lantern sitting on the floorboards a few feet away. There was pitch black all around him, but he could sense that he'd been moved—*driven*—inside some kind of barn or large storage shed. But it was the photographs spread out in a semicircle before him that captivated him.

At least twenty images in all, but they were of the same three monstrous creatures. One of them had to be the thing Millie Delongpre had been turned into. Just as Nikki had written in her journal, the contrast between the creature's scaled face and the huge, staring, death-glazed human eyes stopped Ben's breath in his throat, forced him back onto his haunches.

The others were worse.

All of them had been photographed in death; there was a giant hybrid of a man and what had to be a pit bull that had an almost serene expression, save for its gaping jaws, so huge and so stuffed with giant, almost cartoonish canine teeth, they looked poised to divide the entire creature's head in half. The most human-looking creature of the three was an enormous woman—the combat rifle leaning against the concrete wall next to her gave her scale; Ben figured she was at least ten feet tall—with a giant ridge dividing her head and her twin flaps of greasy, knotted black curls. The flesh of her crossed legs was sealed together as if by hot wax. If she had been mobile, she would have been forced to drag herself around by her arms. Her dangling, teardrop-shaped breasts were striated by spiderwebs of dark blue veins and a lewd, serpentine tongue dangled from her leering clown's grin of a mouth, so big that the entire thing could never have fit between her lips no matter how hard she had tried.

Ten feet tall . . . Mother of God.

And what was she? The nightmare version of some test subject's mother or wife? What crosscurrents of the human mind had literally given flesh to such a horrid thing? *Mind monsters,* he thought. That's what these things were. They were living nightmares, plucked from a person's soul as the material of their soul was drawn from their flesh. No, they weren't just plucked. That wasn't the right word. Jostled. Let loose. Set free. A disturbance in the connection between Nikki and the subject that set these nightmares loose upon the world.

Mind monsters. The term came to him effortlessly. He even whispered it to himself. Then he remembered what Noah had said to him about trying to name and label everything. Clearly, the man had been speaking from his own experience because that was Ben's exact urge. Name, label, categorize. Breathe.

Ben heard movement nearby, then the familiar metallic hum of electricity as several tracks of fluorescent light flickered to life in the rafters above. Noah was standing a few feet behind him at the entrance to what had once been a long boathouse. Walls had been built around the perimeter, and the rails where the boat slips had been rose up out of plywood coverings. On the wall behind Noah, Ben could make out a faded sign in brightly colored print, a series of warnings and notices to the parkgoers who had once lined up for swamp tours and boat rides from this now dark and dank space. The whole place had once been a zoo or an amusement park.

Noah's stare seemed vacant, then Ben heard a swinging chain behind him, and he realized his captor was focused on something just over Ben's shoulder.

Ben screamed when he saw it. Not a short, sharp cry, but a guttural scream triggered by a true belief that he was in immediate physical danger. But after a few minutes of stumbling backward, almost losing his balance a few times, and watching the creature swinging from chains above the floorboards, Ben realized that, even though it was twice his size, the creature swinging from chains strung from the ceiling was dead. A chain had been attached to each large, translucent wing, keeping them spread out behind the slender, malformed body at its center. The wings were patterned like those of a butterfly, but the colors themselves were the greens and browns of the deep swamp. And the body that appeared to be pinned to the very center of both wings was almost humanoid. Infantile, even. Bald, with foreshortened, dangling legs. Covered from head to tiny knotted toes in what looked to be charcoal-colored fur.

And Ben wondered if the reason he hadn't lost his mind entirely was because there was always a part of him that believed the swamp could give birth to such vicious and massive creatures. And to behold one now, to smell the sour-milk stench it gave off, returned him to a state of childlike wonder. But childlike wonder is always accompanied by a child's overpowering sense of helplessness, and so, for the first time in his life, he was fighting not to lose control of his bladder and his hands rested against the nape of his neck as if there was a strand of pearls there for him to clutch for dear life.

"You wanted the whole story," Noah said. "Here's the whole story."

Ben heard Noah's footsteps approaching from behind as he studied the dangling creature before him. And then he realized what was familiar about the creature's blackened face; the deeply recessed brow, and the jutting lips, contorted into a cruel parody of a baby's pout, even in death. They were cartoonish distortions of a face he'd seen just earlier that day—impossible to believe it had been the same day, but it had been—the email a woman named Allison Cross had sent him as he'd pulled away from his apartment building with Marissa and a tiny motorboat in tow.

Millie Delongpre. Yes. You see, she and my husband, they were together before she met Noah, and well, Jeffrey always carried a torch for her. He even talked to her in his sleep.

Her husband, missing. Her husband, one of the only other men to love Millie as much as Noah had. Her husband, here now before him, a shadow in the facial features of this terrible creature.

"Jeffrey Cross," Ben said.

Noah went rigid beside him.

"Jeffrey Cross has been missing for weeks. His wife, she called me today and . . ." Ben pointed at the creature but he couldn't find the right words. "This is . . . Is this . . . ?"

"It doesn't sound like you need my help. You're smarter now. When you were a kid, you were all emotion and temper and—"

"You were trying to reverse it," Ben said. "Jeffrey's wife told me he always carried a torch for Millie. He was there the night you proposed to her. So you re-created Elysium just as it had looked on that night. And you brought Jeffrey Cross here and . . . what?"

In response, Noah lifted his chin and stared directly at the creature.

"Jesus Christ," Ben said. "Is this what Nikki found out? That you were actually going to make a *monster* out of—"

"I was *not* trying to make a *monster.* I was trying to make *her.*"

"Millie. Your wife . . ."

"They're memories. They look like nightmares. But they are memories. *Living* memories. They are fusions of human form and memory and I thought if the process could be refined, we could . . ." His breath left him and he licked his lips desperately, which seemed to bring no moisture to them at all. "Our test subjects were abducted and confined and interrogated; of course they gave birth to monsters. And Millie had suffered the worst trauma of her entire life that night, of course she gave birth to a monster. But what if, what if it could be done another way? What if what appeared to be the great and terrible limitation of Nikki's power could be used to unleash true magic on the world, instead of living hell?"

"You were trying to bring back the dead."

"I was trying to give life and form to a *memory*," Noah said. He pointed to the photographs at their feet. "That woman, she's the mother who molested one of our subjects when he was five years old. That dog, that's the pit bull that attacked our other subject when he was fourteen, the one he could never get out of his head. And my wife . . . my wife ended up merged with the snake Marshall Ferriot put in our car. *Memories,* all of them. Every experiment, every last one. So I picked the man whose memories of my wife were as full of love and longing as mine, and I brought him to a place where she would rise to the surface of his consciousness. And then I reached into his soul. If that qualifies me as bringing back the dead, then so be it. Then that's what I was trying to do."

"And you failed," Ben whispered.

Noah's face wrinkled, and after a few seconds, what Ben thought was a sneer turned into the threat of a sob. He pulled his shirt up over his chest and the wounds Ben saw there were as fearsome-looking as the carcass swinging by chains a few feet away. He'd seen photos of great white shark attacks that looked similar, but the worst parts were the bands of blue and dark green on the perimeter of the giant bite mark that covered half of his chest, his entire side and the lower part of his back. They weren't bruising; they were signs of infection which would explain the weakness and the shivering Noah was suffering from on top of everything else.

"There's no way that thing could—"

"Oh, no. This, this lovely creature was my third attempt. The first was decidedly more reptilian in nature, as you can see from my wounds."

"Your third attempt at . . . what? Millie?"

"No. I'd given up by then. I was trying to turn him back. But he didn't make it."

"You're dying, aren't you?"

Noah let his shirt slide back down over his injuries, and when he turned to face Ben, his eyes were glassy with barely contained tears. "I'm done. There's a difference."

"What do you mean?"

"We're all dying. Every last one of us. Me? I'm actually ready to be dead. And that's fitting, isn't it? I've been legally dead for years." Noah closed the distance between, and in the bright glare of the fluorescent lights, Ben could see for the first time how sallow the man's features were. His lips were so dry they looked ready to slough from his face. "I don't expect you not to judge me. Or not to hate me, even. But whatever choice you make, know this, little Ben Broyard. I am your prologue. And so is Nikki. She used to think we'd hand over everything to you once the time came, or if we were ever discovered or found out. All she wanted you to do was tell our story. But I've been watching you, Ben, and I can see now you have the power to continue it. And I'm going to let you. On one condition."

Noah paused, and despite his stern and aggressive tone of voice, one of the tears he'd tried to contain slipped down his cheek. "You must do what she failed to do, what she lacked the courage to do. You must stop Marshall Ferriot."

A choice, this last thought was still filtering through his consciousness when Ben opened his eyes and found himself staring down at cloudy, mustard-colored water. After a few seconds, like the pixels of an old Magic Eye, the tumbles of flesh-colored particles, many of them flocking together in pulsating clumps, seemed to resolve, and he realized he was standing on the service walkway above a large aquarium tank, another exhibit in the ruined zoo Noah Delongpre had taken as refuge.

There was a service walkway that made a U along the tank's sides and back. Off to his left was a floor that sloped abruptly, probably the ceiling over the walkway tourists had once filed through to get a look through the tank's glass.

Noah had driven Ben to the walkway's far end, and was standing between him and the service door on the opposite side of the tank.

"Why give me the choice?" Ben called out to him.

"Because you won't put it to good use if I force it on you."

And then the door opened on the other side of the tank, and she was there. She was taller, her hair thicker and darker than it had ever been in her youth, no longer the honey shade it had been when he'd used to run a brush through it late at night as she dozed off in his lap. And her face was longer and more angular and there was a hardness to her slanted cat-eyes that hadn't been there before. And when she saw him standing just steps from the tank and the surging, tumbling infestation laced through its cloudy water, her lips parted but no sound came out that he could hear. Indeed, what he heard instead was a shuffling sound, and when he looked to Noah, he saw that the man had taken out a small gun and placed the barrel against his right temple, while balancing his other hand on his cane.

"That's the other thing, Ben," Noah called out. "The other limitation. You can only drive one person at a time. So sometimes, you have to make choices. Hard choices."

Nikki shook her head back and forth, but her expression was one of mild, mature disapproval.

"Enough," she said quietly.

"Of what, dear?" Noah asked his daughter. Then, to Ben, he

said, "She can't decide, you see. Which one of us to stop, that is. And the risks of driving either one of us are already so great to begin with—"

"Enough, Dad. Please."

Still pressing the gun to his own head, Noah looked into Ben's eyes. What he was searching for in them, Ben couldn't be exactly sure.

Was it some roiling evidence of Ben's constant desire, there since the first day he could remember, to be a bigger and more physically powerful man than he would ever be? Was it some evidence of the lifelong terror he'd felt most of his life, always fearing some form of attack on his very being, fearing that his only real defense—his sharp tongue—would offer no protection against pipes and bottles and guns? Or was it Ben's ceaseless desire to change the very flow of the world around him, to alter the course of rivers so that they flowed toward the sunlight of truth? Was it the memories of those ruined and shamed women, clinging to the rafters of their flooded homes in the Lower Ninth Ward or cowering in their attics, terrified to let the floodwaters touch them again, even as Ben and Marissa had goaded them on—*Come on, girl. Come to the boat. It's okay.* Were Ben's lips moving as he remembered those awful scenes, as he thought to himself how the water beneath him now was as clouded and menacing and dark as the water that had blanketed his city that week?

What was her name? he thought. *The one who was too afraid, the one who never swam for the boat. The one who stayed behind because she thought the water would go down soon and she could just walk out of her house as if the levees had never failed. The one who died of dehydration. If only I could have made her swim . . .*

. . . I could make them swim.

He realized he'd said these words aloud only when he felt the breath of them move across his lips. Then Noah Delongpre smiled, and nodded slightly.

"And now it begins," Noah said.

The gunshot knocked him backward , the blood spray painting the wall behind him a split second later, and then Nikki was screaming and racing down the walkway. And Ben felt as if he were floating up and out of his skin and bone. But there was no darkness, no sense of missing time, no sense of having his soul pulled from him by a force he could barely comprehend. All he saw was Noah Delongpre's final, barely perceptible nod. Then the water rushed up to meet him as he dropped himself feet-first into the tank.

27

B en could feel them.

There was nothing quick or predatory about their movements, nothing to suggest they were penetrating his flesh or following some primordial instinct to enter his bloodstream and make their way to his brain. First they drifted toward him, then they formed tendrils down his limbs, up his neck and over his face, and within a few minutes it felt as if a veritable blanket of them had embraced him from head to toe. But there were no pinprick stings, no tiny bites. On their own, they were too small for that, and it was the clumping of them—the *flocking*, as Noah had called it—that rendered them visible at all.

According to her journal, Nikki and Marshall had been in the water together only a few minutes, so that was all it took, right? Just a few minutes was all he needed. But Ben held himself below the surface, just as he used to do when he and Nikki were kids and they would compete to find out who could hold their breath the longest. It was fear that kept him from surfacing, but not fear over what he'd done. Too much of the world had been cracked open during the past few hours for him to be seized by such a childish and reflexive instinct. No, he was simply afraid that if he surfaced too quickly, the little bastards wouldn't have enough time to work their magic.

But then he heard the sound of Nikki sobbing, as familiar to him as if they'd never been separated; the same raw, chesty sobs she'd let loose when choir practice was interrupted and she was told that her grandmother had died. When he broke the surface, gasping for air, feeling wet clumps of the little fuckers sliding down his cheeks and up his nostrils—not sliding, *crawling*—she was cradling her father's corpse in her arms. It looked like she was preparing to flip Noah's body into the tank. But that wasn't it; she was just desperate to hold him, but she didn't want to cradle his gunshot-blasted head on her lap, so she'd slid her arms underneath his lower back, despite the awkwardness of the pose.

Then she saw Ben, floating several feet away, with only his head above the surface. He braced himself for judgment of some kind, but instead, he saw a flash of recognition in her eyes that stalled her violent tears. She was scanning the rippling surface of the tank. The tendrils of Elysium parasite had formed a starburst pattern around his head.

"I knew you would do this." Her voice was choked. "The minute you knew about it, I knew you would do something like this . . . I knew you would want to save the world with it. So I tried to keep it a secret and do my best to save *you*." She was fighting tears again. "It's ridiculous, isn't it? After the life I've lived . . . I'm still so afraid for everyone else. And that's the worst part. You can't use it on the people you love, not even to make them save themselves. It's just too dangerous. You can't. You just can't . . ."

Ben hoisted himself from the tank, did his best to ignore the sensation of a thousand microorganisms sliding down his slick flesh as he made his way to her. Without moving from where she sat, he yanked on her father's body suddenly, until his head was resting on her lap. His face was unharmed and she avoided touching the back of his skull. Instead, she ran her fingers gently down the bridge of his nose, and Ben wondered if she was trying to draw solace from the fact that Noah's death wouldn't be marked by the same hideous transformation as the loss of her mother.

"He was dying," Ben finally said, and he was amazed, a little disappointed, to find that his voice sounded exactly the same. "The thing he turned Jeffrey Cross into, it attacked him. His wounds were infected and he was . . . he was dying, Nikki."

"If only it had been the fountain of youth," she whispered.

Because there was nothing else he could think of to do, he sank down behind her and wrapped his arms around her chest, and in her ear he whispered, "I missed you. I missed you so much." His words felt pathetic and inadequate. He closed his eyes to see if they would resonate, for him, at least. And they did, a little. Nikki shook with more sobs. He gently pulled her to her feet, then he took her hands in his. As her sobs continued, he placed his forehead against hers because he could think of nothing else to do but say her name over and over again.

He was trying for a speech, a strategy, a pitch. But all he kept seeing over and over again was Anthem's apartment building blowing sky high like the redbrick house in Beau Chêne. All he could see was Marissa, possessed, drained of herself, dragging him into that boat propeller. And all his grand plans and clever words kept collapsing in on themselves. There was a great freedom in all of this somewhere, a clarity that would push the shadows from the path ahead.

"It's Marshall, isn't it?" Nikki finally whispered. "He woke up."

"Yes . . ."

She nodded, but she was struggling for breath. Then she took his hand and they started to run.

Ben was astonished that Nikki owned a cell phone and a car. After what he'd just been through, he would have been less surprised to learn she'd spent the last eight years sleeping under bridges and darting between rooftops courtesy of dragonfly wings. But instead she'd been making cell phone calls on the shiny iPhone she passed to him as soon as he asked for it, and gliding along highways in the sleek black SUV that sat parked on the other side of the ruined chain-link fence enclosing most of the property. The Keep Out signs along the fence now looked as mold-bruised and weathered as the once welcoming signs for the old zoo, and the SUV's silver grille glinted in the bouncing beam from Nikki's Maglite.

He'd managed to call Anthem's cell twice by the time they reached Nikki's Jeep Grand Cherokee. Straight to voice mail each time. He couldn't tell if the twisting deep in his gut was just fear, or the first bloom of his immersion's side effects.

Once he'd braced himself against the Jeep, he looked back on the warren of shadows they'd just escaped from. It was the first time he'd seen the place in its entirety, given that he'd been driven through it in a series of forced blackouts. The building they'd just fled was one of several dilapidated one-story exhibit halls that made a semicircle around a courtyard of cracked concrete. The dry fountain at its center sported a giant statue of an alligator dressed up in some sort of festive, plumed hat, its forelegs lengthened into arms that opened to welcome the dark.

"You're going to get sick soon," Nikki said. It was her explanation for shoving him into the backseat, and he didn't fight her, just curled up onto the leather and screwed his eyes shut as the Jeep's engine revved beneath him and gravel and twigs spat out from underneath the tires.

"How long?"

"We're a half hour from New Orleans."

"How long will I be *sick*, I meant."

"Ben, I don't know. It's been eight years. I wasn't in the habit of infecting people."

"How bad?"

"Like the flu, I guess. I mean, you won't be incapacitated but it's not going be pretty and you're gonna want a bathroom . . ." She fell suddenly and abruptly silent, and when he rolled over onto one side, he saw she was struggling to keep her eyes on the road, the sobs threatening to take control of her again. "I wouldn't have stopped you, for Christ's sake. I would have *let* you make a decision. He didn't have do that. He didn't have to—"

"He would have done it anyway. He was planning to do it from the moment he brought me there. Some people are dying, and some people are done. He was done. That's what he said to me, Nick."

"I could have stopped him." In the faint green glow from the dashboard lights, he could see she was focused on the rutted road. "I could have stopped him from going after Jeffrey Cross. He had a *list*, Ben. Did he tell you about that part? We were in Bangkok—"

"He showed me the pictures."

"I found a list in his lab. A list of people who'd loved my mother as much as he had. That's why I left him. We'd been experimenting on psychopaths and he wanted us to come home and switch to his *old friends*."

She was ramping up again, and he was afraid hysteria was about to replace her grief. Chills rippled through his body, and he felt a twisting in his stomach that was resonating down into his bowels. But he reached for her through the shadows anyway, over the gearshift, until his hand came to rest on her right thigh. When he spoke his tongue felt thick.

"Do you remember what you said to me that day on the fly?" Ben said. "We went there after school, just the two of us, and it was a beautiful day. I think it was January but it wasn't too cold and the sky was clear and the river was so high we could practically put our feet in the water. And there was soccer practice going on behind us. Do you remember?"

She was silent, both hands planted on the steering wheel. The road went smooth beneath the tires suddenly and headlights flared over Nikki's face. They were on open freeway now.

"You told me no matter who I turned out to be, you would always accept me. You would always love me. Do you remember that day?"

"Of course I remember," she whispered. "And then I left you."

"You left me with that day. That beautiful, perfect day. And you left me with your kindness and your respect. Those things didn't leave me when you did. They never will. And I'm offering you the same things in return. Always. Always, Nick."

She reached down and took his hand and hers, and brought them to her chest.

"But Nikki . . ."

"Yes?"

"We have to kill Marshall Ferriot."

She brought his hand to her mouth, kissed his fingers gently, and for a few seconds, Ben thought this was the only response he was going to get out of her, then she said, "I know."

28

It was like being atop a floating skyscraper. The borders between river and dry land were hard to discern because the lights of the container and chemical ships passing them on either side appeared briefly as dense as the lights on shore.

After two hours on the bridge, Marshall had managed to commit a map of his surroundings to memory. Exit doors on both sides led to wide exterior staircases that zigzagged several stories down to the main deck. A long bank of radar consoles, a map table and the wheel, which was currently being manned by a tiny Southeast Asian quartermaster, took up the center of the room. Every few minutes Anthem would call out a new direction—*Port 10, Midships, Starboard 10*—and the quartermaster would repeat it in a chirpy, heavily accented voice that suggested these nautical terms might be the only English words he knew.

Just behind the ship's glowing, flickering nerve center, a pull curtain hid a messy navigation area that contained a battered gooseneck lamp and two computers that looked older than any of the three men currently on the bridge. Both computers were off, and a nicotine-stained dot-matrix printer was attached to each one. Right behind this cluttered area, the ship's main interior staircase entered the bridge. Next to this entrance, the door to the small bathroom drifted and swayed with the giant ship's almost imperceptible motions.

In front of the wheel, radar screens and empty pilot's chair, there was enough walk-through space for Anthem Landry to stand and devour a plate of hamburger patties and sliced potatoes brought to him by the ship's cook. His view of the river wasn't perfect. Four giant cranes lined the ship's hull, perpendicular to the bridge, and Marshall figured the long, swaying hooks and chains attached to each one were used to open the grain containers that filled the ship's hull.

There was enough room at the long counter lining the windows for Marshall to sidle up to him, but he chose to stay back. No video cameras were visible; he didn't even see any protrusion in the ceiling. But there was no telling where they might be hidden. Best to hang back and play as small a role as he could, just in case the whole thing ended up on film. "You okay?" Marshall said.

Anthem nodded. His eyes were saucer wide in the glow from the brightly lit cranes outside. But his mood seemed morose, distant. It was just the two of them on deck with the quartermaster now. The jovial Greek captain had disappeared after introducing himself when they first came aboard. The chief mate had poked his head in a few times, but it was clear they were all resting up before they took to the Gulf of Mexico on their own.

"You bored?" Anthem asked.

"Nah uh," Marshall answered.

"Should be about another half hour before we reach the base of Canal Street. Then we'll hand off to the next pilot at Chalmette. You sure you don't want coffee or anything?"

"I'm good."

"Thank you. For coming. I appreciate it."

"It's good. It's all good."

"It's funny. When it's light out, we've got pigeons all over the hull, eating at the grain. Dancing around like they're all hopped up on crack."

"What do you do? Chase 'em off with a broomstick?"

Without a smile, Anthem said, "You heard about Deepwater Horizon, right? I mean, you were probably still . . ."

"The big oil spill. Yeah. I read about it."

"Friend of mine worked with the cleanup efforts out in the Gulf. He said they used these big booms to corral all the oil and then they'd light it up to burn it off. Most times they did it, they'd have birds and turtles and stuff caught in the oil. But they didn't give a shit. They'd light 'em all up anyway. Sometimes I can't get it out of my head, that's all."

"Can't get what out of your head?"

"The thought of those birds trying to take to the sky, oil all over their wings, flames racing after them, taking 'em down just when they got airborne. Sometimes I close my eyes, and they're all I see."

"Never thought you'd turn out to be some animal rights guy, Landry."

Anthem managed a weak smile, but his eyes were still locked on the hull below, like he was seeing the dancing, grain-drunk pigeons that typically flocked there when the sun was out.

"Sometimes I just wonder if there's always gonna be a price for living here," Anthem whispered. "That's all."

"There's a price for living anywhere, isn't there?"

"True. But it's getting steeper here."

Marshall said, "I'm gonna take a leak."

"Don't fall in."

Once he was behind the pull curtain in the messy navigation area, Marshall removed the pistol he'd been carrying in the back of his jeans and tucked it in between one of the ancient computers and its accompanying printer. He made sure the barrel pointed toward the wall, and the handle was extending slightly out from the edge of the shelf, as poised and ready for action as a ripcord.

Everything had fallen into place and nothing else mattered. So what if Anthem's soul burned more brightly than the others? Marshall knew he could get his hooks into the man—he'd already done it once that night—and now that all the pieces had fallen into place, that was all that mattered. Because if things kept going as well as they'd gone for the past few hours, he would only need to drive Anthem for a short time to bring about a perfect ending for a not-so-perfect hero.

"Hey, Ferriot? You seen my phone?"

29

G et down!" Nikki cried.

They were flying through Jefferson Parish on Interstate 10, passing the broad off-ramps to various shopping malls, cavernous hangarlike buildings where Ben had done last-minute Christmas shopping in another life. He'd been dialing numbers so frantically he'd missed the flare-up of police lights behind them. Now he lowered his head and watched as Nikki looked into the rearview mirror and let her foot off the gas.

"No, no, no!" Ben protested. "C'mon. You gotta—"

"Hush."

The police car was gaining on them, lights flaring, siren wailing. They'd been doing ninety since hooking up with the interstate behind the airport. Ben had been curled into a ball for the first twenty minutes of the drive until he realized the nausea was actually more bearable when he was sitting up. By the time he got his bearings they'd been cutting through the sea of cypresses that cradled the 310 Freeway, leaving the towering Luling–Destrehan Bridge in their wake, and crossing behind the airport's runways. Wherever Noah had taken him, it had been on the west bank of the river.

But now they were just a few minutes from the best off-ramp to get to Anthem's apartment and Nikki was letting a cop car get within inches of their rear bumper. "Gotcha," she whispered.

The cop car suddenly swerved to one side and slammed nose-first into the concrete divider. She hadn't just let the car gain on them; she'd been letting the driver get within range.

"You have a test question, right? If you get him. You understand what I mean, don't you? In case Marshall's already—"

"Yeah. I've got one."

"You need to throw up?"

"No."

"Are you lying?"

"Yes. Nikki . . . how long until I can . . ."

"I don't know, Ben. It was days with me, but I didn't know what had really happened to me. It could be sooner. I don't know."

"*Jesus!*"

"Just open the door, I'll slow down and—"

"No, no, no. It's not that. He's on *call.* I forgot. He's probably on a ship right now."

"He's safer on a ship."

"He wouldn't go out on one without his phone. He needs it. He uses it to communicate with the relief pilot."

The great hulk of the new pumping station they'd installed next to the broad, flood-prone dip in the interstate flew past the left-hand side of the Jeep, then they were passing under the train trestle, and two expansive aboveground cemeteries appeared on either side of the freeway. The city was within sight now, the South Carrollton off-ramp dead ahead.

"Do I get off?"

"I don't . . ."

"*Ben.* Should I get off?"

"I don't know. Just wait. Just hold on—"

A call to information put him through to Vessel Traffic Control, the small bunkerlike building where all the bar pilots monitored their own river traffic. Each station was manned by an off-duty pilot, and chances were high at least one of those pilots would be a member of the Landry family. A gruff male voice answered before Ben could rehearse his words. So he went with his first instinct.

"Are any of the Landry brothers working a shift tonight? I have to speak to them immediately. There's been a family emergency."

"And who's this?"

"My name is Ben. I'm a close friend of their brother, Anthem. There's been an accident."

"There's been an accident, you say?"

"Yes. I'm trying to get in touch with any of the Landry brothers. Merit or Greg or—"

"Hold on," the guy said. The curtness of his response suggested that either Merit or Greg was working one of the computers in the other room, maybe within sight of the guy's desk, and he wanted nothing more than to pass off this crazy dead-of-night caller to one of them as soon as he could.

"Ben?" It was Greg Landry. The last time they'd spoken had been at a family crawfish bowl a few weeks earlier, where the family was shot through by a wary optimism over Anthem's newfound sobriety. Radio calls squawked in the background; Greg must have picked up in the central control room.

"What accident? Anthem's on a ship."

"Where's the ship?"

"Uh, sheesh . . . I don't know. I know it's grain and it's headed south for a handoff to a Crescent City pilot at Chalmette. One of its containers is cracked . . . What the hell's going on, Ben?"

"Find out if he got on alone. If he didn't, we have a very serious problem."

"What kind of problem?"

"Find out, Greg. You said he's headed south? Toward downtown?"

"Yeah. I can give you his exact position . . ."

"I need to know if he's *alone,* Greg. He's not answering his cell phone."

"Now just hold on a second. Okay? Hold on! He's got his radio with him."

Nikki said, "Where am I headed?" Ben gestured dead ahead, toward the mushroom swell of the Superdome and the brightly lit skyscrapers of the Central Business District. The radio noises continued in the background. Greg Landry must have been sitting at his station when he answered the phone, and he didn't even bother putting his hand over the receiver as he asked the guy next to him, "You talked to A-Team since he boarded?"

"Wait, wait, wait!" Ben cried. "Don't radio the ship!"

"Well, how in the hell do you expect me to—"

"Listen to me, Greg. And I promise you, I am not fucking around here, okay? So you have to listen to me here—"

"I'm *listening,* for Christ's sake!"

"If he didn't get on the ship alone, then he's in danger—"

But Greg was talking to the man next to him in the control room again, his tone urgent.

"Greg!"

"He's not alone," Greg said into the phone. "Guy next to me just talked to the pilot who handed off to him at Destrehan. He said some . . ." To the guy next to him, Greg said, "What frickin' cousin?"

Greg's simple question—What frickin' cousin?—resounded over and over again in Ben's head like cannon fire.

"You want to tell me what the hell's going on here, Benny?"

"There's been a threat against Anthem," Ben said.

"A threat against— What kind of threat? Like terrorism?"

"Something like that."

What frickin' cousin? What frickin' cousin? What frickin'—

"You think somebody got on with him?" Greg said, dropping his voice so as not to be overheard. "Benny. Are you saying what I think you're saying?"

"Yes."

"Mother of Christ. I'm calling the ship, for Christ's sake!"

"No! Don't do that! You'll tip him off."

"Then he'll use the code word we've got for hijackings."

"Just tell me where the ship is!"

"Ben, you're not making any goddamn—"

"Tell me where he is!"

His scream frightened Nikki so badly she winced and brought one hand to her mouth. There was a stunned silence from the other end. But Ben didn't care about any of it. He was trying to strategize in his head. *Can't go behind the floodwalls 'cause we might miss the ship and then we'll get trapped. And how much range do we have anyway and what good can I do if I can't see inside of the ship or the bridge or where they are? I've got to get high up and the whole city's below sea level. Have to get downtown. One River Place. The Hilton. Or the bridge. That's it, that's it. The bridge. Have to get on the bridge. But what will we do then? Something. That's all. That's all anyone can ever do. Something, goddammit.*

"They passed the Upper Nine about fifteen minutes ago," Greg said, sounding stunned by Ben's eruption. "That's Audubon Park. They'll hit the base of Canal Street in a few minutes."

What frickin' cousin? What frickin' cousin? What frickin'—

"If you have a terrorist protocol, activate it. Activate it now."

Greg inhaled sharply, but before he could respond, a familiar, static-spiked voice echoed through the room on the other end of the line, sending a spike of cold fear through the center of Ben's gut.

"Heeeeeellllllooooo everyone? Is anyone theeeeeerrrrree?"

There was a rustle against the phone, probably because Greg was setting it down on a table. But Ben could still hear everything: the click of Greg answering the radio call from the man he thought was his brother, and then Greg's voice saying, too softly, too controlled, "Hey, man. It's your brotha. How's everything going out there tonight?"

"My *brother*, huh?" came the coy, probing response.

He doesn't know his name, doesn't recognize the voice. He doesn't know his name because it's not him anymore.

"Yeah, man," Greg answered, trying to play it cool even though his voice had the tension of a high wire. "How's that Panamax treating yah, A- Team?"

"Oh, it's just fine," Anthem's voice said, and then in the background, Ben heard something else. Crying. A man crying. Not just crying. A pathetic, terrifying and yet somehow universal sound: a man pleading for his life. "Listen up, *brotha*"—and this snide ridicule of Greg Landry's Lakefront accent was all it took to confirm Ben's most horrifying fear— "there's something I want y'all to hear!"

The gunshots came so close together it was impossible to tell how many there were.

30

G unfire swallowed the quartermaster's cries for mercy.

Amazing how the body just drops like that, Marshall thought. He was crouched in the back corner of the deck. He had, only seconds before, closed the interior entrance to the main deck, and now he was studying his handiwork with a calming sense of satisfaction. No grasping at the chest, no arms opening to God above. Just sudden deadweight hitting the floor like a ton of bricks.

And now Anthem Landry towered over the crumpled form of his third and final victim, the gun in his right hand, the walkie-talkie in his left; the latter erupting with terrified demands for information from Vessel Traffic Control.

Marshall saved the quartermaster for last not because he was the smallest, but because he'd been alone at the wheel while the captain and chief mate had been huddled in discussion close to one of the exits.

Four shots had taken down both men, then Anthem had crossed the deck in several long, effortless strides, aiming the gun at the terrified, screaming quartermaster as he threw the lock on both doors. All these tasks had been completed effortlessly by the blood-lashed, gun-wielding pilot, probably because a man whose arm wasn't aching from the gun's recoil was controlling his every move.

And now the call had been made, the final murder recorded for posterity's sake. The interior entrance was locked, which meant anyone who tried to break in from the side staircases would be exposed to gunfire on the landings outside. It had all come together so beautifully; he allowed himself several moments to just savor it. Even the blood splatters throughout the bridge were just a faint, delicate glisten in the radar screen's green glow.

Up ahead, the Crescent City Connection blazed high above the rippling black waters.

He couldn't wait too long. The clock was winding down. The heart of the city that had stupidly declared Anthem Landry a hero would soon be exposed to the ship's giant prow.

Anthem Landry raised the walkie-talkie to his mouth, pressed the button and began to speak. "Answer me a question, brotha, motha, and whoever else can hear me on this beautiful night. Don't you have days when you're just ready to be done with this place? With this whole fuckin' city, I mean. Don't any of you get tired of pretending this place wasn't meant to fall into the fucking sea? Anyone? Anyone?"

Could they get there ahead of the ship? Were they ahead of it right now? There was no getting Greg's attention back. He was too busy trying to break in on his brother's full-scale mental breakdown. And he was failing. Anthem wasn't interested in being interrupted. Marshall Ferriot wasn't interested in being interrupted.

" . . . You know how fucked up it feels to have everyone call you a hero, only to turn around and realize you're the hero of a giant shit pile full of niggers and drunks? It's like being handed a medal and realizing it's covered in piss. A piss medal. Hey, maybe I just invented a new term. How about that?"

"What the fuck, man?" Greg Landry wailed into the phone. "What the fuck is happening?"

"It's not him, Greg."

"What do you mean it's not—" Voices on the other end of the line interrupted him. They were gruff, authoritative, trying for a sympathetic tone and failing in their eagerness to get Greg Landry out of the control room. He was losing his shit.

"Who is this?" a new voice said.

"My name's Ben Broyard. I called about a threat we received against Anthem Landry at our offices earlier tonight—" When the guy didn't ask all the questions he should have been asking, like What office? and What does threat mean? Ben understood the level of terror that now gripped everyone at Vessel Traffic Control.

In the background, the venomous diatribe continued. " . . . Fact is, we ignored our own history. No city ever should have been built here. This damn river! It's just a giant toilet for the rest of the country. And we're the sewer! And do you know what that means? Do you know what that means for every last one of us? We live in shit! That's what!"

When the stranger spoke again, his attempt to enunciate every syllable only caused his voice to wobble even more. "I've known Anthem Landry most of my life. And that's Anthem Landry's voice we're hearin'. So tell me, just who in the hell is this threat against?"

Shouts erupted in the control room and, after a few seconds of this melee, Ben heard a recurring phrase: He's turning. He's turning the thing. He's turning.

"Where?" Ben shouted. "How's he turning it around so quickly?"

"He's not turning it around. And it's empty."

"Empty. Isn't that good?"

"No. It means its got no weight. It'll ride up over anything it hits and just keep on going. And they were just starting to drain the ballast so the bow's still sticking up out of the water and . . . Aw, Jesus . . ." The man groaned. "Aw, no, no, no . . ."

"What?"

"He's turning for the east bank. He's headed for Spanish Plaza."

Spanish Plaza. The spot where Marshall Ferriot's death plunge had been broken by his own father. How fitting. *How fitting, you monster. And that's what this is about, isn't it?* You're not just taking out Anthem. You're sending Nikki a message. And Ben had no choice but to relay it.

To Nikki, he said, "Spanish Plaza. The Hilton."

Her eyes flashed, but then her icy calm returned, even as she drove like a kamikaze pilot.

"Have you evacuated the riverfront?" Ben asked.

"A tactical alert's been sent out. NOPD's been mobilized. But we've got the Hilton, One River Place . . . It's the middle of the night. Those folks are asleep."

"Then wake them up!"

The Jeep rocketed down the long expanse of the Ernest M. Morial Convention Center, and then Nikki pulled a hard right, tires screaming, before she could plow into the sidewall of Harrah's Hotel and Casino. Cabs swerved out of their way as she careened into the large circular carport of the Hilton Hotel and Riverwalk Shopping Mall.

A woman in a bathrobe was staring into the Jeep's headlights. Nikki slammed on the brakes, came within a foot of hitting her. The woman didn't care. She took one look at Ben and kept running. She was too busy trying to get away from the Hilton's entrance. And she wasn't alone. Several bright lights were flashing above the hotel's entrance doors, and more guests—most of them sleep-rumpled and in their nightclothes—were pouring out into the night while security guards directed them away from the entrance and the fire alarm let out a series of bloodcurdling, automated screams.

Several NOPD cruisers squealed into the turnaround behind him, but they didn't give two shits about the speeding Jeep that had beaten them there by a heartbeat. The uniformed cops sprang into action, directing guests away from the building.

Ben struggled out of the car, grateful that adrenaline had caused his nausea to wane. But his head was spinning, and the crowd of evacuees from the hotel was threatening to throw him off balance. Nikki was calling out to him from the other side of the Jeep, but he ignored her, focusing instead on a dazed-looking man in a half-unbuttoned plaid shirt and loose-fitting jeans. Plaid Shirt was doing a half-stumble, half-trot away from the lobby doors, because he was scanning the crowd around him for someone important.

. . . and then he was a ten-year-old boy, standing at his mother's bedside, reaching for her hand, and she was pale and gaunt and bald from chemo, but her fragile smile and her reach for her son's hand was enough to comfort him . . .

He felt Nikki's hand on his shoulder, but the world had gone silver, the crowd surging through the hotel's circular driveway casting off ghostly impressions, and Plaid Shirt stood frozen, awaiting Ben's commands.

"Let him go," Nikki whispered into his ear. "Let him *go*, Ben!"

It wasn't ego that had made him hesitate, but the same rich, delicious pleasure she'd described in her journal. It was like the peak of an orgasm, softened and sustained. And letting it go felt like yanking a half-chewed bite of ambrosia from his mouth.

The world returned to its normal, everyday colors in a seamless instant. And then it was just him, and his nausea, and the screaming fire alarm, and his best friend, back from the dead and glaring at him with a schoolteacher's anger and intensity.

"I think I'm good to go," Ben whispered.

She started pulling on his shoulder, then she ran for the opening in the concrete floodwall up ahead that served as the entrance to the Riverwalk Shopping Mall.

As soon as they entered the courtyard, they saw the ship. Its wheelhouse was tall enough to block out part of the glimmering Crescent City Connection bridge it had just left in its wake, and it was on a direct course for the riverbank, its approach silent but undeniable. The fire alarms from both the Hilton and One River Place, the condo high-rise just west of the hotel, sounded eerily distant now, like sci-fi sound effects from a neighbor's television. The fountain behind him was off. And the plaza around him was just an expanse of empty concrete. No one to scream, no one to warn. Just wind-rattled tree branches and the deceptively gentle swish of the river water breaking across the approaching ship's giant bow.

"We can't drive him," Nikki gasped, struggling for breath. "We'll turn him into something so much worse than what he is now."

"Then what the hell are we going to do?"

Nikki started to spin in place, surveying their surroundings. He couldn't tell if she was looking for something specific, or if it was panic that propelled her now. Then she went rigid. It couldn't be the ferry landing that had stilled her. What could they possibly do with— Then he saw what was just beyond it and rising over the ferry landing's elevated concrete walkway; the great parabolic sweep of green glass that enclosed the jungle exhibit at the Audubon Aquarium of the Americas.

"Sorry, folks. I wish I could do this another way. But I guess y'all just don't want to get the message. Hell, if Katrina didn't deliver it, I'm not sure I can. But I'll try. I have to try. So here's what I say to all those folks who called me a—" But Anthem's voice sounded weak, and a small seizure shook Marshall's sternum in time with Anthem's every stammer.

Something was wrong. His ribs wanted to burst from his chest, he was sure of it.

Their speed had been over fifteen knots right before they went into the turn. Now they were crossing the current, which was slowing them down, but not by much. And he'd been fine then, his fears about Anthem's overpowering soul flash seemed to have been for naught.

Then suddenly, it was all gone. Marshall had fallen to his knees on the metal floor and the world had been returned to its bleak, everyday colors, and several feet away, Anthem Landry's entire body was shuddering, so severely it was visible even in shadows. It looked as if his shoulders were about to jerk up and out of their sockets, and Marshall realized the chattering sound was the man's teeth knocking together. And his hold on him was gone. And when Marshall went to hook him again, the shadow that had been Anthem Landry turned on him, and in the green glow of the radar screens, he saw that the shoulders poised to lift free from Anthem Landry's body had blossomed into impossible, dual swells that surged upward from the man's arching back. Anthem's eyes were gone, caverns of blackness that seemed to be devouring his entire face. But there was a channel of suddenly molten flesh pouring down the bridge of the man's nose, lengthening it. And his stooped pose wasn't correcting itself. He was standing upright. In fact, the man's silhouette was expanding, lengthening.

It's his spine, Marshall realized. *His fucking spine is getting longer. That's why he's not standing up.*

And then there were two clattering sounds, sharp and subtle given the nightmare unfolding before him, and in the radar screen's glow, Marshall saw what had made them; two giant, matching talons that had slapped to the floor of the bridge in unison. And that's when Marshall could no longer deny what the twin surges of shadow emerging from Anthem Landry's rapidly lengthening back actually were.

"Wings," he muttered aloud, before the wave of shadow surged toward him across the deck, emitting a piercing, shrieking sound that emptied Marshall Ferriot's bladder instantly. And then it felt as if he was being dragged across the metal floor by darkness itself.

The police officer had just finished shooting out four of the glass doors in the entrance to the Aquarium of the Americas when the ship's great bow slammed into one corner of the ferry landing. The two-story skeletal steel structure gave way like kindling. And then, just as the pilot on the phone had predicted, the ship's bow jerked upward, riding up and over the descending maelstrom of struts and support beams, driving them down into the maelstrom of muddy water. The ship kept going, the giant chains attached to its four loading cranes swaying.

Nikki drove the police officer to run in the opposite direction, toward Woldenberg Park, away from where Ben and Nikki now stood clutching each other just outside the now shattered entrance doors to the aquarium. The ground underneath their feet was trembling as the ship tore through yards of red bricks emblazoned with the names of the aquarium's donors. Its approach across the water had appeared so lazy, it was almost impossible to believe that the deafening sounds of splintering wood and collapsing concrete were the results of its hull devouring the dock front.

Ben glanced over one shoulder, just as Nikki drove the cop to toss his gun over the railing into the river. Then, once he was a good sprint away from them, she released him and he literally spun in place, he was so disoriented.

Then he was knocked off his feet, and before he could think twice, he pulled Nikki down with him. The ship's bow had slammed into the two-story wall of green glass that enclosed the Amazon Jungle exhibit, and the vast sweep of shattering glass was so loud and piercing, it was like a thousand children screaming at once.

Now that it had been stopped at a forty-five-degree angle with the bank, Ben scanned the length of the ship. The wheelhouse was still a good two hundred feet out into the river. A dark shape was trying to fight its way out through the broken windows, but it was caught on a long series of empty metal window frames. Then, with one powerful thrust, the dark shape hurled itself forward and the entire row of empty window frames popped free and somersaulted through open air down to the main deck.

A pair of wings pushed their way through the new, elongated opening, unfurling suddenly to a span of at least fifteen feet, as dark and solid as the hull of the ship itself. Then the creature dropped from the front of the wheelhouse, revealing two legs shaped like those of a giant human but covered in the same glittering, obsidian feathers that plated its enormous wings. On its way down the thing buoyed itself with several awkward wing-pumps, then it landed feet-first atop the grain hatches.

Ben glimpsed the creature's foreshortened arms, crossed against the chest as if it wasn't quite sure how to use them, enormous talons latticing each other. Five curving nails on each claw? Could it be possible? The same number as fingers on a human hand. Then the giant creature raced down the length of the ship, wings spread to keep the disproportionate body upright as it ran.

Nikki had seen it too, and she was getting to her feet, slowly, using both hands to brush her hair back from her forehead, as if she thought the creature might be a trick played by her bangs.

He was visited again by the same two words that had coursed through his brain when he'd seen those awful photos. *Mind monster.* And Nikki was shaking her head, her hands gripping the top of her skull now.

"Come on," she said.

When he didn't move right away, she grabbed him by the hand and pulled him to his feet, then she turned and kicked out the remaining glass in the bullet-pierced door, all the while holding his hand as if he were a child who might try to flee.

31

Marshall had been so sure the creature was going to drop him in the river, he started kicking the second he hit the water, determined to keep himself floating above the treacherous currents that flowed just beneath the surface. But now his feet brushed sand and when he broke the surface, he heard screaming emergency alarms all around him, along with the wet, thwacking sounds of debris slamming against concrete.

He was inside the aquarium. The damn thing had flown right into the soaring Amazon Jungle exhibit and dropped him into one of the open-air fish tanks. The glass wall had been cracked in a dozen places, and water was spewing out onto the debris-strewn walkway so fast the level inside the tank was dropping. Marshall threw his arms over the steel rim in an intact portion of the glass wall and managed to swing one leg over the side, then the other. When he dropped to the walkway, he sensed a great movement high above him. A shifting of something massive and not quite steady. It was up there, somewhere, perched atop the giant thatched tree house that hung high above the exhibit; a dark shadow, wings folded against its newly formed back.

Silent, watching.

There was a sharp, high-pitched crash from high above. Marshall thought it might be the creature, until he saw the thing's shadow jerk in startled response. A quadrant of steel framing and shattered glass had pulled free of the shattered ceiling, sending daggers plunging into the jungle foliage a few feet away. He heard a soft pop nearby, another tank giving way. But the creature was still up there, the creature that had been Anthem Landry just moments before. It was still Anthem. It had been made from him. He'd watched it happen. What would happen if he—

Something seemed to explode in the air right in front of him, and his first thought was that the creature had descended on him, and he was preparing to hook the damn thing when there was an explosion of white-hot pain in the center of his skull, piercing and flowing. Feathers slapped his face and there was a blast of wild, rank stench. A bird. A real bird, normal size, and it had just taken a bite out of his face. There was another explosion in the air a few feet away; this one right behind him. Feathers slapped his neck. And another. He was still spinning. They were attacking silently, one after the other. Three were as many as he could count from the blasts of their wings. He focused on their blasts, tried to hook them, but he couldn't. It was like scraping his hands against a steel door. Because they were already hooked.

Another one landed a searing, direct hit, tearing a chunk of flesh from his eyelid. He screamed despite himself, felt his knees slam to the concrete. *They're going for my eyes. She's here. She's here and she's trying to blind me.* Then he heard one of them slap to the concrete next to them, and then another. And a third, and the air around him felt still suddenly.

He was wiping the blood from his eyes, blinking furiously, telling himself they hadn't pierced his eyeball, that he would be in agony if they had, and that when he was able to see again, he'd see them littering the walkway around him, their skulls exploded like all the animals who were subjected to a power like his own.

"Nikki Delongpre?" he growled.

But once he said her name aloud, realization hit. Three birds at once. There'd been three birds at once, and unless she was infinitely more powerful than him, there was no way she could have hooked more than one animal at a time. He'd tried countless times and failed. She wasn't alone.

He was still wiping the blood from his eyes when he felt sudden movement around his legs, then in between them, the brush of cold, tensile skin. His vision cleared just enough for him to see the giant snake coiling itself around his knees. The exhibit's star attraction, freed from its tank and coiling around his waist now. He managed to lift one arm above his head, but the other was pinned underneath the sudden constriction, and immediately his lung cried out in protest as he felt the squeeze. The son of a bitch was ten feet long uncoiled, so thick he probably wouldn't have been able to fit both hands around its body.

And now its expressionless eye was level with his, its giant head sliding over his chest, and when he went to scream, there wasn't enough breath left in his lungs to give voice to its terror. He had one free arm, but when he went to claw the thing's eye out, the mouth opened and swallowed his hand. And the knowledge that it was human intention—*her* intention—driving the snake's seemingly emotionless movements only added fury to his terror. He tried to say her name, but what came out was a slurred perversion of it that made him sound brain-damaged. And he prepared himself to die, on his knees, splinted by the snake's unnatural constriction, his vision finally cleared of his own blood.

Then the snake's head exploded, and its suddenly lifeless body lost its coil, sliding down him gradually. He pulled his hand free of the mass of gore that had once been its head and used it to push himself out of the snake's ghostly coil. The last few movements needed to free himself made him look like a bride stepping out of a wedding gown she'd let puddle on the floor.

Another sharp crack from high above, but nothing animal about it. Another rain of glass from the shattered ceiling. Only there was a disturbance in the high mound of jungle foliage a few feet away in advance of the impact. A startled movement that was all too human. The fresh rain of glass was about to expose someone's hiding place.

Ben Broyard somersaulted to the walkway in front of him, head slamming to the pavement just as the giant wet leaves that had concealed him were torn to pieces. His body went limp and Marshall was wondering if the little fucker had been knocked out cold when suddenly, for the first time, his own world was wiped away from him as if by a giant hand.

Someone was calling his name. His head was spinning and everything he heard sounded like it was coming to him through a thin tube. But he could hear his name, laced with another word he couldn't make out. A woman's voice. Screaming . . .

Nikki.

His eyes popped open. Marshall Ferriot stood over him, wide-eyed, blood streaming from the bites across his forehead and the bridge of his nose, his expression as vacant as Marissa's had been earlier that day when she'd almost torn his head off. Nikki's voice was blending with the squealing emergency alarms. They'd spread out the second they hit the jungle exhibit, both of them trying to get different vantage points on Marshall, as far away from him as possible.

But now he'd been exposed and . . . she'd hooked him! That's why she was screaming. When he'd fallen right in front of Marshall, she had no choice but to hook the guy, and that was the other word she was screaming: *Now Now Now Now Now.*

Ben reached out for a giant shard of glass lying a few feet away. He ignored the fact that it had sliced into the flesh of his palm. He knew if he looked right into Marshall's eyes, he would hesitate, so he closed the distance between them without looking at his face. When there were only inches between them, he slashed the jagged pieces of glass at Marshall's throat. And it was as if it had moved through water.

Because Marshall Ferriot's skin had become fluid and black. It looked as if he was bending backward at the waist, but his torso was actually lengthening, his legs fattening, and then his mouth opened so wide it appeared to consume his entire face, turning his head into a featureless, gelatinous black mass that looked like crawling lava after it has dived under the surface of the ocean. His neck was lengthening and taking on the patterning of a snake's smoke-colored scales. His arms had opened as if he were about to take Ben in an embrace, then they sealed themselves to both sides of his narrowing trunk, sprouted into something that looked like a millipede's legs. Then the matching rows of dripping fangs took shape inside the creature's giant, crescent-shaped mouth, and it was now ten feet long, level with the floor, its blazing eyes focused on Ben.

Ben wasn't sure what terrified him more, the thought of staying put or the thought of what the thing's soul would look like if he tried to drive it a second time. So he turned and ran. And that's when he felt an incredible gust of air behind him, heard a deafening, pained hiss and looked back in time to see the winged beast Anthem Landry had become seize the giant serpent in its great avian beak and lift it off the ground. Doglike, the winged monster swung its head back and forth, wings pumping madly, and the giant serpent's entire body jerked and spasmed as it was hefted up into the air. Then they both dropped.

The serpent's limp body smashed into the emptying remains of one of the open-air tanks. Now that it was pinned to the floor, the winged creature landed talons-first on the serpent's back, and then tugged lightly on each talon to make sure it had pierced its scales. Then, wings pumping to give it balance, it pulled its talons in opposite directions and tore the son of a bitch in half.

One after the other, it yanked it talons free from the blood, gore and shredded scales. When it turned and looked back at Ben, he collapsed on the walkway, just inside the tunnel that lead to the rest of the aquarium. The creature stood up on its hind legs, its talons tucked against its feathered chest, and despite the inhuman shape of its blood-splattered beak, the eye that it focused on Ben was Anthem's. And when the creature opened its beak and let out a piercing scream that sounded like a woman's cry filtered through a torrential thunderstorm, Ben thought it might be parroting the terrified sobs he couldn't fight any longer.

Having exhausted itself, the creature picked up the serpent's severed head in its talons, then kicked itself into the air with its powerful legs, the pumping wings giving it flight. It took a few minutes for Ben to gather his courage and walk to the spot where the serpent's shredded lower half lay strewn across the walkway. Once he was there, he looked up and saw Nikki standing on one of the thatched, elevated walkways that passed just below the tree house overhead. She was staring up through the shattered glass ceiling of the exhibit, probably at the spot where the creature had flown away. By the time he had joined her on the walkway, they could hear the footfalls of approaching police officers, too many at once to drive off, so he took her hand and they sped off down the walkway in the opposite direction.

32

MADISONVILLE

They crossed Lake Pontchartrain in silence, and by the time they reached the old push boat outside Madisonville, they had three hours until dawn. Nikki used her Maglite to guide the way toward the ship's remains, which now seemed tiny to Ben in comparison to the leviathan that had almost run them down earlier that night. For a while, they stood at the edge of the empty parking lot as Nikki ran her flashlight beam over the push boat's glassless windows, waiting for the eruption of some unnamable creature cowering inside, Ben scanned the night sky. But the boat was empty and so was the sky. The dock had mostly rotted away, so they were forced to wade through waist-high water to get to its back deck.

They searched the lower deck for any signs of talon marks, any stray obsidian feathers. But there was nothing, just a hollowed-out steel-walled cavern. The situation on the upper deck was the same. That left the wheelhouse. And when the beam of Nikki's flashlight traveled across the pile of red Mardi Gras beads Anthem had piled there every year after the Krewe of Ares parade, she sank slowly to her knees and ran them through her fingers.

Ben turned his back on her, allowing her this private moment at the graveside of her adolescence, and surveyed the sweeping view of the lake. In the near distance the causeway twinkled, though not with its usual energy given the lateness of the hour. But the world around them was flat, silent and dark, devoid of monsters and seemingly drained of magic. And this sudden peace made him feel dizzy and light-headed. He had the sense that he was about to float away, as if all that truly tied him to the earth's surface over the years was his belief in the inevitable orderliness and decay of the human body.

He was exhausted, and he smelled awful, so awful he was tempted to douse himself in more lake water. But that would only make it worse. Having taken her moment with Anthem's makeshift altar, Nikki sank to the floor, knees to her chest.

"The way to keep from losing your mind is to see them as extensions of the person, rather than . . . you know, a separate thing. Something from another dimension. It sounds horrible, but it actually makes it easier. The eyes . . . They're always there, in the eyes."

Ben nodded, and for a while, neither of them spoke, just listened to the gentle howl of the wind moving through the ship's hollow, rusted skeleton.

"I never told him," Ben finally said.

"Never told him what?"

"That I thought Marshall caused the accident. That I knew you two had gone to Elysium together."

"What does it matter, Ben?"

"If I'd given him some reason to . . . suspect, I don't know. Some reason to hate him or fear him, even, maybe he wouldn't have let him get so close . . ."

"Marshall didn't need permission to use his power on anyone. That's not how it works. You know that."

"I know, but . . . he brought him on the ship."

"He could have been driving him all night long."

"Then he would have changed earlier. Look how quickly Marshall changed. No, they were . . . They were together, Nick. For a while before Marshall did anything. And if I had told Anthem what I . . ."

"Why didn't you?"

"Because I thought he would kill him. Now that doesn't seem like such a bad thing."

"No, of course not. Marshall would be dead and Anthem would be on trial and you would have no real idea of what you'd been spared, just that your best friend was going to go to jail for murder. And all because I was still out there, letting everyone believe I was dead. You're not going to beat me at the blame game, Benny."

Another silence fell, and then she whispered, "I never thought he'd wake up. You have to believe me. I never . . ." And then a tremor took control of her voice, and Ben sank down to the floor beside her and laced his arm around her leg and held it there until she seemed to have regained her composure.

"Of course you didn't," he whispered.

He gave in to the urge to rest his head against her shoulder, and when she relaxed under the weight, leaning back against the wall and spreading her legs out in front of her for support, he leaned in further and she curved an arm around his back.

"I've never turned one back," she said. "You know that, right? I mean, not into anything that's . . . livable."

"But you've never loved any of them either."

"That's true . . ."

"Do you still love him?"

"What I feel for him, I've never felt for any other man."

"Me too . . ."

"Did you guys ever . . . You know, after I left . . ."

"No. Oh my God."

"I don't know. I just thought, maybe . . ."

"You thought he'd get wasted and I'd get desperate."

"Not exactly that. But something like it."

"I would never."

"All right, fine." She ran her fingers through his hair gently. "Has there ever been anyone?"

"You mean besides the guy you drove out of my apartment that night?"

"You're welcome, by the way."

"No. No one who . . . mattered. As much as you or him."

Her touch was soothing and hypnotic.

"Ben . . ."

"Yeah?"

"I don't know how they are when they're . . . loose. What if he doesn't come?"

"Then we look for him."

Or someone else finds him first, and the entire world changes. She must have heard the exhaustion in his voice, because she slowed the gentle movement of her fingers through his hair, and for a while, they said nothing. It was long enough for the weight of sleep to sand away the edges of his thoughts.

"Ben?"

"Yeah?"

"I really thought you'd get a little bit taller."

He laughed into her chest, and then she tightened her arm around his back, and after another few minutes or so, he slipped away. But it was the kind of fitful sleep he typically had after too many drinks, where the brief snippets of dreams seemed raw and close to the surface of wakefulness; he dreamed that he was awake and they were talking to each other when they really weren't, and then the images from the aquarium played rapid-fire across his mind, each one too quick to startle him awake. But the high-speed-download quality of it left him with the awareness that he wasn't slumbering so much as processing, and underneath this realization was the vague fear of who he would be once the impossible events he'd witnessed that night became a part of his memory.

Then Nikki was shaking him awake, and there was a noise outside like a low, crackling fire. "Ben," she whispered fiercely. "He's here."

He could barely walk upright, not without the support of his wings pumping the air behind him, and the effort seemed to be exhausting him as he shambled across the empty parking lot. He switched to all fours but his forearms were ill designed for the task. In order to take a step, he had to flatten his five-nailed talons entirely against the asphalt, then take them up high into the air with each step, like a cat pulling its paws out of something sticky, all the while making sure the long curved nails didn't fold together on each retraction, preventing him from taking another step.

Ben realized what was so awful about the creature; there was no evolution to its form, no logical physical adaptations to environment that had been refined over millennia. He remembered the photograph of the giant, deformed woman, whose giant tongue had been too big to fit inside her mouth. This creature had the same lunatic quality to it; its giant, protruding beak didn't close entirely and the huge, ovular eyes—too full of human-shaped iris and pupil to look anything like those of a bird—didn't blink because there were no eyelids to go with them.

If they left him like this, if they didn't do *something*, he would not survive for long. Ben was sure of it. And the more he studied its imbalanced form, the more he realized why the creature seemed exhausted. Its massive wingspan made it more suited for flight, but the weight of its heavy, humanoid body must have created incredible drag. There was no way this creature could survive in the wild, if it wasn't killed by a human. What choice would it have if it went on like this? Fly itself to death?

As he and Nikki crouched against the railing outside the wheelhouse watching its approach, Ben was grasping to figure out what memory of Anthem's could have given rise to this thing. Then he remembered a drunken late-night phone call, right after Deepwater Horizon blew. *They're burning birds, Benny. In the oil. They're caught in it but they don't get them out before they light the fires to burn it off, and they're all just going up. Are you going to write about it, Benny? You got to write about it, Benny.*

The creature jumped down into the water with a great splash and began walking down the side of the boat, away from the wheelhouse, toward the yawning opening in back. The push boat's weight shifted beneath them as the creature crawled inside the lower deck, and that's when Nikki turned to Ben and looped several strands of red Mardi Gras beads around his neck. Then did the same to herself.

"I'll get as close as I can," she whispered. "You stand by, and when I'm ready ... you drive him. But not until ... not until ..."

"Not until what?"

She bent forward and whispered words into his ear. They were short and sweet and simple enough to remember, but he was still sure he'd forget them in the terror of the moment, so he started whispering them to himself over and over again.

"I don't know how much of him is still in there, Ben. I don't know if—"

"He came here, Nikki," Ben whispered. "Remember that. He came *here.*"

Nikki turned from him and started slowly down the exterior staircase that lead to the lower deck. He followed a safe distance behind. When they reached the lower deck, they found the creature slumped against one corner of the shadowy steel cavern, its feathered chest heaving. From the way it had jammed its wings up into the corner of the ceiling, holding them there by leaning his upper back against the wall, Ben could see what a terrible compulsion they made for the thing; a giant, undeniable invitation to take to the air, even though the rest of the thing's body wasn't properly crafted for flight.

Ben stood his ground outside the door to the lower deck.

Nikki entered the shadows. The creature didn't seem to notice her approach, then, when she was eight feet from it, she said, "You know, you're not going make a lot of friends around here with that T-shirt you got on."

The avian head jerked back on its neck. The beak opened and closed, but no sound came from it.

"True," Nikki continued, taking several slow steps toward the thing. "You did meet the two of us today, so I guess that's something. But maybe after school, we can run you by Perlis and get you some of those polo shirts with the crawfish on them. You know, help you fit in a little bit more. What do you say to that, huh, Anthem Landry?"

The creature leapt forward, talons slapping to the metal floor inches from Nikki's feet. Ben gripped the door frame, prepared himself to take the creature under his command, but when its beak opened, the sound that came ripping out of it had the tinge of a man's wail in it. Nikki had held her ground and lifted one palm.

"After all," she continued, but her voice was trembling. "You are the most beautiful man I have ever laid eyes on, so you can't blame me for coming up with an excuse to get close, now, can you?"

The creature lifted one talon off the floor, and slowly extended one sharp, curving nail. "Nikki . . ." Ben said quietly.

Nikki shook her head, but she was having trouble keeping her eyes open, and her chest was heaving as the creature's one nail traveled slowly up the length of her torso. To Ben, it looked like he was searching for a target, and he prayed it wasn't Nikki's beating heart or her carotid artery.

"You know . . . Mardi Gras is coming up soon, and we like to watch the parades from Third and St. Charles. It's not too far from my house. Maybe you could join us, Anthem Landry. Would you like that? Would you like to watch the Ares parade with us?"

The nail found its target, the plastic medallion attached to the beads hanging from Nikki's neck. A soft, gentle whine escaped from the winged beast. And Nikki said, "Would you like that . . . my hero, my God, my angel?"

Having heard the signal, Ben opened, and just as the scene before him turned silvery and luminescent, the creature's soul sent him stumbling backward. He felt his ass hit the steel staircase, and then all sense of up and down, all sense of a bordered, orderly world was lost as he was battered by the nightmare-gnarled images pouring through him. The writhing body of the serpent Marshall Ferriot had become, Nikki shrinking from view as the creature rose up through the jungle exhibit's shattered ceiling. And then there was a soft, radiating glow, beating like a heartbeat within the chaos. And Ben recognized the twirling knots of flame blossoming throughout his consciousness. He could hear the music, he could smell the spilt beer. He could feel the memory of a long-ago Mardi Gras parade coursing through him, and that's when he realized Anthem Landry was moving through him too.

VII

MARISSA

33

H ow 'bout you fuck yourself?" Marissa finally said to the lawyer. "How's that sound?"

Hilda Lane's lackey and henchman had been lecturing her for a good fifteen minutes on how her actions had violated the standards clause in her contract, giving the Lanes grounds to fire her as editor in chief of *Kingfisher* without severance.

The man hadn't even bothered to inquire after her physical condition when he'd forced his way into her room, even though she'd just been moved out of post-op recovery two days before after running a high fever for the three days. He'd been droning on about how even though there were no witnesses to her shooting, the simple fact that an officer of the law had seen fit to put a bullet in her—God rest his soul; the poor man hadn't survived his injuries—combined with the slanderous allegations she made against Hilda Lane during their last phone call gave *Kingfisher*'s owner ample cause to—and then she told him to go fuck himself and things got real quiet all of a sudden. She'd said it brightly and casually, as if she were suggesting he try adding a little Tabasco to his scrambled eggs every morning.

"I take it this is your way of saying you don't intend to—"

"I'm real tired and I don't feel that well and you're a jerk. So no, it's my way of saying you should go fuck yourself is what it is." Maybe it was fatigue that kept her tone breathy and casual. Or maybe she really thought it was good idea for the beady-eyed prick to use some blunt object on one of his orifices. She'd lost track of which pain meds they were giving her. "Seriously, take that contract in your hand, roll it up real narrowlike and see how far up it'll go. I'll wait right here till you're through. And I've got some pills lying around if it starts to hurt too bad."

"Okay," the lawyer muttered. He sprang to his feet, placed the contract in question back in his briefcase and closed it with a punctilious snap. "Ms. Lane asked me to inform you that she appreciates the time you gave to her—"

"*Her*? Her newspaper? Is that what you were going to say? Well, you tell Ms. *Lane* I was working at that paper when she was doing PTA. And I'd rather mop floors before I go back to being her house negro. She's not getting any fight out of me. Don't you worry your bald little head."

"I wish you a speedy recovery, Ms. Powell."

"Then get outta here and let me get back to it."

And then she was alone again with rebroadcasts of that morning's WWL *Eyewitness News* and the endless photos of Anthem Landry that kept rolling across the screen, along with the now familiar helicopter shots of the giant grain ship he'd allegedly been at the helm of when it speared the Audubon Aquarium of the Americas. There were more tearful interviews with Landry's relatives, some of whom looked vaguely familiar to her from birthday dinners and crawfish boils where she'd been the token black lady over the years. And she prayed that whatever had happened with that damn ship, whatever had caused Anthem to go missing, was the real reason Ben hadn't come to visit her.

Indeed, her only visitors over the past five days had been Mr. Suit and a bunch of police officers who were desperate to find out why one of their own had put a bullet in her, even though she insisted to kingdom come, and despite the influence of all manner of tongue-loosing medications, that she couldn't remember a damn thing that happened out there on that river after the corpse of Danny Stevens had bobbed to the surface. She'd gone from being included in their collective head-scratching sessions to being flat-out accused of all manner of crimes; all of which only served to convince her the cops didn't have a damn clue what had happened out there either. Not with the murder of Danny Stevens and his wife, not with the explosion at the house, and not with the bullet some cop had seen fit to put in her. But she was a lot more willing to put up with their nonsense than she was some prick Uptown lawyer who'd been dispatched by a boss too cowardly to fire her in person.

The doctors came about an hour later, told her she would be free to go in the morning, and she put on her best game face, tried to look grateful over the news, and then they were gone and she was back alone with the news. She dreamed fitfully that night, dreams with Anthem Landry's face in them and corpses tumbling through green water.

The map was there when she woke up, folded neatly and resting on the tray table she'd been eating her meals on.

When she opened it, she saw a thick red line that went from the hospital she was in, across Lake Pontchartrain, then west on I-10 before meeting up with 310 Freeway just past Louis Armstrong International Airport. She traced the line with her finger, past Destrehan, over the Mississippi River on the Luling–Destrehan Bridge, and then on some crazy unfamiliar spur that appeared to lead right into the swamp, to a fat red dot. And right next to the dot, Ben's handwriting: *As soon as you can.*

Then she saw her own car keys, tucked underneath the map.

She'd pocketed both by the time she was ready to leave a few hours later. A silent assemblage of most of the cops who had questioned her during her stay were waiting next to the nurses' station as she walked past, and she wasn't quite sure how to read their brusque nods and penetrating stares. But there was no sliding out from under the terrible weight of the feeling it left her with. An accomplished journalist and writer, a graduate of one of the best universities in the country, one of the hardest-working girls ever to come out of her neighborhood, and now what was she? A black lady with no job, nursing a gunshot wound in her left side, leaving a hospital under a cloud of criminal suspicion.

Once she was in the open-air parking lot, she hit the button on her remote and the headlights of her Prius flashed several rows away.

This better be good, Uptown Girl. Please, Lord. Make this good.

Fifteen minutes after she turned off the highway, Marissa came to a ru-ined chain-link fence surrounding what looked like an abandoned zoo. The Keep Out signs along the fence were as stained and perforated as the chain link itself, and in the center of the concrete courtyard, a ridiculous statue of a smiling, humanoid alligator with a plumed hat welcomed her with open arms, even though the fountain basin around its feet was dry and choked with vines. Past the old ticket booth, with its shattered front windows, there were three one-story wooden build-ings around the courtyard, each with a steeply pitched roof, and sign-age that was no longer legible.

The door to the center building was standing open, and when she entered, she found herself staring at the glass wall of a giant aquarium tank, filled with cloudy green water. The tank's glass panel had once been bordered by carved wooden alligators and snakes, but the paint had faded away entirely, leaving behind a jumble of dark wood that looked more like the outline of a dark lava flow.

She kept walking, waiting for Ben to show himself at any moment, too exhausted and too dispirited to marshal anything close to fear. So often in her life fear had taken the form not of self-regard, but of concern for those who'd first receive the news of her car accident or stabbing or immolation in a house fire. But now her mother, the same mother she'd returned to New Orleans for, had been in the ground for years. There'd been no real man (or woman, for that matter) in her life for some time. (Unless you counted Ben.) This realization felt strangely liberating, but it also left her feeling hollowed out.

She passed the aquarium and stepped into the room at the end of the hallway. Once, long ago, it had been a gift shop of some kind. Many of the shelves were still there, a couple of rusted metal spin racks still leaning against the walls. There was enough pale daylight coming in through the door she'd left open behind her that she almost moved on without noticing the single gooseneck desk lamp, new-looking and startlingly out of place amidst the decrepit surroundings. It had been set on what had once been the cashier's desk, and positioned right under its halo was a scored, leather-bound journal, with a single note-card on top that said READ ME.

She glanced up briefly when Ben entered the room, but when he didn't say a word, she went back to reading. As soon as she turned the last page, he began to tell her the rest.

34

P rove it," Marissa said.

"What? On *you*? No way. You heard what I just said—"

"Ten seconds, fifty seconds. What's it gonna hurt?"

"You! It'll hurt *you*."

Ben rolled his eyes, brushed past her and threw open the back door. A few seconds later, a tiny sparrow zipped into the room and landed on the cashier's desk right next to the journal.

"Left," Ben said. The sparrow fluttered up into the air, then dropped to the table a few inches to left. "Right," Ben said.

The sparrow complied, and Marissa felt a strange heat spreading through her abdomen, then turning to icy chills as it ascended her spine, and suddenly her hands were going to her mouth against her will. Ben continued to manipulate the tiny bird. *Left, right, left, right . . .* And then the thing's skull collapsed into a tiny little spill of gore and it fell to one side with a soft plop and all Marissa could hear was the sound of her own breaths rasping against her sweaty palms.

Ben walked toward the aquarium, holding the door open until she found the wherewithal to follow him, and then they were standing before the cloudy, moss-dappled glass, and finally she saw it, pulsing in floating tendrils through the water. And even though she wanted to bring her hands away from her mouth, she couldn't, and this made her feel both terrified and terribly self-conscious at the same time.

"We wouldn't have to hurt anyone," Ben finally said. "Not physically, anyway. We'd never have to spill a drop of blood. Not one."

"*We?*"

"Think of the potential, just for a minute. Before you freak out. Think of the confessions we could force from their lips when the cameras were rolling. Think of what it would mean if we married it to our investigative skill. Vultures will start to feed off an animal just because it's stopped moving. And they've been feeding off this city for years, Marissa. If we scared the vultures away, this city could walk again. Hell, it could *run*. We could—"

"I need to go. I need to . . . just . . ." She started for the open doorway to the courtyard. "This is . . ."

"We don't have time," Ben called out to her. "Isn't that what you said to me that day, after the pipeline blew? This city lost its margin of error fifty years ago. That's what you said, Marissa. And somebody's supposed to be telling the truth. Even when no one wants them to."

"Ben . . ."

"Not one drop of blood. Not one. Words, Marissa. We'd be working with words. Only, instead of ours, we'd be working with *theirs*. We couldn't go after the ones we hated directly, you see. The risk of changing them would be too great. But we could take away the environment they used to thrive in, piece by piece. Crook by crook. Thief by thief. Liar by liar—"

"Ben, this is absolutely. You just can't—"

"We could take away their *luck*. Their good fortune. Their culture of corruption. Don't tell me you can't see the potential. Don't tell me that you weren't sitting there wondering what kind of *good* this could have done if some little privileged white family from Uptown hadn't kept it a secret for eight years."

"*You want to go there with me*?" She whirled on him, finger pointing, words flying from her faster than she could think. "You want to play that card while you talk to me about the casual enslavement of other human beings? Because that's what this is, Ben. This is a violation of everything anyone who values the human mind believes in. Including me. A person's ability to think for themselves. Free will, for the love of God. Where would I be without those things? Where would *you* be?"

"Small moves with a giant hand," Ben whispered. "Small moves with a giant hand, Marissa. That's what this would be. Precise, specific, brief. And just enough to advance a bigger objective."

"What bigger objective?"

"Our city, Marissa! The same one the rest of the country is ready to cut loose into the sea as soon as they're done with their wild weekend. The same one they want to blame for their racism and their addiction to oil because they can't manage to care about most of the people here because they're black and they're poor. It's the same objective we've had for eight years, Marissa, and only now we wouldn't have mountains of lies standing in our way."

"This is insane," she whispered, her vision blurred by tears she couldn't bring herself to fight.

"You're right. Maybe we should have given up a long time ago. But we didn't."

"Tell me," she said quietly. "Do you really believe *this* is the only way to do any good here anymore? After everything you've been through, after everything you've seen, is that really what you believe?"

"After everything you've taught me. Yes. Yes, I do."

"Okay . . . Then I quit. If this is truly what it takes, then I'm out. I can't do it anymore."

His eyes fluttered shut as if he had tried to brace himself against the blow a second too late, and she could see he was fighting tears as well. But now that the words had left her mouth, she was backing away from the tank's sweep of glass and its terrible, pulsating potential.

"Marissa . . . please . . ."

"No, I'm sorry, Ben. That's it. I'm done. But don't worry. Your secret's safe with me and I'll be long gone by the time you get to *work*. So don't you worry . . ."

"Marissa!"

She expected him to call after her again, but there was only the sound of her shoes crunching twigs as she hurried to her car.

She got almost as far as the freeway when her foot slid off the gas pedal and found the brake, and her hands left the steering wheel and ended up bunched together in her lap. For a few seconds, she thought he'd followed her and was using his power on her. But wouldn't she have blacked out? Wasn't that how it worked? But here she was, alone in her car, the rutted road behind her empty save for shadows cast by branches and moss. And she suddenly wished that he had forced it on her instead of leaving her with this bitter litany of all the sacrifices she'd made for her profession, for her city.

But was that why she was hesitating now? Not because she truly wanted what he'd offered her, but because she wouldn't be able to face the sacrifices she had already made if she gave up on everything now. And why did she have to give up? Why did she have to leave? Did she truly think he would hurt her if she didn't?

But the question that had brought her to a standstill was the one she'd just asked him a few minutes ago, a question so pointed and absurdly leading she never would have been able to include it in a professional interview in good conscience. Did Ben truly believe his newfound power was the only way to help New Orleans?

Maybe not. But you sure do.

You prayed for courage and you got an opportunity to be courageous. That was what the true believers in her mother's church had always preached. You didn't get to pick what the opportunity would be. That wasn't how the universe worked, or seemed to work, anyway.

You didn't get to pick your miracles You could either lean into them or run the other way. And that's all she was doing. Running.

Ben must have heard her car coming back down the road because he was standing in the middle of the courtyard when she returned. He held his ground as she approached, as if he thought any sudden moves might spook her again, but his eyes were bloodshot and every muscle in his body appeared to tense with each step she took in his direction, as if she were a fearsome wind he was determined to lean in to without loosing his balance. The tiny building behind him looked too forlon to be harboring such an earth-shattering secret, and for a while she studied it as Ben studied her.

"Come inside, Marissa," Ben finally whispered. "Come with me. Please."

And then she felt him take her hand, and together they stepped out of the cypress-filtered sunlight and into the shadows.

FROM THE JOURNALS
OF NIQUETTE DELONGPRE

*L*ast night he asked me to drive him to the Luling Bridge, and I said yes, even though I knew the risks were high. It's possible someone could have recognized him, although he more closely resembles what he looked like as a teenager than the man they've been showing on the news constantly since the accident.

It's funny what he remembers, and as much as Ben and I have tried to outline some logical process to figure out which memories are returning first, we can't seem to identify one. The guilt over keeping him a secret from his family started to go away when he didn't recognize any of his brothers in the photographs we showed him. That's part of why I agreed to take him to the bridge, because I knew it meant he wanted to see the ships on the river. Another memory returning.

The bridge feels monumental for being so far from a densely urban area.

At its height, you can see the entire sweep of Jefferson and Orleans Parishes to the east, and the great black bowl of Lake Pontchartrain to the north. The river banks directly below it are sparsely populated, lined by a smattering of grain docks.

It was the middle of the night and he leapt from the Jeep as soon as I slowed down, even though he was shirtless. Dressing him isn't the easiest. He is almost seven feet tall. And there are some other concerns. By the time I stopped the Jeep, I realized what he was about to do. By the time I called out his full name, he had leapt up onto the railing and the wings at his back had extended, two smooth flaps of flesh with slender, exposed ligaments securing them to a ridge along his spine that inflated almost like parachutes as he dropped over the side and into the darkness.

Of course, I'd seen him fly before, but never by dropping from such a great height, and my heart was in my throat as he shrank in size, plummeting toward the dark river. There is much of Anthem in him, but this split-second, wordless impulsiveness is entirely new. Or at least it's not the Anthem I remember. That Anthem announced everything he planned to do, and often didn't do very much of it. There are aspects of this creature, this being that are entirely different. And then there's the physical. The impossibly perfect muscles. The incredible height. The idealization of his teenage features.

It was not just my words that created him—my hero, my God, my angel. It was the marriage of those words and the collective images they inspired inside his imagination each time I whispered them to him over the years. And in that fateful instant on the old push boat in Madisonville, my words met the history of his dreams, and he was reborn.

By the time I saw him rising up from the darkness, it was too late for me to move, and in a dizzying instant, he had taken me in his giant arms and we were rising up alongside one of the bridge's massive copper-colored towers, until we had passed the blinking red light at its very top, and I could see New Orleans aglow on the dark, watery horizon. And as my screams turned to laughter, I thought of Ben and the work he and Marissa would begin soon.

He has asked me to help, and even though I have asked for time to consider it, I know I will say yes for one reason. I have learned that magic withheld gives birth to nightmares, and so I have no choice but to stand back, open my heart and let the heavens rise.

ACKNOWLEDGMENTS

This novel exists in its current form largely due to the generosity of a man named Cory F. Heitmeier. Cory is a pilot with the New Orleans–Baton Rouge Steamship Pilots Association, an organization that hasn't always been treated kindly by writers in the past, and even though he'd never read any of my books, he agreed to take me out on a ship with him. We traveled the exact same journey Anthem and Marshall take in this novel, only no one got shot or transformed into a great winged beast by the time we reached the relief pilot in Chalmette. I'm eternally grateful to Cory, his Coast Guard commander and the other pilots at Vessel Traffic Control who took the time to answer my technical questions.

As always, I'm grateful to my best friend, business partner and co-host of *The Dinner Party Show*, Eric Shaw Quinn, who demanded that I get over my terror of boarding and disembarking a giant, moving ship by way of a glorified rope ladder and a swaying platform atop a crew boat. It was one of the scariest experiences of my life but I'm glad I did it and I think the book is all the better for it. (And if you haven't listened to our Internet radio show, you should, because we're funny. It's always streaming at TheDinnerPartyShow.com. Special thanks to our team who kept the show running so smoothly while I was working on this novel's revisions: our sound guy, Brandon Griffith; our computer genius, Brett Churnin; and our guest-relations dudes, Billy McIntyre and Nick Cedergren.)

New Orleans is a profoundly changed city as a result of Katrina, and I moved away several years before the storm hit. I was able to get a fine-tuned sense of her new, bruised spirit from friends who opened their homes and their hearts to me during the multiple visits I made there to research this novel. The book is dedicated to two of my good friends, Sid Montz and Christian LeBlanc, because they both played a major role in this process. But I also owe similar debts of gratitude to Spencer Doody, Phin Percy, Joyce Hunter and Ralph Mascaro, who did a wonderful job of driving me up and down the rivers and bayous of Lake Pontchartrain's North Shore while I searched for the right location for Elysium.

I wrote several drafts of this novel before I submitted it to a publisher, and those drafts were given invaluable, probing reads by my agent Lynn Nesbit and my friends Marc Andreyko, Gregg Hurwitz, Becket Ghiotto and Eric Shaw Quinn. This was the first time my mother read an early draft of one of my novels and it was an interesting experience for both of us. Thanks, Mom. I hope I wasn't too difficult. Thank God for email, huh?

I'm incredibly grateful this book found a home with Mitchell Ivers and Louise Burke at Gallery Books, two individuals who have made great contributions to my career as a novelist. With the gentlest of hands, Mitchell guided me through one of the most challenging processes a novelist can face—the total elimination of two major characters I had tried, in vain, to keep alive through various drafts.

I am also profoundly grateful to my attorney, Christine Cuddy, and my film agent, Rich Green at Resolution.

I'm blessed to have over 100,000 Facebook followers and whenever I post anything about my writing, they're incredibly supportive. According to their various posts, they've been waiting for this book for quite a long time; I thank them for their patience and I hope it meets their expectations. I wonder if they'll let me call them "mind monsters" now.